Like whales brea

directions, frost giants burst from the gleaming white surface ahead. Some sorcery, or perhaps just their natural affinity for winter and all its works, had enabled them to lurk submerged in the low place and smooth away all sign of their presence as well.

Had the Asgardians floundered deeper into the snow, they would have been helpless to defend themselves. Even though they'd stopped short, the situation was dire. Roaring, eight frost giants tramped forward. Enormous clubs, swung low to the ground, smashed into men and women in the front ranks and hurled their pulverized bodies through the air.

"Shoot!" Ivar bellowed to his troops.

Heart pounding, Heimdall drew and loosed, drew and loosed. He aimed for the eyes and hoped others were doing the same. It was what Asgardian warriors were trained to do.

BY THE SAME AUTHOR

FORGOTTEN REALMS
The Reaver
Queen of the Depths
The Black Bouquet
Dissolution
The Shattered Mask

FORGOTTEN REALMS:
BROTHERHOOD OF THE GRIFFIN
The Captive Flame
Whisper of Venom
The Spectral Blaze
The Masked Witches
Prophet of the Dead

FORGOTTEN REALMS:
THE HAUNTED LANDS
Unclean
Undead
Unholy

FORGOTTEN REALMS:
THE YEAR OF ROGUE DRAGONS
The Rage
The Rite
The Ruin

PATHFINDER TALES
Called to Darkness
Lord of Penance

IRON KINGDOMS:
THE BLACK RIVER IRREGULARS
Black Crowns
Black Dogs

ARKHAM HORROR
Ire of the Void
The Blood of Baalshandor

THE IMPOSTOR
Half a Hero
Blood Machine

THE NIGHTMARE CLUB
Joy Ride
Warlock Games
Party Till You Drop

SCARRED LANDS:
DEAD GOD TRILOGY
Forsaken
Forsworn
Forbidden

The Paladins: Arrival
The Shadow Guide
This Sword for Hire
Murder in Corvis
Blind God's Bluff
The Enemy Within
The Vampire's Apprentice
The Hand of Rasputin
Children of Gaia & Uktena
Undercity
The Ebon Mask
On a Darkling Plain Stormtalons
The Ghost in the Stone
Citadel of Gold
X-Men: Soul Killer
Dark Fortune
Dead Time
Fright Line
Deathward
The Tale of the Terrible Toys

MARVEL LEGENDS OF ASGARD

The Head of Mimir

RICHARD LEE BYERS

FOR MARVEL PUBLISHING

VP Production & Special Projects: Jeff Youngquist
Assistant Editor, Special Projects: Caitlin O'Connell
Manager, Licensed Publishing: Jeremy West
VP, Licensed Publishing: Sven Larsen
SVP Print, Sales & Marketing: David Gabriel
Editor in Chief: C B Cebulski

Special Thanks to Wil Moss

First published by Aconyte Books in 2020

ISBN 978 1 83908 054 8

Ebook ISBN 978 1 83908 055 5

Cover art by Grant Griffin

Distributed in North America by Simon & Schuster Inc, New York, USA
Printed in the United States of America
9 8 7 6 5 4 3 2 1

ACONYTE BOOKS

An imprint of Asmodee Entertainment Ltd

Mercury House, Shipstones Business Centre

North Gate, Nottingham NG7 7FN, UK

aconytebooks.com // twitter.com/aconytebooks

For Duane and Dolly at the Comics Club,
my suppliers of Marvel Comics for...
it can't possibly be that many years, can it?

Prologue

The sun of Asgard gleamed on the armor and blunted double-handed swords of the boys and girls facing one another in pairs around the grassy field, each duo with an adult referee hovering to oversee the bout and award points. Some of the children looked tense as drawn bows, others were confident and relaxed, and still others grinned with the excitement of competition. Massive, with a bushy beard the tawny red of fox fur, clad in a scarlet doublet trimmed with cloth of gold, Volstagg was one of the parents relegated to the ring of spectators around the tourney area.

Like the other fathers and mothers, Volstagg was watching his own child with a mixture of pride, hope, and anxiety, so intent on young Bjarke that despite a legendary appetite that often provided fodder for his friends' jests, a half-eaten goose pastry hung forgotten in his hand. Bjarke very much wanted to win the tourney, and so his father wanted it for him. Tall for his age, strong, and aggressive, the lad had eliminated his first two opponents, but now only the better competitors remained. He was likely to have a more challenging time of it moving forward.

"Begin!" the referee said.

Blunted practice sword raised high, Bjarke instantly charged. His opponent, a slim girl a head shorter than he was, didn't move. Some people might have assumed Bjarke's sudden assault had startled and frozen her, but Volstagg had survived centuries of combat, albeit often by keeping his head well down, and his instincts told him she was inviting the attack. He wanted to call out a warning, but that wasn't how things were done. Besides, it might simply distract Bjarke at a critical moment.

Bjarke's blade swept down at the top of her helmet, and sure enough, the girl spun out of the way and cut to the flank. Her weapon clanked on mail as it bashed Bjarke in the ribs.

"Halt!" the referee called. "Point for Ulrika!"

Now it was acceptable for Volstagg to shout, and he did so. "It's all right, son! It's only the first point!"

The children returned to their starting positions. The referee again gave the command to commence.

Bjarke advanced a little more cautiously this time, with Ulrika giving ground before him. Even circling, though, she couldn't retreat too far lest she step over the chalk line defining the limits of the dueling ring. When he'd backed her up as far as she could go, Bjarke began a rapid series of cuts. Steel rang as Ulrika parried but seemed unable to riposte. Perhaps, Volstagg thought, the boy's attacks were coming too fast, or the jarring impacts of sword on sword were weakening her grip on the hilt of her weapon, with its cross guard and heavy steel disk of a pommel. He hoped that was the case even as his instincts warned the girl was setting a trap.

Screaming a battle cry, Bjarke made a horizontal cut. Ulrika dropped to one knee, and the boy's blade glanced off her helmet. She cut at the same time, and her weapon clashed against her opponent's high boot with its reinforcing strips of metal.

"Halt!" the referee shouted. "Point for Ulrika!"

Scowling, Volstagg doubted he would have made the same call. Still, he resisted the impulse to call out to the official and argue. That wasn't done either and would accomplish nothing beyond quite possibly embarrassing his son. It was for the referee to judge whether the attack that skipped off the helm would or wouldn't have penetrated armor had the sword been an actual weapon of war, and to his credit, though he too frowned, Bjarke didn't try to argue either. As he and the girl returned to their starting positions, Volstagg called, "Be careful, son! You can still win if you use what you know!"

The official set the children at one another again. Bjarke tried compound attacks to penetrate Ulrika's guard, but the feints didn't deceive her, and her blade was always in position to block the true cut. After a few such exchanges, she attacked *while* Bjarke was feinting, and he jerked his arms back just in time to avoid a stroke that, in a real fight, might well have severed a hand.

To Volstagg's dismay, that was the end of Bjarke attempting finesse. The boy struck hard, fast, relentlessly until Ulrika skipped out of the way of a downward cut as she had before and landed another clanking counterattack to the flank.

"Halt!" the referee shouted. "Point to Ulrika! Match to Ulrika!"

Bjarke saluted her with his sword and shook the girl's hand as he was supposed to. He even managed to smile. But as he pulled off his helmet and trudged toward Volstagg, the smile slumped into sullenness. Volstagg felt a corresponding disappointment but did his best to hide it lest the boy think he was disappointed in *him*.

Instead, he tousled his son's sweaty hair, red like his own, but of a more coppery hue. "You did well."

The boy twitched away from his father's touch. "Not well enough," he said.

"There'll be other tourneys," Volstagg told him. "Do you want to watch the end of this one?"

"No," said the boy.

"As you wish. But there's a stand over there selling cherry tarts. A warrior needs sustenance after a battle." Volstagg noticed he was still holding the half-eaten goose pastry and tossed what was left to somebody's wandering elkhound. The dog caught it in the air and gobbled it down.

"Can we just go home?" Bjarke asked.

"Leaving the poor vendor bereft of our coin? We're thanes of Asgard, lad. It's our duty to help the commons prosper. Now come along, and don't let the blade of your sword drag on the ground. A man-at-arms respects his weapons."

Father and son sat down to eat on a bench some distance from the action of the tourney, although they could still hear cheers and the clangor of metal. The warm cherry pastry was as tasty as Volstagg had hoped, the perfect juicy blend of tart and sweet, but Bjarke only nibbled, even though such treats were one of his favorites. By all indications, the lad was even more demoralized than Volstagg had initially realized, and his father determined to set things right. Perhaps he could do so by giving Bjarke reason to believe he'd fare better next time.

"Very well," Volstagg said. "If you can't forget about the tourney, let's talk about it. See what there is to learn."

Bjarke gave his father a look that suggested he knew he *should* learn from the experience but was reluctant to suffer through a dissection of his mistakes and deficiencies. "All right."

"When Ulrika wasn't fighting a bout herself," Volstagg said, "she watched those who were. She watched you. Did you watch her?"

"I guess," Bjarke said. "I did watch some of the other bouts."

To Volstagg, that sounded like an evasion. "But did you study her as she studied you?"

Bjarke frowned. "I don't know."

"If you didn't, you weren't prepared for her tactics and favorite techniques, while she was ready for yours."

"I still should have beaten her. She didn't deserve that second point."

Although Volstagg had thought the same himself, that was the wrong lesson to take away from the bout, and he didn't want it to take root. "Whether she did or didn't," he said, "it was one point out of three. When something doesn't work out as you thought it should on the battlefield, are you going to dwell on it or set it aside and move on?"

Bjarke sighed. "Move on, I guess. But I tried! What else was I supposed to do?"

"You're bigger and stronger than most children your age – you can thank your mighty father for that – and you rely on it too much. In a bout, you make the same basic attacks over and over again, counting on power and fierceness to carry you through."

Bjarke frowned. "The way I fight won me the first two bouts."

That too was the wrong lesson. Volstagg wished fleetingly that his beloved wife Gudrun were here. She was sometimes better at correcting the children than he was. She wasn't, though, so he had to find a way. "But it lost you the third one," he said.

"I *did* change –" the boy began.

"For a bit," Volstagg said. "Then you grew impatient and went back to your old moves. As Ulrika wanted you to do."

"Well, Thor's the strongest of anybody, and he always wins."

That remark prompted a thought, an idea of how Volstagg might get through to Bjarke. "Not *every* fight," he said, "and when he does win, which is indeed mostly, it isn't by dint of strength alone. A victorious warrior *thinks.* He observes and plans. He's patient and persistent enough to see a plan through to the finish, but adaptable enough to change what isn't working. Maybe a story will convince you."

Bjarke finally perked up. He had always liked his father's stories. "Is it about Thor?"

"Not this one," Volstagg said. "It's about Heimdall long ago, long before he was the guardian of the Bifrost, when he was barely grown to manhood, in fact, and Asgard had fallen on dark times."

ONE

A final volley of arrows put the two frost giants to flight. They'd attacked by surprise, seemingly hoping that this – coupled with their strength, size, and ferocity – would carry the day, but Asgardian marksmanship had disabused them of that expectation.

The Jotuns were as tall as trees. They were blue skinned, wearing only horned helmets, other scraps of armor, crudely made iron and ivory ornaments, and loincloths, but mostly naked in the cold they didn't feel. They fled down the defile that ran between a pair of hills. Their crunching footsteps left holes in the snow long enough for a man to lie in like a grave.

"After them!" Captain Ivar bellowed. He bore a battle-axe in one hand and a round shield on the other arm, and his yellow beard hung in three plaits.

Other members of the Asgardian patrol brandished their weapons and roared their eagerness to obey. Several months ago, at the command of its king, Skrymir, a mighty warrior, sorcerer, and illusionist, Jotunheim had invaded Asgard, and the two worlds were at war. Yet, in their weeks scouting this province on the outskirts of the Realm Eternal, the patrol hadn't hitherto had the chance to strike a blow against the enemy. They meant to make up for that now.

Yew bow in hand, another arrow nocked, Heimdall, though he tried, couldn't share their enthusiasm. It seemed to him that the frost giants had run away too easily. As if their intent was to lead the Asgardian warriors into a trap.

But then again, what did he know? He and his sister were the youngest warriors in the company. Ivar was by far the more experienced warrior and the war leader. It was his role to give commands and the role of callow recruits like Heimdall to obey them, preferably with the boldness that was the hallmark of an Asgardian warrior.

The boldness embodied by his sister, Sif. As she strode along beside him in her red war gear with white trim, her black hair hanging down her back in a ponytail, the fierce gaze of her blue eyes and the set of her jaw revealed her eagerness to pursue and to fight, to prove she was valiant and skilled as her older comrades. He told himself to be more like her.

The company trotted forward. Sif glanced over at Heimdall and evidently noted worry in his expression. "Cheer up, brother," she said. "It will be fine."

Heimdall hoped she was right. Certainly, the frost giants weren't known for laying cunning traps or employing subtle tactics. In past conflicts, they'd generally charged into combat like berserkers.

Like the path before them, the wooded hillsides were

cloaked in snow with icicles dangling from branches. Much of Asgard enjoyed a perpetual summer. Out here near the borders that wasn't the case, but winter should have already given way to spring, and it hadn't. Maybe that was because the invading Jotuns had brought their own preferred climate with them.

Or perhaps Odin's will and magic were necessary to turn the wheel of the seasons, and with him inexplicably lost to the Odinsleep for months on end, it was stuck. In which case, unless the All-Father woke, it always would be.

Heimdall scowled and pushed such dismal reflections aside. Even if he'd been in any position to do anything about such high and mysterious matters, now would not have been the time to brood about them. He, Sif, and their comrades were heading into a fight, and he needed to concentrate on that.

Or *maybe* a fight was imminent. He wasn't certain, but other than their footprints, there was no further sign of the frost giants. Maybe they simply had run away, their long legs allowing them to outdistance their pursuers. Maybe any danger was long gone.

But suppose, just suppose, the Jotuns had run to join more of their kind. In that case, perhaps the creatures were waiting where the terrain favored them. Heimdall had never been to this particular bit of the Realm Eternal before, but he had studied the maps, and he sought to recall the specifics of what lay ahead.

The warriors in the front ranks of the company slowed because they'd blundered into deeper snow. Cursing, they pushed onward, and it was at that point that Heimdall saw something that sent a jolt of alarm through him.

For an instant he hesitated, still reluctant to be the warrior who questioned his thane's commands or looked timid in any way. But he couldn't let his sister and his comrades advance obliviously into danger and *not* speak up.

"Stop!" he shouted. "Everyone, stop!"

Ivar looked over at him. "What?" the war leader asked, impatience in his tone.

"If I remember the map of this area correctly," Heimdall replied, "it shows a long slope ahead. If we push down it, that snow will be over our heads."

"Then we need a way around," Ivar said.

"But that's not all of it," Heimdall replied. "The giants' footprints stop here. Which way did *they* go? Maybe they didn't go anywhere. I think–"

Like whales breaching, showering snow in all directions, frost giants burst from the gleaming white surface ahead. Some sorcery, or perhaps just their natural affinity for winter and all its works, had enabled them to lurk submerged in the low place and smooth away all sign of their presence as well.

Had the Asgardians floundered deeper into the snow, they would have been helpless to defend themselves. Even though they'd stopped short, the situation was dire. Roaring, eight frost giants tramped forward. Enormous clubs, swung low to the ground, smashed into men and women in the front ranks and hurled their pulverized bodies through the air.

"Shoot!" Ivar bellowed to his troops.

Heart pounding, Heimdall drew and loosed, drew and

loosed. He aimed for the eyes and hoped others were doing the same. It was what Asgardian warriors were trained to do.

To his surprise, the volleys of shafts slowed the frost giants long enough for the few survivors in the front ranks to fall back. The creatures flailed their hands in front of their faces like men trying to swipe away clouds of midges. One of the blue-skinned Jotuns even toppled backward when Sif shot an iron-tipped length of birch so deep into his eye that it disappeared completely.

"Ha!" she cried. "One down!"

"Fall back!" Ivar bellowed. Unfortunately, the chance vanished before he finished speaking.

A frost giant with hammered gold and enormous crudely cut blue gems among his ornaments charged despite the flights of arrows, and the other Jotuns followed their leader's example. They only needed a moment and a couple strides, and then they were looming over Heimdall, Sif, and much of the Asgardian patrol.

A huge spiked club swept down. Sif grabbed hold of Heimdall's arm and yanked him out of the way of a blow that might otherwise have killed them both. She then dropped her bow and drew her blade. Meanwhile, Heimdall was slower to reach for the great sword hanging down his back.

He was a skilled swordsman. His father's master-at-arms and pretty much everyone else on the estate had been surprised that the odd boy, who liked books and asked questions about what everyone else accepted as simply the way things were, had possessed the knack. Heimdall had been surprised himself.

But there was a vast difference between training bouts

and fighting in earnest for one's life. He'd done almost none of the latter, and what sane person would want to engage a foe as terrible as a frost giant at close quarters?

Still, it was unthinkable to hang back while Sif and his other comrades risked themselves, and he only hesitated for an instant. Then he dropped his bow, drew the twohanded sword, and bellowed "Vanaheim," the war cry of his native realm, to banish fear and send him charging into the fray.

He and Sif hacked at an enormous foot clad in a goatskin shoe tied at the ankle. Their swords sliced through the covering, and the frost giant roared. The Jotun jumped back from his foes, small as mice to him, and swung his club straight down.

Heimdall and Sif dashed between the Jotun's legs, and the club splashed up snow and jolted the ground behind them. They cut at the same foot they'd already bloodied, and the giant stumbled away.

As the creature struggled to regain his balance, Heimdall cast about for the frost giant with the gold and blue-gem ornaments. He didn't *want* to engage the Jotun leader, who might well be the fiercest of them all, but perhaps that offered the best hope of the Asgardians surviving the ambush. Sneering as he advanced, the creature swung a war club studded with sharp pieces of flint like a farmer using a scythe and reaped an Asgardian life with every strike.

"That one!" Heimdall said, dashing toward the leader.

"The other one–" Sif began. She likely meant to say the other wasn't dead or incapacitated, and they turned their backs on him at their peril. But when it was clear her brother wasn't stopping to listen, he heard her running after him.

They came up behind the leader and attacked a blue-skinned leg. The frost giant picked up his foot and stamped. They dodged out from underneath and kept on cutting.

Despite the thick leather of the frost giant's calfskin boot, Sif's broadsword slashed deep. When she yanked it out of the wound, blood spurted across the snow. The Jotun leader screamed and fell to his hands and knees.

"Retreat!" Ivar shouted, and he and his surviving warriors turned and ran.

One man fell behind immediately. A blow from a giant's maul or hammer had bloodied but somehow not killed him. Discerning his plight, Sif dashed back and, using her Asgardian strength, picked him up and carried him.

After a time, Heimdall risked another glance backward. The frost giants weren't pursuing yet. When their leader fell, lamed, it had balked them.

But he and Sif hadn't killed the towering creature, and he had little doubt their Jotun foes would take up the chase soon enough. To his relief, though, the Asgardians soon came to a thick stand of pines and gray alders growing on the hillside to the right. The woods would slow them, but they'd hinder enormous creatures like frost giants even more.

Plainly thinking the same, Ivar changed course. "Up the hill!" he shouted.

The ploy worked as Heimdall had hoped. As he and his comrades raced through the forest, the crashing and bellowing attendant upon the Jotuns' pursuit grew fainter and fainter. Around dusk, it fell silent entirely.

Two

Half of Ivar's command survived, but the slaughter of the other half led to the company returning to the Realm Eternal's capital city, likewise known as Asgard, there either to fill its ranks with new recruits or combine with another band of warriors as his superiors deemed expedient.

Though he recognized the practical reason for it, Heimdall hadn't wanted to return. He'd always been determined to do his utmost to defend Asgard, for the sake of his people and to make his family proud, and that determination had only strengthened now that he was grieving for so many comrades, warriors he'd come to know well.

That grief was fed in turn by guilt. What if he'd communicated his misgivings to Captain Ivar sooner? Perhaps everyone would still be alive.

Once she wormed the cause of his brooding out of him, Sif told him he was being ridiculous. He'd noticed what no one else had, and if he hadn't called out when he did, the *entire* patrol would have perished. He should be proud.

He wasn't, though, and when Sif thought no one was looking, he sometimes saw a mournful cast to her countenance and a slump to her shoulders that revealed she felt the loss of their fellows more keenly than she liked to let on.

Even so, however, it seemed to him that she was better able to accept the deaths as an inevitable consequence of war and put them behind her. It might be one more indication that she was better suited to a warrior's life than he was.

In any case, on the march back she'd argued that they'd been in the field for months and believed he could be forgiven a period of rest and relaxation however grim the circumstances providing the opportunity. Ultimately, somewhat persuaded, he'd resolved to enjoy his sojourn to the best of his ability.

Sadly, conditions in the city made it impossible to forget the war raging in the provinces. Perpetual summer prevailed here – so far, anyway – and purple saxifrage, blue speedwell, and white mouse-ear bloomed in the many parks and gardens. The golden spires and palaces gleamed as splendidly as ever. But large portions of the city were given over to military encampments. Builders were busy erecting new fortifications, artisans were fashioning new catapults, and the streets echoed with the clangor of swordsmiths laboring at their forges. More disheartening still were the hospital tents stinking of blood, sweat, and fever, and the haggard refugee families begging and sleeping in the streets.

Sitting across from Sif in a tavern crowded with other warriors – many sporting bandages, slings, and crutches

– a flagon of beer in his hand, Heimdall said what seemed obvious to him. "We're losing."

"Not so loud!" his sister replied, glancing around at the occupants of the nearer tables. When it seemed clear no one had overheard, she glowered at Heimdall. "You're liable to end up in a brawl, and I might not be inclined to stand with you."

Heimdall sighed. "You know I'm not impugning anyone's courage or prowess. The problem – well, one of the problems – is that the frost giants are fighting differently. The ambush they sprang on our patrol was just one small example. According to the sagas and chronicles, there was a time when they just came straight at us with nothing in the way of strategy and only the crudest tactics. Now it's different." It sometimes seemed to him that the Asgardian side might have benefited from a similar infusion of craftiness, but that was something he wouldn't say aloud. It would feel disloyal and likely annoy Sif more than what he'd said already.

"We'll beat them anyway." Sif took a drink from her flagon and wiped foam from her upper lip. "We always do."

"*Always* only holds until it doesn't. I wish the All-Father would wake. He'd know how to win the war. He might even be able to break the connection between Asgard and Jotunheim."

Asgard and Jotunheim were two of the Nine Worlds hung on Yggdrasil, the World Tree, but their relative positioning was more complicated than that fact might imply. Sometimes it took magic to journey from one to the other, but there were also conjunctions when one linked with the other as though they were simply two adjacent kingdoms on a continent. Such a conjunction currently existed between Asgard and Jotunheim, and this fusion, combined with Odin's protracted slumber and the giants' newfound cleverness, resulted in a situation as disadvantageous to Asgard as Heimdall could readily imagine.

Sif nodded to indicate that on this point at least she and her brother were in accord. "I'm sure he'll wake soon," she said.

Heimdall felt a pang of anger, although he wasn't sure at who or what. Sif's declaration of blind faith, perhaps. "Are you?" he asked. "In times past, the Odinsleep lasted a week, always. This time it's lasted months."

Sif snorted. "You're quite the expert, considering you'd never even set foot in Asgard until a few months ago."

She was of course right. He'd grown up in Vanaheim prior to pledging his sword to the legions of Asgard. Still, he wasn't willing to let the matter drop. "I read books," Heimdall said. "I talk to people."

"In short," Sif said, "you think too much, and that's always been your problem. The All-Father will wake when he wakes. There's nothing you can do to speed the process along."

Heimdall frowned. He'd actually had an idea about that. It was an idea he'd pushed away several times as possibly foolish and certainly above his station It kept coming back, though, and now he was experiencing something he'd occasionally experienced when he and Sif were growing up. Someone else's obvious belief that he'd be a fool to proceed with a certain notion fed a stubborn desire to try it out. "Maybe there is," he said.

Three

Heimdall was having second thoughts, though – eleventh or twelfth thoughts, really – three days later when the royal guards opened the tall double doors for him to make the long walk down the central aisle of the throne room. He'd been in that enormous space with its high vaulted ceilings twice before, but only as a member of Captain Ivar's company on ceremonial occasions. He now found it was one thing to stand silent in the ranks and something else entirely to approach the ruler of Asgard alone and on his own initiative.

While Odin slept, that ruler was Frigga Freyrdottir, his wife, governing as regent in his stead. A tall, blue-eyed woman with strong features and white hair piled high on her head, she'd left most of her jewelry in the coffers and wore a pale-yellow gown less splendid than those Heimdall had seen her in previously on state occasions. She was dressed to work, to direct the affairs of a land at war.

The boil of activity around the dais on which she sat, her

husband's empty high-backed golden throne beside her, attested to the need for such direction. Advisors offered their counsel. Warriors hurried in and out, making reports and carrying away orders. Clerks scratched away with quill pens, recording the queen's decrees. Either meek and nervous or shifting from foot to foot with impatience, commoners waited until she could spare a moment to hear their petitions.

Heimdall wondered if he shouldn't just turn around and slip out the way he'd come in. Frigga was manifestly extremely busy, and she was the Queen of the Gods. He too was a god, but only as per the loose usage giants, dwarves, elves, and mortal men accorded to any inhabitant of Asgard. Whereas she was *truly* a deity, one of a handful of people either born with extraordinary powers, invested with them by Odin, or both. Who was he, a common warrior – a recent addition to the ranks, no less – to take up any of such a personage's time?

But, having successfully requested an audience, he couldn't just run away without looking ridiculous and without thoroughly annoying Captain Ivar, whose recommendation had helped him gain entry here. Besides, what if he truly was seeing something important that no one else had seen? If so, wasn't it his duty to speak up?

His resolve somewhat bolstered by such thoughts, he started toward the throne. His mouth was dry, though, and the magnificence of all he saw before him fed the fear that he was presumptuously intruding where he didn't belong. He had of course cleaned up thoroughly and put on his best clothes for a royal audience, but suspected he must still look drab – if not lowly – compared to all the courtiers in their splendid attire.

It was truly too late to back out now, though. He would have looked and felt a fool had he turned and fled while still back by the doors, but perhaps few people would have noticed. He was now far enough into the room that everybody would. Perhaps that was the reflection that gave him the final bit of courage required to walk on to the foot of the dais, drop to one knee, and wait to be recognized.

After the queen finished conferring with a minister, he was. "Rise," Frigga said. She glanced at a list resting along with a cup of water on a little table beside her. "Heimdall, is it?"

He swallowed. "Yes, Your Majesty."

"Of the Vanir."

"Yes."

Frigga smiled. "It's always nice to meet a kinsman." She too was of the Vanir, before her marriage to Odin sealed the treaty ending the all-but-forgotten war with the Aesir of Asgard. "Captain Ivar credits you with preventing the calamity that befell his company from being even worse."

Heimdall felt embarrassed. Whatever he'd accomplished, it didn't seem like much compared to the high matters of state that were Frigga's concern. "There was a moment when I may have said something helpful, Your Majesty. But it was all of us working and fighting together that kept the frost giants from killing us all."

"Well, Ivar made more of it than that, and that's why I granted you an audience. But you see how hectic it is this afternoon." The queen waved her hand at the waiting ministers, warriors, clerks, and petitioners. "Forgive me if I ask you to come straight to the point."

"Well..." Heimdall began. He'd planned what he meant to say, but now that the moment had come, he felt nervous and tongue-tied nonetheless. "The Odinsleep has lasted months longer than ever before."

Frigga sighed. "I *have* noticed."

"Odin's warriors need his leadership." As soon as the words left his mouth, Heimdall felt a surge of anxiety that they might give offense. "Even though Your Majesty is doing a fine job!"

"I'm also aware that I am not my husband," Frigga said. "I won't have you thrown in a dungeon for saying so. I *will* ask if this parade of the obvious is going anywhere."

"It is, Your Majesty. I mean, I hope it is. Has anyone considered that the All-Father's slumber may have been unnaturally prolonged?"

Frigga frowned. "What do you mean?"

"Well, by sorcery, perhaps?"

The queen looked to the group of advisors. "Lady Amora. Have you been listening?"

A woman dressed all in patterned green leather stepped forth. A headdress confined her blond hair, and high boots sheathed her legs. She smiled a condescending smile. "I have, Your Majesty, and I assure you, this young man is being foolish. Odin is the mightiest of all. No one could cast a spell on him."

That, Heimdall thought, should be that. Lady Amora was a mage, he wasn't, and now that she'd said his idea was without merit, he should accept her judgment and escape this place where he had no business as soon as possible.

But it wasn't quite that simple. Once a notion occurred to him, he'd always had trouble letting go of it until he'd tested it thoroughly, even when his continued questioning – occasionally arguing – irritated others. And thus, against his own better judgment, he said, "No one could cast a spell on Odin when he was awake. But isn't he more vulnerable during the Odinsleep? Isn't that why he shuts himself away? What if he was already asleep, and then the enemy struck?"

"Even assuming that would make any difference," Amora said, "no one can get into the chamber. That's the point of the defenses."

Frigga spread her hands. "Lady Amora knows whereof she speaks. She's one of the wisest mages in Asgard."

That, Heimdall knew, was certainly her reputation. As he understood it, Lady Amora had studied magic with Karnilla the Norn Queen and then with other sorcerers throughout the Realm Eternal and beyond.

Still, wasn't there always more for any person to learn about any subject? Presumably that even included witchcraft, which meant there might conceivably be a warlock somewhere who knew tricks Amora didn't.

"I bow to Lady Amora's wisdom," he said. "Truly. Still, might it not be a good idea if someone entered the vault and checked? That way, Your Majesty would know for certain."

Frigga's blue eyes widened in shock. "Odin expressly commanded that no one is to enter under any circumstances. Disobedience would constitute high treason."

"Even if Your Majesty commanded it? Until someone does go in, can we even be sure the All-Father is still alive?"

"Young man!" Frigga snapped. "Before, I warned you to avoid treason. *That* remark was little short of blasphemy. Odin is not only our king but also a primordial being. He and his brothers shaped the Nine Worlds. Which is to say, he, his will, and his mysteries are beyond you. Stick to your place and your proper concerns."

FOUR

Despite Sif's stated intent to relax and enjoy her time in the city of Asgard, it hadn't taken her long to grow restless and resume practicing her martial skills. It was a sign, perhaps, that despite the air of confidence she put on, underneath she was as worried about the progress of the war as Heimdall was. This afternoon, on the day following his audience with the queen, she'd sought out an archery range, and, for want of anything better to do, he'd tagged along with her.

She nocked, drew, and loosed in one smooth motion, seemingly without taking the time to aim. Like the ones before it, her arrow, with its red and white fletchings, arced at the target far down the range and plunged into the bull's-eye. "Stick to your place and your proper concerns," she said. "Excellent advice."

There were unopened crates of arrows behind the shooting line, and Heimdall had appropriated one to use as a seat. To sit on and sulk, as Sif had put it. Unfairly, he thought. Or somewhat unfairly, at any rate. He realized that in the wake of the royal audience, he was experiencing an untidy tangle of emotions that included worry, disappointment, and frustration. A little sulking might be somewhere in the mix. "I thought my own sister would be more sympathetic," he said.

"I can't imagine why," Sif said, picking up another shaft. Farther down the line, two other archers clasped hands to seal some sort of wager. "If you'd told me you were going to bother the queen – the queen! – with your wild notions, I would have done my best to talk you out of it."

He didn't doubt it. Throughout their childhoods, she'd always done her best to look out for him, which, in her view, sometimes required pulling him back when he was doing something harebrained. He loved her and was grateful for her protectiveness yet also often found it stifling and resented it.

"I probably wouldn't have listened," he admitted.

"Of course not. When do you ever?" Sif loosed and scored another bull's-eye. "At least you escaped with your head still attached to your shoulders. Now forget about it, come, and shoot."

Heimdall remained sitting. "I know what you think, but I'm not angry that the queen didn't take my advice."

Sif smiled a skeptical smile. "You're not?"

"I'm not. Well, not exactly. Who am I that Frigga Freyrdottir should take direction from me? But I'm upset that she and those around her rejected my thoughts without really even considering them. They were blinded by this haze of reverence for Odin."

"Deafened," Sif replied.

"What?"

"If they couldn't hear you," his sister said, "they were *deafened* by their reverence. As only makes sense. Don't *you* revere the All-Father?"

"You know I do. But if you read the histories, even Odin's not omnipotent. He's not the only mighty being or force in all the Nine Worlds. It's at least possible that the right enemy striking under the right circumstances could lay him low."

"And who might that *right enemy* be? Do you really think a frost giant could reach the vault of the Odinsleep in the very heart of Asgard undetected?"

"King Skrymir might, with his command over illusions."

"As far as I've heard, Skrymir has yet to take the field at all. He's still in Jotunheim. Even if he does come to Asgard, sneaking into the citadel alone doesn't seem like the sort of a mission a king would undertake himself."

"Fair enough," Heimdall said. "But what if he enlisted the aid of a traitor in the court? Unlike a frost giant or some other outsider, a traitor would have a big advantage. He could move freely around the citadel, and no one would think anything about it."

Sif made a spitting sound. "Now you're truly just making wild guesses. Who are you accusing? Who's been acting suspiciously? Who has anything to gain?"

"How can I know when I'm not a member of the court myself? I haven't had the chance to observe anybody."

"Exactly. Frigga has and evidently sees nothing amiss, and then we come back to the matter that Odin's magic protects the vault. Brother, those who are older, wiser, and higher-ranking say no one could have gotten in, so there's an end to it."

Heimdall felt a flash of irritation. He'd like to accept the idea that those in authority above him knew best – life seemed easier for those who did – but was it truly *always* so?

"I'd let go of my idea if it was about anything less important," he said. "I swear I would. But please, just consider for a moment. What if I'm right, and because no one would listen to me, Jotunheim wins the war?"

Sif turned to glare at him. "The frost giants *won't* win if warriors like us attend to our proper business!" Her expression softened. "Brother, I know you don't think yourself a perfect fit for Ivar's company. I know you've wondered if the Norns intend you for a different destiny. But–"

"You're wrong," Heimdall said. "Or rather, maybe there's truth in what you say, but this isn't about that. Truly, it's about protecting our people. I think…" The presumption and the danger, the sheer lunacy, perhaps, of what he was about to say came crashing down on him, and he had to pause and take a breath before proceeding. "I think someone should try to enter Odin's chamber whether Frigga agrees to it or not."

"Someone meaning you? That's madness!"

"I don't *want* to do it, but who else is there?"

"Even leaving aside the fact that trying would be the death of you, what could you do if you did get in?"

"I could at least look around," Heimdall said. "If someone has been there before me and I discover signs of the intrusion, evidence of dark magic, perhaps, I can report my findings to Frigga, and maybe then she, Lady Amora, and the other royal mages can undo the enchantment."

"You can't risk your life on *ifs* and *maybes*."

"Isn't that a warrior's job?" Heimdall asked.

"As the warrior's commanders and oaths dictate. Brother, I won't *let* you do this."

There was that overprotectiveness again. It rankled, and Heimdall realized he no longer liked his sister looking down at him. He rose, and they glowered at one another eye to eye.

"Are you going to inform on me?" he asked. "That's the only way to stop me. Then I'll rot in a dungeon or go to the block, and there'll be a blot on our family honor forever after."

Sif stared into his eyes for a few more seconds before snarling, "Curse you!"

"Does that mean you won't tell?"

"It means I'm going with you, idiot!" Her expression softened, and she put her hand on his shoulder. "Where one would surely die, perhaps two can survive and sneak in and out without being caught. So clearly I won't let you go alone."

FIVE

Heimdall and Sif had decided they might as well attempt their incursion into the vault that very night. With no way to know what awaited them, there was really no way to make elaborate preparations, so why wait? Waiting, he knew, would only scrape at his nerves and undermine his resolve.

And now the moment was at hand. He peeked around the corner and down the corridor beyond, felt a twinge of dismay at something he hadn't expected to see, and pulled his head back. "There's a guard posted beside the door," he whispered.

Sif frowned. "If the way beyond is deadly, what's the point?"

"The pomp that's Odin's due? Or maybe the guard's there to keep folk from going through the door by accident. The castle is something of a maze. You got lost the first day we were here."

"I only got turned around for a second," Sif replied, plainly nettled by the reminder. "Anyway, magical defenses are one thing. If there's a living, breathing sentry, we can't do this."

The relief in her voice irritated Heimdall. He suspected that was because it mirrored a relief he felt, at least momentarily, himself. But the stubborn part of him rejected the excuse for turning back.

"I can get rid of the guard," he said, hoping it was so. "You wait here."

He pulled up his hood to shadow his face and wrapped his scarf around the lower portion as a man who'd ridden hard might have done to keep from breathing road dust along the way. His pulse beating faster, he then hurried around the corner and down the hallway. "Found you!" he called.

The guard, a burly fellow equipped with a spear and round shield emblazoned with the ravens that were one of the All-Father's heraldic devices, gave him an inquiring look. "What?"

"I just delivered a dispatch to the thane of your company. Then he told me to find you and tell you to report to him."

"I can't leave my post," the sentry replied.

"The thane is ordering you to."

The burly man eyed Heimdall suspiciously. "Is he, now? What's my captain's name, if you truly come from him?"

Heimdall's heart was beating even faster. He could feel his pulse ticking in his neck, and sweat breaking out under his arms. "Friend, I've been riding since yesterday. I'm dull-witted for want of sleep, and I can't remember. But–"

"This doesn't smell right," said the guard. "Unbuckle your baldric and lay your sword on the ground." He started to point his spear.

In another moment, the weapon would *be* leveled, and

Heimdall reacted by instinct. He lunged, punched the guard in the face and kept on hitting him until he slid down the wall unconscious.

Sif hurried down the hallway. "What have you *done*?" she cried.

"I couldn't persuade him to step away."

"And so you *attacked* him?"

"I know," he said, "it was stupid. But it was my stupidity. He doesn't know anyone else was with me. You can still walk away from all this."

"Meaning you're pressing forward?"

"Yes." He felt bad, and perhaps even ashamed of striking the warrior, but in a strange way it had also shored up his intent. It was as if the transgression had so committed him that turning back was no longer an option.

"Then I'm still coming too," said Sif, her voice now less angry than grimly resigned. "At least you had the sense to mask your face, and as you say, the man hasn't even seen me. With luck, he won't be able to describe us."

Under the scarf, Heimdall smiled. Now, with the unknown perils of the crypt immediately before him, he realized just how grateful he was for her company.

"And if we do discover something important in the vault," he said, "the fact that I knocked out the guard won't matter any more. See if the door's locked."

Sif pushed down the golden handle, and the door clicked ajar. "It's not. I'm surprised."

"If the way beyond is deadly, maybe no one thought it needed to be." Heimdall dragged the guard inside onto the landing at the top of a steep flight of stairs descending deeper underground. Once Sif closed the door after them, darkness engulfed the space.

Heimdall touched the amulet he'd purchased late that afternoon from a seller of petty magic in an open-air marketplace and willed the enchantment to life. White light glowed from the brass disk on its leather thong.

A second light flowered as Sif roused the medallion she'd bought. "Let's get on with it," she said.

They crept down the stairs without incident. At the bottom, another corridor smelling of old stone stretched away into shadow. They prowled along it for perhaps a dozen paces, and then Heimdall spotted rusty brown discolorations on the walls ahead and the floor beneath.

"Stop." He pointed. "Do you see that?"

"Yes," Sif replied. "Someone bled out. But the person or thing who killed him isn't here now."

"I wonder," Heimdall said. "Imagine blades or spikes jumping out of the walls to stab and then retracting. That would leave spots of blood on the walls, and the blood would drip down and make streaks underneath. Which matches what we're seeing."

"What I *don't* see," said Sif, "is any slots or holes for blades to pop out of."

"But if this place is magical, maybe there don't have to be any holes."

Sif grunted. "Let's say you're right. How do we get by?"

"The spots are either waist-high or higher," Heimdall said. "I think that if we crawl, we'll be all right." He dropped to his hands and knees, and his sister did the same.

As they crawled forward, the walls above them made

snapping, cracking noises. Long, pointed protrusions sprang from the stone itself and then back in again. Had Sif and Heimdall tried to walk, the vertical stalagmites would surely have impaled them.

As it was, he tensed at every crack and crunch. He *believed* he'd figured out how to get past the spikes, but what if he was wrong? What if they could stab out just above the floor if they needed to, to kill an intruder? He heaved a sigh of relief when he and his sister left the last of the brown discolorations, and the jabbing of the spikes subsided behind them.

When he judged he and Sif were well clear of the trap, he stood up, and she followed his lead. They stalked on and came to an open doorway.

In the vault on the other side, a mountain of a man with an eye patch, the golden ring of kingship called Draupnir on his forearm, and a white beard lay on a bed that bore an unpleasant resemblance to a bier. The remaining contents of the space, however, attested to Odin's expectation that he would in due course rise from the Odinsleep, refresh himself, and return to his subjects presenting a majestic appearance proper for the King of Asgard. There were handsomely carved chairs sized for a man of his bulk, a freestanding polished silver mirror with combs and brushes laid out on the table beside it, and a haunch of beef, golden apples, and a pitcher of beer on a table elsewhere. Confronted with the spectacle, Heimdall felt a shivering awe in the presence of the King of the Gods.

Sif let out a long breath. "I can't believe it was this easy," she said.

Heimdall made an effort to stop gaping and resume thinking, for, after all, there was work to be done, work better accomplished before the unconscious guard awoke. "Apparently," he said, "the tales of impenetrable defenses grew with time, and stories were all it took to keep intruders out."

"Until us."

"Well, until the enemy – the traitor, perhaps – who sneaked in shortly after the Odinsleep began, and now us." Or so he hoped to discover. If there'd really been such an enemy, there were no signs of that intrusion so far. Heimdall quashed a flicker of doubt and told himself he and Sif hadn't really started searching yet.

They headed for the sleeping god, and, with a jolt of alarm, Heimdall thought he glimpsed a flicker of motion from the corner of his eye. He instantly looked around and was relieved to see there was nothing. The glow of his medallion, swinging slightly at the end of its cord, had merely stirred the shadows.

But, in searching for what was moving, he had perforce returned his gaze to one of the All-Father's ornately carved chairs. The seat looked enticingly comfortable, and he was suddenly aware of just how much the tramp through the castle, down the stairs, and along the subterranean passageway had wearied him. He was breathing hard, and his limbs were leaden.

Why, he thought, not sit for just a moment? He'd search better when he recovered his strength. Eyelids drooping, smothering a yawn, he headed for the chair.

As he did, though, Sif's words came back to him. *I can't believe it was this easy.*

It truly shouldn't have been, nor should his walk have left him exhausted. Any healthy mortal could have made it easily, and an Asgardian warrior was stronger and hardier than any man of Midgard.

Dread welling up inside him, cutting through the strange fatigue that had briefly numbed his thinking, Heimdall stopped in his tracks and gave himself a stinging slap in the face. Weariness and the urge to sit in the chair fell away from him.

With his mind clear, he realized Sif was no longer at this side. When he'd headed for the chair, she'd gone elsewhere. He turned, and she was standing in front of the table laden with food. Smiling, she picked up a shining yellow apple.

More alarmed for her than he had been for himself, Heimdall rushed across the room and struck the fruit from her grasp as she was raising it to her mouth. He shoved her away from the table, upended it, and sent the food and drink crashing to the floor.

Sif glared at him. "What's wrong with you?"

"It's what's wrong with the food!" he said. "Think about it! Even if Odin only expected to sleep for a week, would he want a meal that had been sitting out that long?"

"I…" Sif looked down at the items scattered on the floor. The food was black with rot and crawling with grubs, the beer sizzling and steaming. "It would have poisoned me, wouldn't it?" she asked, a tremor in her voice. "Until you roused me, I was so hungry I couldn't think straight."

"I believe now," Heimdall said, "the obvious trap in the corridor was to make us think we'd gotten through the defenses and were safe. The real traps are here."

Sif took a breath, and when she spoke again, any trace of a quaver was gone. "Was that all of them?"

Heimdall looked around. For a moment, he didn't spot anything else threatening, and then, staring in fear and amazement, he spied his reflection in the silver mirror. Or rather, partly still in the mirror. That other Heimdall was stepping out of the gleaming metal, head bowed to pass through a portal a bit too short for him. Once out, the counterfeit reached over his shoulder for the hilt of the great sword hanging down his back.

Heimdall's warrior impulse was to draw his own sword, but he had a terrible suspicion he wouldn't be able to outfight himself. Glad it took such a long weapon a moment to clear the scabbard, he charged, grabbed his counterpart, and shoved him into one of the suspect chairs.

Metal clanged and clattered as the chair revealed its true form. Chains reared and struck like serpents, snapping the shackles on their ends shut on wrists and ankles. A different chain coiled around the false Heimdall's neck and jerked tight with a spine-breaking *crack*.

"Heimdall!" his sister called.

He whirled to discover Sif dueling herself. As the two blades flashed through the air, cutting and parrying so quickly that only a trained swordsman could follow the exchanges, the warriors in red and white appeared equally fast, equally skilled, equally fond of the same combinations. He froze, knowing he had to act to help his true sister but uncertain of which was which. It was a paralysis resembling ones he'd occasionally experienced in nightmares.

"I'm facing the mirror!" one of the women snarled. "She

has her back to it! So who just stepped out of it?"

Convinced, Heimdall pulled his two-handed sword from its scabbard and edged into striking distance. Over the next few seconds, it became apparent that while the counterfeit was fully a match for the real Sif, Sif and Heimdall together were too much for her. He caught her blade with his own, opening her guard, but then, gazing at what certainly appeared to be his sister, found himself incapable of making the killing stroke. Taking advantage of his hesitation, the counterfeit spun her sword free and poised it for a chest cut. Then, however, the true Sif shouted a battle cry and thrust her blade into her double's torso. The counterfeit collapsed.

Brother and sister looked toward the mirror. Two more Heimdalls and three more Sifs had emerged. Seemingly the supply was endless. Swords in hand, they moved to surround the originals. The true Sif placed herself at her brother's back.

It was a good idea. It would keep either of them from being struck down from behind and ensured that neither would become confused as to which combatant was which.

But, breathing heavily, fear gnawing at him, Heimdall realized it wasn't a good enough idea. An endless stream of attackers, each fighting as well as they did, was bound to overwhelm them, and in all likelihood sooner rather than later.

"Tell your amulet to stop shining!" he said, meanwhile giving that silent command to his own. The lights dangling from the necks of the imitation Heimdalls went out at the same moment.

"What?" said Sif. "We won't be able to see!"

"Trust me!"

The remaining lights went out, and darkness swallowed the vault. Heimdall listened, but no matter how he strained, couldn't hear a ring of foes creeping around his sister and him. He extended his arms and swung the great sword in a horizontal arc. It didn't bump into anything.

"I'm going to move away," he said. "You stay where you are. I think everything's all right now, but stay on guard."

"I didn't need you to tell me that."

Feeling his way with the two-handed sword, he crept toward what he judged to be the location of the mirror. Once, the probing weapon touched one of the enchanted chairs and woke the magic inside. Chains rattled and manacles clashed shut repeatedly, and he recoiled from the sudden clatter, but as he himself wasn't in range, the chair didn't catch him.

A few steps later, the great sword touched a different object, and he used it to trace what was surely the frame of the freestanding mirror. He took hold of the looking glass and laid it on the floor facedown.

With that accomplished, he hoped it was safe to draw light from his medallion once again. He did, and all the counterfeits were gone.

Lowering her broadsword, now cleansed of blood, Sif woke the light that lived in her own amulet. "Explain," she said.

Heimdall smiled. Maybe Sif was right that it had been idiotic to venture here at all, imbecilic to assault the sentry, but even so, there wasn't just relief but a certain satisfaction in figuring out how to neutralize the mirror creatures and save both their lives. "Reflections can't exist in the absence of light."

For a second, Sif stood as though awaiting more. Then she said, "That's it? You couldn't know the magic had that weakness!"

"Well," he said, her reaction leaving him less smug than he'd felt a moment before, "I was listening. As soon as I heard one of the things move or breathe in the dark, I would have known I'd guessed wrong and brought back the light."

"By that time, we could have both been dead."

"But we're not, and now, with its face to the floor, the mirror can't reflect us any more."

Sif sheathed her broadsword. "I suppose not. And thank you. For saving me from the foul feast and for this too." She turned toward Odin. "Anyway, you can look him over now. See if there's anything to see."

"Maybe, maybe not."

Sif scowled in irritation. "What does *that* mean? Why else did we come here?"

"I'm just realizing," Heimdall said, speaking slowly as he thought it through, "this room is full of defenses, but an enemy of the All-Father could still shoot arrows or cast spells through that open doorway. It seems a strange vulnerability unless that isn't really Odin on the bier. Perhaps it's a decoy. Maybe it's even another creature of magic made to look like him, something that will rouse and attack if we disturb it."

"But everyone knows this is where the All-Father comes when it's time for the Odinsleep. There's nowhere else he could be." Sif hesitated. "Unless there's a hidden vault beyond this one."

"We're finally thinking alike."

"I hope not." Sif gave him a smile that took some of the sting out of her reply. "Look for a secret door, and be wary of more traps. If we don't find another chamber, then you can look closely at the Odin in this one."

Heimdall stayed close to Sif as they felt along the walls. That way, if one of them fell into another magical daze, with luck the other would notice immediately. Neither did, however, and in due course, Sif found a concealed catch. She pulled it, and a section of stone wall pivoted.

Beyond the hidden door was another vault where a second Odin, identical to the one behind them, lay sleeping on his own bier. The space was reassuringly bare compared to the one behind them, with no enchanted chairs, food, or mirrors to destroy intruders. There was, however, one long table, on which reposed a triple-pronged spear forged of the magical metal uru, a scepter fashioned of the same material that doubled as a mace when the King of the Gods saw fit to wield it as such, and a long-ship currently no bigger than a man's hand. They were Gungnir, Thrudstok, and Skidbladnir, treasures the All-Father had evidently brought with him for safekeeping while he slept the Sleep of Life.

Sif took a deep breath and let it out slowly. "There he is," she said. "Do what you came to do."

Now that the moment had arrived, a fearful reverence welled up again, and it took an act of will for Heimdall to advance. It was like approaching Frigga in the throne room only worse. This felt like lese-majeste, if not, indeed, outright blasphemy.

I'm doing it for Asgard, he reminded himself. If the All-Father knew what was happening, he'd want me to do it.

He circled the bier looking for runes written on the floor or on the sides of the platform. There were none. Then, his heart thumping, he approached the platform.

As he looked down at the huge figure lying atop the marble bier, he could tell that at least Odin was still alive. The All-Father's barrel chest rose and fell, and the snowy hairs of his mustache stirred minutely as the breath went in and out of his nostrils. But there were still no runes in evidence, sinister fetishes laid upon his breast, or any other indications the King of the Gods had fallen victim to a curse.

Heimdall had heard that warlocks sometimes used incense in their rituals, but, increasingly fearful that this intrusion was indeed a fool's errand, that he'd risked Sif's life and his own for nothing, he sniffed and could catch no trace of any such scent. He listened just in case the enchantment gave off some sort of faint but audible sound, and that didn't work either. He sought to feel some sort of crawling or prickling on his skin, and that too availed him nothing.

He raised his hand, hesitated for a moment, then gripped Odin's shoulder and gave him a shake.

"Heimdall, no!" Sif cried.

He ignored her. "Your Majesty! Odin! Wake up!"

The All-Father slumbered on.

Heimdall gave Sif an apologetic look. "I can't find any sign of evil magic, so I thought, try the obvious. Maybe it's just simple enough to work."

"You mean stupid enough to work," Sif replied. "If you haven't found anything, it's time to leave."

She might well have been right, but having come this far he was loath to give up until he was satisfied he'd done absolutely everything he could. "Just one more moment," he said.

Sif heaved an exasperated sigh. "*One.*"

Heimdall walked to the long table. There were the Spear of Heaven, the mace, and the shrunken long-ship, and nothing else. Still no runes, sigils drawn in blood, or other evidence of hostile magic.

"All right," Sif said, "you had your moment, now come on. I'll drag you out of here if I have to."

Feeling defeated as he had after pleading with Frigga – no, worse, because now it seemed he had no choice but to accept that he truly was a fool who'd involved his sister in his dangerous folly – Heimdall started to turn to follow her out. Then, however, he realized there was something else on the tabletop after all. There was dust, and a clear oval space within it. "Come look at this," he said, his voice vibrant with excitement.

Scowling, Sif strode up to the table. "What?"

Heimdall pointed to the oval. "Something else was here, and now it isn't." He should have realized before, but better late than never.

"Well… all right. So what?"

"What are the magical treasures of Odin?" he asked.

Sif frowned. "I know the spear and the ship…"

"There's also the scepter, which is here, and the cask containing the head of Mimir, which isn't."

"Mimir?"

"Famous for his wisdom," Heimdall said. "By all accounts,

he understood things even Odin didn't. During the war between the Aesir and the Vanir, the All-Father sent him to our people in an exchange of hostages meant to seal a truce. The Vanir grew unhappy with the bargain, however, killed Mimir, and sent his head to Odin. Our king embalmed it, woke it with necromancy, and seeks its counsel still."

Sif shook her head. "I'm still having a hard time with all your conjectures. If someone truly got in here before us, why didn't he just stick a dagger in Odin?"

"I don't know yet," Heimdall said.

"And why wouldn't a thief take all the treasures? Why the head and the head alone?"

"There's a limit to how much one person can easily carry. Perhaps he stole the one item he deemed most precious of all, or the one he knew how to use."

"Well … maybe."

"The point is," Heimdall said, smiling at the vindication of at least one of his ideas, "we now have evidence of an intruder. It's time to tell the queen what we discovered."

"And hope she doesn't cut off our own heads for our pains." Sif smiled back at him. "But even if she does, brother, you acquitted yourself well here tonight."

Six

Heimdall and Sif crawled back under the stabbing stone spikes and then hurried up the stairs. They stopped short, however, when the landing at the top came into view, because the guard Heimdall had knocked unconscious was gone.

"He woke," said Sif. "We should have tied him up."

That gave Heimdall a pang of anxiety, but perhaps it wasn't catastrophic. "Well," he said, "we were going to Frigga anyway. The important thing now is to go immediately so it's clear we're coming of our own volition and not because warriors arrested us and dragged us there."

"Right." Sif opened the door and balked a second time. Heimdall peered past her. The guard he'd struck was sprawled on the floor outside.

"He must have woken," Heimdall said, "stumbled out the door, and passed out again." He simultaneously felt relief that the man had made it no farther and a fresh twinge of guilt for striking down a brother-in-arms.

"We should check him," said Sif. Brother and sister stepped into the hallway, and Sif knelt down. She pressed her fingers to the side of the guard's neck, cupped her hand in front of the man's nostrils and mouth, and then cursed.

Heimdall suddenly felt cold. "What's wrong?"

Her expression full of shock and sorrow, Sif looked up and said, "His heart isn't beating, and he isn't breathing. You killed him."

"No!" Heimdall said, horrified and disbelieving. "I didn't hit him that hard!"

"Apparently you did," Sif said grimly. "Or he had a weak skull. Poor fellow."

Guilt came crashing down on Heimdall. He had the same feeling he'd had in the crypt, that he'd somehow stumbled into a nightmare, only this time it was worse. "I'm a murderer," he said. "I murdered a comrade."

Sif stood up. Heimdall had no doubt she was still aghast at the warrior's death, but, as was her way she'd quickly locked that feeling away to attend to practicalities. Her example reminded him he needed to do the same. "Does this change things?" she asked.

Heimdall took a long, steadying breath, and though guilt and horror didn't fall away, the paralysis they'd engendered did. "No," he said. "The queen still needs to know what we discovered, that Mimir's head is gone and it's at least possible that it was a traitor in the citadel who stole it. I'll accept whatever punishment she exacts for taking the man's life."

Sif frowned. "I don't like hearing you say that, but it's what I'd say in your place. Let's go, then."

The tramp of feet, the creak of leather, and the clink of mail announced the approach of warriors. A moment later, ten men-at-arms rounded a corner farther down the hall. Heimdall supposed they were either on a routine patrol of the citadel or on their way to perform some other duty. Either way, their appearance at this moment was the worst of luck.

The newcomers faltered for an instant when they spied Heimdall and Sif standing over the guard's body. Then they aimed their spears.

"Wait!" Heimdall called. "This isn't what it looks like!"

Their faces either angry or set with grim resolve, the spearmen trotted forward.

Evidently surmising the patrol meant to kill her and Heimdall out of hand – based on their expressions and actions it was an impression he shared – Sif whipped her broadsword from its scabbard and pointed it at the fallen guard's throat. "Stop," she said, "or he dies!"

A narrow-eyed, black-bearded warrior in the lead raised his hand, and the men under his command halted. Looking from a distance, the war leader couldn't tell the guard Sif was threatening was already dead.

"You're in the heart of the citadel," he said. "No matter what you do, you won't escape. I won't let you escape."

"We don't want to escape," Heimdall said.

"No," said the black-bearded warrior, "you want to go where everyone is forbidden to go on pain of death. Be glad we caught you. You'll likely die easier up here than caught in a trap below."

"We've already been below," Heimdall said, "and

discovered something of the utmost importance to the Realm. Come with us and I'll show you." He tried to twist the door handle.

To his surprise and his horror, the door wouldn't open. Sif must have engaged a locking mechanism without noticing it was there.

"I give you my word," Heimdall said. "Sif and I truly did visit the All-Father's vault. The head of Mimir–"

"Liar and traitor," the black-bearded warrior said. He advanced, and his men followed. Evidently, he'd decided the duty to deal with treachery was more important than protecting Sif's supposed hostage.

For a heartbeat, Heimdall considered surrender. With luck, it would bring him before the queen again, albeit in chains, and wasn't that what he wanted?

But would he truly be afforded that opportunity? The faces behind the poised spears suggested otherwise. It still seemed likely the angry warriors meant to strike down his sister and him no matter what they did, and he didn't see how they could even fight back. He didn't want to kill still more Asgardian warriors who were only doing their duty as they understood it, and even if he were willing, he and Sif were heavily outnumbered.

"Run!" he said.

He and his sister bolted in the opposite direction from the patrol. A lance flew between them and clattered on the floor several strides farther along. The long weapons were made for thrusting, not throwing, and perhaps that was the only reason it didn't find its target.

Desperate, his thoughts now focused solely on escape,

Heimdall led his sister up another flight of stairs, then along another passage. It was more crowded, with functionaries and servants scurrying about in the performance of their duties, and the pair had to shove through them and even knock some aside. But the congestion would slow down the spearmen too and likewise keep them from throwing any more of their weapons. Or so he hoped.

Another turn brought an arched doorway and the stairs beyond into view. These steps led down into a courtyard. He and Sif dashed down them and found themselves facing a company of horsemen climbing down from their mounts. By the looks of it, the riders had just come back from a patrol or some other errand. They turned to peer in surprise at the two Vanir rushing into view.

Heimdall picked out a bow-legged warrior with long brown hair. The man's air of authority suggested he was in command no less than the golden badge bearing a stylized image of Sleipnir, Odin's eight-legged steed, gleaming in the torchlight illuminating the courtyard.

Heimdall rushed up to him. "Impostors!" he cried. "Disguised as Asgardian warriors, but they're not! They're right behind my sister and me!"

The cavalry commander frowned. "What?"

"There's no time!" Heimdall said. He was lying, but there was no need to manufacture whatever frantic urgency was manifest in his voice and expression. That was altogether real. "If your men are going to defend themselves, they have to do it now!"

The war leader looked around at his warriors. "Swords out! Shields up! Make a line facing that door!"

Heimdall had caught the cavalry commander by surprise, but the confusion was unlikely to last more than a moment when the two groups of warriors came face to face. He and Sif ran towards the steeds the horsemen had been riding and the grooms who had taken charge of them. Fresh mounts would be preferable, but there was no time to procure them.

He fixed on a gray stallion simply because the groom hadn't yet begun removing its saddle and tack. He jerked the reins from the startled attendant's grasp and swung himself into the saddle. The warhorse, which had no doubt assumed he was all done carrying a rider for a while and had nothing but feed and rest in his immediate future, turned back his ears and stamped a hoof.

"That's–" began the groom.

"I'm in a hurry!" Heimdall said, and that at least was true enough.

"Go!" Sif called. She was astride her own purloined steed, one dappled brown and white.

Brother and sister kicked back with their heels, and unhappy though they were the two warhorses sprang toward the gate in the wall around the courtyard. Still fearful as he was, Heimdall half expected someone to jump in his way and try to stop him, but nobody did. His ruse still had everybody flummoxed. He and Sif thundered through the gate of the citadel, across the clear ring of ground encircling it, and into the city beyond.

They turned down one cobbled side street, then another, following a route that, in his estimation, was *not* the fastest, most direct route for two runaways to take. Once Odin's palace disappeared behind them, and Heimdall felt a *little* relief, he and Sif allowed their reluctant mounts to slow lest a full-out gallop suggest to onlookers that they were fugitives in flight. The slower pace also made it easier to converse.

"They'll chase us soon enough," said Sif.

"I know," Heimdall said. "We aren't on the most obvious escape route, but there is a way out of the city up ahead. We just have to get there."

They rode on through a square with a pale marble centerpiece – a statue of a stalwart Tyr putting his hand in the jaws of the Fenris wolf – then skirted an open-air gathering where, in seeming defiance of the peril hanging over the Realm Eternal, people were dancing or singing along to the music of a bone flute, a goat horn, a lyre, and a skin-headed drum. They then headed down a street of smiths where the air smelled of smoke and burning, forges glowed red, and hammered metal rang as the artisans labored into the night to fill their orders. Low doorways and squat buildings indicated that many of the smiths were dwarves, they or their ancestors having immigrated to Asgard from Nidavellir.

Now that the need for immediate desperate action had come and gone, all that had gone wrong weighed more and more heavily on Heimdall. He'd killed a brother-in-arms and in all likelihood would never even have the chance to tell Frigga of his discovery. He'd allowed Sif to join him in his reckless scheme with the result that she was now a hunted outlaw too.

Sif guided her horse up beside his own. "Do you hear that?" she asked.

Lost to despondency, Heimdall hadn't. Now, he realized, a different metallic clangor was offering a counterpoint to the hammering of the smiths.

"Those are the castle bells," he said. "Someone's ringing the signal to close the city gates." Once again, the need to act and act now drove guilt and regret to the back of his mind.

Sif sent the dappled courser racing forward. Heimdall's steed was less cooperative. He had to kick the gray three times before it resumed a gallop, but then he hurtled after his sister.

Men and dwarves hurried into the street to see if they could determine the reason for the alarm. The stallion tried to balk when confronted by the sudden congestion, and Heimdall kicked it forward once again. "Royal messengers!" he shouted. "Get out of the way!"

People did, either because they believed the lie or simply feared being trampled. The gray pounded onward, veering to one side or the other when necessary to avoid obstacles, but then a dwarf drove a cart drawn by two mules into view from the cross street immediately ahead. The cart was piled high with charcoal to feed the smelters' furnaces.

Sif was already on the other side of the intersection. Heimdall, however, saw no alternative but to stop short if he hoped to avoid a collision. He started to haul back on the reins and then discerned that the gray, though it surely recognized the danger, was still charging forward. On impulse, and desperate with the need for haste, he allowed the horse to continue.

As the people of Asgard were stronger than the mortal folk of Midgard, so too were their horses. Tired and grudging though he was, the gray leaped high into the air and cleared the cart and its load. Cowering in expectation of a crash, the dwarf on the bench shouted an obscenity as Heimdall passed overhead.

Farther along the street, Sif had stopped to wait when she realized the cart had rolled into Heimdall's way. As he caught up to her, and she urged her mount into motion once again, she asked, "How did you know your horse was a jumper?"

"He told me."

"What?"

"I'll explain later. Just keep going!"

Another turn brought one of Asgard's gates into view. It wasn't the main gate, but it was still high, wide, and deep, a tunnel burrowing through the massive stone wall. The valves at the far end were slowly closing, the enormous windlass mechanism that controlled them rumbling.

As he and Sif raced forward, Heimdall bellowed, "Royal messengers! Let us through!"

A woman in a silver-chased helm and mail – the officer in charge of the gate, most likely – replied, "You hear the bells!"

"Our errand is urgent!" Heimdall said.

"Stop and show me your credentials!" she replied.

Heimdall only wished he could, but, of course, there were none. He and Sif hurtled past the woman in the silver armor and into the tunnel.

"Drop the portcullis!" the officer shouted, but it was too late for that. The metal grille banged down when Heimdall and Sif were already past.

Unfortunately, though, the gap between the massive

valves ahead was still narrowing. Heimdall kicked the gray and shouted, "Hyah!" Beside, Sif was shouting something too. The riders cleared the space with barely a dagger-length to spare on either side.

On the other side of the wall were newer and, in most cases, humbler dwellings and the fresh fortifications the engineers were building to at least slow the frost giants if they ever came this far. Beyond those were forests and farmland.

Sif turned to Heimdall. "We should get off the road."

They headed through someone's barley field, and rode onwards for much of the night. The horses started breathing hard, and eventually, the gray stumbled.

"The horses need to rest," Heimdall said, "or we're going to hurt them." Unlike him, whose folly had produced an unmitigated disaster, the steeds deserved better.

Sif pointed to the right. "There's a farm with the barn a bit of a distance from the house. There'll be food and water for the horses. We can all rest and be gone before daybreak."

SEVEN

Heimdall and Sif had unsaddled the horses and put them in vacant stalls where they stood crunching oats the farmer had stored in the barn. Sif was at the barn door they'd left open just a crack, spying across the distance that separated the structure from the farmhouse. "I don't see any lights being lit," she said, "or anybody moving around. I don't think we woke anyone up."

"That's good," Heimdall said, although, in truth, nothing seemed good now that the excitement of desperate flight had worn off. He remembered how, for just a few moments in the vault, he'd felt jubilant when the absence of Mimir's head seemed a vindication of all he'd thought and done. Now that he knew he'd killed the sentry and ruined his sister's life along with his own, the recollection seemed a bitter mockery.

He slumped down on a bench. "I don't understand how things could have gone so wrong."

Dimly illuminated by the trace of moonlight the door

admitted, red armor gray in the gloom, Sif turned her head to give him a sour look. "I have a few thoughts on the subject."

"I'm sorry," he said, knowing even as he spoke that the words were useless and inadequate.

"Ever since I was a child," she said, "all I ever wanted was to be a warrior of Asgard and bring honor to our family."

"I wanted that too."

She snorted. "Did you?"

He had. It was the path his father expected him to walk, and he'd been happy enough to do so. It gave him a chance to serve and to put at least some of his talents to good use.

But there were other abilities he *hadn't* had much opportunity to use. He'd always been a thinker, a questioner, and young warriors weren't supposed to do either. They were supposed to follow orders and fight bravely. If they did, they might one day rise to positions of command, and that would be time enough for thinking.

But Heimdall hadn't been willing to wait, had he? He'd decided he knew better than his superiors, and, as a result, here he was, a disgraced murderer, and Sif a hunted fugitive along with him. He despised himself for that.

"I truly am sorry," he repeated, the words feeling as weak and contemptible as before. "I wish you hadn't come with me."

Something in his contrition or his overall misery seemed to touch Sif, and her angry scowl gave way to a gentler expression. "I'm not *really* sorry I did. You'd be dead now if I hadn't."

"Maybe I deserve to be."

"Stop it! You didn't mean to kill the guard, and you were right. We *did* find something in the vault. Something important."

Her forgiveness made him feel a little better. "I suppose we did."

"Of course we did. I'll take first watch, you sleep, and we'll figure out our next move in the morning."

"I am tired," Heimdall said. But he realized he was also starting to consider the future again. "Still, maybe I'll sleep better if I know we already have a plan."

Sif smiled, perhaps to see him rouse at least to some degree from his despair. "That's fine," she said. "*I'm* not losing sleep at the moment."

"All right," Heimdall said. "Let's look at what we know. We didn't find any *direct* evidence that anyone, a traitor or someone from outside the castle, cast a spell on Odin to prolong the Sleep of Life. But we did discover Mimir's head is missing. That at least proves a trespasser sneaked into the vault."

"Only to you and me," Sif replied. "Everybody else thinks we killed the guard but couldn't get through the door, and they won't go down and look on our say-so because we're murderers and traitors and the All-Father forbade anyone to enter."

"Only I'm a murderer. I hit the guard."

"You have to stop dwelling on that," his sister said. "Any good man would feel the guilt you feel. But in war or even just in training, warriors occasionally kill comrades accidentally. You know it's so. Don't let regret cripple you."

"It won't." He hoped. "I was just thinking that if you're not the killer, you're not as bad in the eyes of the world as I am. Maybe you could go back to Asgard alone, throw yourself on Frigga's mercy, and present our case."

"*They* don't know which of us delivered the fatal blow, and do you truly think it would matter if they did? Trying to enter the chamber where Odin lies sleeping is punishable by death all by itself."

He sighed. "You're right."

"Besides," she said, "I'm not leaving you. There's room for two on that bench, so bring it over here. Standing feels good after all those hours in the saddle, but I'll want to sit eventually."

Heimdall stood, carried the bench to her, and then gazed out at the night. "If neither of us is going back to the city," he said, "what do we do instead?"

"I thought of sneaking back to Vanaheim," his sister replied, "but Odin's writ runs there too, and we can't ask our family to shelter us. That's the first place hunters will look, and we can't let our kin share in our ruin. The disgrace will be bad enough as it is."

"I know," Heimdall said, "and maybe we shouldn't simply run and hide in any case. I hate the way things have turned out, but everything we did, we did because we're loyal Asgardians and want to protect our people from the frost giants. It doesn't matter that no one understands. My feelings haven't changed."

"Nor mine."

"Then maybe we should do what we set out to do."

"But how?" Sif asked. "We can't fight in the army when the army will no longer have us."

"Someone crept into the vault and stole the head of Mimir. It's hard to say who. Someone who knew it was there. Someone who could slip past the sentry without him even realizing anything was amiss and deal with the magical traps afterward. Whoever it was, the head is a source of wisdom. Now the giants fight with a newfound cunning. What does that suggest?"

"They have the head," said Sif.

"So someone needs to take it back. If the Jotuns know how to make it serve their purposes, I'll wager Frigga and the royal mages can too. Even if they can't, retrieving it would deprive the giants of its use."

"And possibly redeem our honor," said Sif. "But if I were the king of the frost giants, I'd have the head in my stronghold for safekeeping. Is there any hope of we two alone stealing it back from there?"

"Why not? Somebody took it from the citadel of Asgard." He smiled. "And if we succeed, think of the renown it will bring you. The queen will make you the leader of your own war band."

Sif scowled. "I don't care about that." Then the scowl gave way to a grudging smile of her own. "All right, I care a little. But I mainly care about saving our people. Anyway, I'll help you, brother. It's a mad scheme, but I don't see any other path forward."

"Thank you."

"That sounded so heartfelt! As if you had any doubt I'd come along. Lie down and try to sleep. You'll need it."

Heimdall shed his two-handed sword, armor, and boots and lay down in the straw in an empty stall. For a time, he saw the guard he'd killed, relived the fateful moment – had he truly struck that hard? – but eventually he drifted into slumber.

EIGHT

The following morning, the barn left behind, Heimdall twisted in the saddle to scan the hillsides and low places, the farmland, pastureland, heath, and woodland. It was all well and good to plan a bold foray into Jotunheim, where who knew what perils awaited, but first he and Sif would need to escape their own outraged people.

The red sun had barely cleared the horizon. Shadows were long, the gloom still thick beneath the spruces, pines, and birches. White dots in the distance, sheep grazed in a meadow to the east, but otherwise, nothing was moving.

"I don't see anyone chasing us yet," he said.

Sif was looking around as well. "I don't either. Asgard does still have a war to fight. Maybe those in charge decided they have more important concerns than running us to ground."

"Maybe, but we shouldn't count on that." Heimdall urged the gray onward. After being afforded water, food, and at least a little sleep, the steed was less balky, and, if not fond of his new rider, at least resigned to him.

The day was a bit farther along when his mount and Sif's crossed a shallow stream, the coursers' hooves splashing up frigid droplets that glinted in the morning light. Despite Sif's advice and his own wishes, Heimdall was thinking again of the man he'd accidentally killed. Would paying the wergild make things right? Well, no, not *right*, plainly, but would coin be sufficient atonement that the fellow's kin wouldn't demand bloody retribution? And was he cowardly and selfish even to consider whether there was anything that might spare him the most severe punishment for what he'd done?

Heimdall told himself that everything to do with the guard was tomorrow's concern. He wrenched his attention back to the here and now. His surroundings still appeared tranquil and devoid of danger, the only change to the scene a tiny speck of a bird floating high in the sky.

He and Sif rode on, and she cursed. Feeling a jolt of alarm, Heimdall turned his head to look where she was looking. A company of riders was cresting a ridge off to the right.

Apparently, Sif had been wrong when she'd conjectured that the forces of Asgard might not look for them too vigorously. The attempted violation of the All-Father's vault, if not the death of the guard, had stirred them to serious effort.

To Heimdall's surprise, the bird swooped toward the riders who followed it, perhaps to resume its accustomed place on the gauntlet of a falconer. Evidently it had been flying high to spot the fugitives and, having done so, had summoned them in the right direction. Heimdall had no idea how anyone could train a hawk to do such a thing, but it seemed someone had, and he felt a flash of anger at himself for not suspecting the threat when he first spied the bird.

But he was glad the riders had stopped to await its return. It gave him and Sif the chance to lengthen their lead. They kicked their horses into a gallop.

As they fled, he glanced backward to see if their pursuers had started down the hillside, and so he saw the bird reach its destination. To his astonishment, it didn't perch on anybody's arm, perchance to be hooded or rewarded with a tidbit. Rather, as it swooped the last few feet to the ground, it became a green-clad woman with blonde hair who took a nimble step to steady herself. Perhaps at Frigga's command, Lady Amora herself had joined the manhunt. Heimdall felt an upwelling of dread to realize that his plight and Sif's were even more desperate than he'd initially imagined.

He kicked the gray once more, exhorting the animal to even greater speed, and for a few seconds, it gave him what he asked of it. Then, however, a crooning, wordless song in a sweet soprano voice sounded from the air. The melody stayed just as clear and loud as his steed and Sif's galloped onward, as if the invisible source was moving right along with them.

Sif's courser turned unexpectedly, and she shouted in surprise. The warhorse started running *toward* the riders on the hilltop. Heimdall's mount began to turn a moment later.

"No!" he shouted, hauling back on the reins. Eyes rolling, tossing his head, the gray struggled to do what the ghostly crooning was presumably telling him to do. As Heimdall strained to control him, the steed started rearing and bucking like a wild horse that had never had a man on its back before, doing his utmost to fling his rider out of the saddle.

Barely keeping his seat, Heimdall looked around. Sif was in the same plight as he was, lurching from side to side and bouncing up and down as her horse sought to cast her off. One crimson-booted foot flew out of the stirrup, and he was sure her courser would throw her, but somehow she remained astride her mount.

"What do we do?" she called to Heimdall.

Deafen the horses? No, not feasible even if it would help and even if he'd had the stomach for it. "Jump off!" he yelled.

He kicked his feet from the stirrups and heaved himself from the saddle. Just as Asgardians were stronger than the folk of Midgard, so too were they more agile, but, even so, the gray's bucking made it difficult to leap off gracefully. He staggered a step and fell to one knee. As he looked up, Sif landed on her feet, seemingly with no more trouble than a cat springing off a chair. The entranced horses galloped toward the hunters riding down the hillside. Amora was now astride a steed someone had presumably led for her to mount when she was ready. Or maybe she'd simply snapped her fingers and it appeared out of thin air. Heimdall had no real idea of her limits and capabilities.

He *did* know that a person could outrun a horse, for a little while at least, or anyway, someone had once told him so. He grimly supposed he and Sif were about to put that bit of supposed knowledge to the test. They fled before their pursuers, farther along the heath with its mottling of white clover and yellow meadow buttercups.

When Heimdall glanced back, to his dismay, the hunters

were closer. They'd reached the bottom of the slope. He felt a fresh surge of desperation at the thought of what it would mean to be caught. Death, either on the spot or after being condemned by a tribunal, for him and his sister both.

He and Sif dashed onward. He was exerting himself to the utmost, heart pounding, sweat periodically stinging his eyes until he swiped it away. He wasn't slowing down yet, and racing along beside him his sister wasn't either, but as they kept fleeing across the open moorland the chase could end in only one way. He cast about and felt a surge of hope upon spying a place where a forest of pine, spruce, and a scattering of other trees met the heath. Reaching it meant running uphill, but still it was a potential haven, the only one within reach.

He turned, Sif followed, and they dashed up the rise. They were still a bowshot away from the tree line when a second group of horsemen appeared on their flank. Amora had either called them with magic or the new hunters had simply showed up at an especially inopportune moment. Their arrival was horrifying, infuriating, just when it had begun to seem plausible that he and his sister might actually get away.

As Heimdall had previously exhorted the gray stallion to press beyond his limits and give him a final burst of speed, he now strained to do the same himself. Javelins rained down around Sif and him, thrown by the oncoming riders.

The fugitives passed among the first trees but weren't safe yet. They needed to penetrate deeper into the forest, where the pine and spruce grew more thickly, where there were thickets and deep shadows, where horsemen would have difficulty following and two people on foot could throw them off their trail. Heimdall glanced to the side and saw that he and Sif weren't going to make it there without another confrontation. Possessed of the fastest horses, each with a sword in hand, three of the hunters were about to catch up to them.

After the sentry's disastrous death, Heimdall dreaded another confrontation with men who by rights should be his comrades-in-arms. Unwilling to draw his sword, he looked around and found a fist-sized chunk of stone at his feet. He threw it and struck one rider in the chest. The warrior's mail clanked, and the impact knocked him from the saddle.

Sif hadn't drawn her blade either. Even so, she stood beneath a gray alder in the poised manner of a foot soldier waiting to receive a rider's attack. Leering at the expectation of an easy kill, the hunter rode in with his blade raised to cut her down.

Sif leaped into the air, caught hold of one of the alder's lower branches, and swung. Her legs straight, she booted the grinning hunter in the face, and he too flew from the saddle. Pounding on by, his mount whinnied in surprise.

The remaining horseman's eyes widened to see his two comrades abruptly lying stunned on the ground, but after a moment's hesitation he kicked his steed toward Heimdall. Heimdall looked for a second stone and, to his dismay, couldn't find one.

Sif dropped to the ground and rushed the remaining rider on his off-hand side. He saw her coming and hacked at her, whereupon she dodged the somewhat awkward cross-body cut and grabbed his wrist before he could lift the blade for another try. She yanked him out of the saddle and kicked him in the head. Heimdall was glad she'd once again neutralized a pursuer without resorting to lethal force, but the two of them weren't out of danger yet.

Brother and sister dashed on into a patch of forest where the tree trunks made a maze, and the morning sun barely pierced the thick mesh of branches overhead. Roots tripped them, and branches swiped and scratched at them. They forced their way into a thicket, and the thorns on the briers snagged their clothing and bloodied their skin.

The important thing, however, was that – much to Heimdall's relief – the cries and curses of the hunters grew faint behind them. When they deemed them faint enough, brother and sister stopped charging along in favor of a stealthy, wary advance, treading lightly and peering in all directions as they made their way. Eventually they came upon a cloudberry bush bearing ripe pink fruit, and Heimdall raised his hand for a halt.

"We could use a chance to catch our breath," he said, keeping his voice low.

"Agreed," said Sif, "and while we're here, we should eat and pick more berries to carry with us. Since we lost what meager provisions we had with our saddlebags."

"At least we still have our lives and our freedom." He picked a cloudberry and bit into the tart fruit.

"Yes," Sif said, "there's that. But are you all right? I don't mean physically. I saw the look on your face when the riders were coming at us. You really didn't want to fight them."

"I wasn't afraid," he said. Not afraid in the way that kept a warrior from fighting, anyway.

"I know," she said. "It wasn't that." She sighed. "Fighting them felt wrong to me too. But we didn't kill them, and they didn't kill us either. Things worked out as well as they could. Now we have to figure out how to keep away from them and continue the mission."

As it had before, her commonsense attitude and focus on practicalities helped him feel somewhat better. "Do you have any thoughts on the subject?"

Sif frowned, considering. "Our situation could be better. Hunters skilled at woodcraft will track us. On foot, they can go wherever we can, and apparently Lady Amora's magic can summon reinforcements to enter the forest from all sides."

"Like a noose drawing tight," he said.

"More or less." Sif paused to eat a cloudberry and wipe juice from her mouth with the back of a red-gloved hand. "I assume that if she takes a mind to, Amora can also turn into a bird again, fly high, and spot us if we do slip through the circle and leave the forest."

"I know you better than to think you're giving up."

Sif snorted. "Of course not. But you fancy yourself the clever sibling. If you are, it's time to finally come up with a *good* idea. Something to see us safely out of the wood and along our merry way to Jotunheim."

As Heimdall picked cloudberries and put them in his belt pouch – still watching out for pursuers – he turned his mind to the problem. Specifically, he sought to remember details of maps he'd seen Captain Ivar consulting of the lands surrounding the city of Asgard. There must be *some* path out of the forest where the hunters wouldn't think to intercept the hunted.

Eventually he hit on something, and some change in his expression must have alerted Sif that he had. "Tell me," she said.

"It's risky," he replied.

"This has all been risky," she said. "We might as well go on as we began."

He supposed she had a point. "All right then. You said the hunters can go wherever we can. But what if we go somewhere they *won't* go? The Realm Below."

The Realm Below was an enormous and labyrinthine network of caverns underlying much of Asgard. Few Aesir or Vanir had ventured far inside and fewer had returned. The caves contained the Domain of the Trolls and were home to their even more ferocious cousins, the wild trolls, creatures famously inimical to all those who dwelled aboveground.

Sif undoubtedly knew as much, but if it fazed her she didn't let on. "I take it you know of a way in somewhere here in the forest."

"Yes," he said. "We simply have to get there."

"How hard will it be to get out again?"

"Hard. I know where there are other exit points scattered across Asgard, but what I don't know are the tunnel routes connecting one to the next. No one has ever mapped them." He pushed his misgivings away. "But we'll have to figure it out once we're inside."

"We will, and at least Amora and her friends won't be able to guess which one we're going to pop out of." Sif squared her shoulders and drew her broadsword a finger-length before sliding it back, making sure it was loose in the scabbard. "Lead on."

They skulked in what Heimdall reckoned to be the proper direction. At one point, they heard voices and crouched motionless in a stand of pines. Heimdall's heart pounded with anxiety until the hunters passed by.

The outcome might well have been different if the searchers had hounds to sniff them out, and he assumed someone would fetch packs of bear dogs soon enough. He and Sif had better be belowground before the animals arrived.

They crept on, and after what seemed too long and nerve-wracking a time, Sif touched his arm and pointed. "*That* looks like the way in to someplace no one with sense would want to go."

Just barely visible through the ranks of trees that still stood between them and it, the cave mouth yawning in a rise in the ground did indeed have a forbidding aspect. Even in daylight, or the dusk-like gloom that passed for it here in the deep forest, it looked as ominous as the entry to a haunted barrow where wights and draugr held sway. Some creature had heaped human skulls on the ground outside, perhaps to warn that intruders would be slaughtered.

Still, forbidding as the cave entrance appeared, what Heimdall primarily felt was relief, relief that he'd found the way this far before the Asgardian pursuers found Sif and him. Surviving the caves of the Realm Below was the *next* problem. He and his sister would address it when the current one was through. They pushed forward, but Amora's sweet soprano singing sounded once again.

"Curse it, not now!" Sif snarled. She drew her blade and quickened her pace. Heimdall did the same while grimly wondering what creatures the melody was intended to control. There were no horses in view, no animals of any type big enough to pose a threat to anyone, let alone an armed warrior.

The trees in the fugitives' immediate vicinity lashed their branches like whips. Limbs snapped loose and showered down. Some were big and heavy enough to strike Heimdall and Sif with bruising force. Others, large and small, littered the approach to the cave mouth to make the footing treacherous.

Amora's song became more strident. Its substance creaking and groaning, a birch swatted one of its branches at Heimdall. Aghast but determined to defend himself, he sidestepped and hacked the limb off short, but that didn't deter the birch. It struck with other limbs, and he evaded and cut at those as well. When the tree gave him an opening, he stepped in and swung the great sword at its trunk with the full measure of his Asgardian strength.

The heavy blade pierced the bark and drove deep into heartwood, but, to his dismay, even that didn't stop or even slow the birch. Another branch struck at his head, and he jerked the sword free and dodged just in time to slip the blow.

Fighting a birch of her own, Sif was faring no better, her broadsword an even less adequate weapon than his own two-handed sword. Even dwarf-forged blades were made for cutting flesh, not hewing wood, and where did a tree keep its vital organs anyway?

Meanwhile, the creaking and groaning of tortured wood came from all around, and the smell of disturbed soil mingled with that of forest verdure, as other trees uprooted themselves. Swaying, their gnarled roots alternately reaching, clutching, and releasing the ground to drag themselves along, some converged on the embattled Heimdall and Sif. Others crept with the evident intention of combining into an impenetrable wall in front of the cave mouth.

Brother and sister tried to escape before it became inaccessible, but trees bunched together and bashed with their branches to bar the way. Attacks came from all directions now, and the two warriors turned and hacked to keep from being pummeled. A pair of limbs belonging to two different trees caught Heimdall by the forearms – immobilizing the two-handed sword – lifted him, and started to pull in opposite directions. Enraged, terrified, he bellowed a war cry, jerked his arms down, and broke free before the branches could tear him apart.

But, he wondered grimly, in the long run, would it matter? The blows he and Sif were striking weren't stopping the trees, and even if they figured out how to kill one, there was no reason to doubt Amora's song could wake as many as required.

It occurred to him, however, that maybe she needed to be close to direct the attack. After all, the cursed trees didn't even have eyes. And maybe if he silenced her song, they'd stop moving.

Still turning, dodging, and chopping branches off short, he looked for a blonde figure in green peering out from the more distant and still rooted and slumbering trees. There was no one. Dividing his attention simply resulted in a savage blow across the back. If not for his mail and

Asgardian hardiness, it likely would have broken his spine. As it was, it stunned him and knocked him to his knees. Sif stood over him, slashing, defending them both until he took a deep breath and drew himself to his feet.

As he desperately resumed swinging the great sword, it occurred to him that Amora didn't have to be present in human form, if she was indeed present at all. Chopping apart a gnarled tree limb that was reaching for Sif's head from behind, he looked for a bird perched on a branch above. He didn't find one of those, either.

Sif cried out. Alarmed, he spun around. Her winged helmet was gone, she had a bloody scrape on her brow, and her black hair was swinging loose and free. "I'm fine!" she gasped, making another sword cut.

If Amora could turn into a bird, could she change into other animals too? Heimdall looked for one, whilst a tree limb that divided into several smaller ones like fingers on a hand grabbed his knee and yanked his leg out from underneath him. He slammed to the ground, and the tree dragged him toward other branches poised to hammer down.

He frantically heaved himself into a sitting position, swung the great sword, and cleaved the branch that had hold of his leg. At the same instant, now that his sight line was lower, he spied a fox peering from the shadow under a pine. It looked just like a normal fox, but wouldn't any natural animal run away from the unnatural commotion close at hand?

He scrambled up and looked for a path to the fox. The animated trees weren't quite as thick in that direction. Thinking she would go undetected, Amora – if it was Amora

– had apparently been more concerned with blocking the way into the caverns.

"Follow!" Heimdall shouted. Winding his way through the obstacles, no longer hacking with the great sword, depending on his armor and agility to keep him alive, he charged the fox. Branches battered him and knocked him staggering.

After a moment, he realized his sister wasn't with him, hadn't succeeded in breaking free of the innermost circle of trees. Fighting alone, she was in even greater danger, and his every instinct cried out for him to turn around and help her. Still, he resisted the impulse. Rushing the fox was the only real hope for either of them.

He brushed past a tree trunk, and one of its roots writhed across the ground and tripped him. As he stumbled, he suffered another hard blow across the back. He stayed on his feet, though, and then the last of the attacking trees were behind him, and the fox was only a few more strides away.

With a sweep of its bushy tail, the animal whirled, bounded away, and disappeared into the forest. At the same instant, the singing stopped.

Deprived of the sorceress's magic, the uprooted trees stopped attacking and toppled, crashing into one another and then to the ground. Some ended up leaning against trees the spell hadn't animated, the branches of the two tangled together.

Sif had been fighting in the very middle of the falling trees, and, with them on the ground Heimdall couldn't see any trace of her. Terrified that one had crushed her beneath its bulk, he called her name.

For an awful moment, nothing happened. Then she climbed and squirmed through the branches of a fallen birch.

"Why didn't you answer?" he asked, nearly as annoyed as he was relieved.

"I had to catch my breath and find my helm," she said. "I'm standing in front of you now, aren't I? That's your answer."

Heimdall smiled a grudging smile. "I suppose."

"Don't think I'm complaining, but what did you do to stop the trees?"

He told her about the fox.

Sif said, "You're lucky Amora didn't turn you to stone or something."

Heimdall felt a reflexive pang of dismay even though the danger was, for the moment, past. "Maybe she could have. Frantic as I was, I didn't even think of that at the time, and perhaps, with me charging to cut her to pieces, she didn't either."

"Mages are all alike," Sif said. "No stomach for close combat."

"Odin and Frigga are mages. Among other things."

"Don't nitpick."

Heimdall grinned. "Sorry. We should get belowground beyond the hunters' reach before something else happens."

The jumble of fallen trees was especially dense in front of the cave mouth, but not *quite* impassable. Brother and sister clambered through it and eventually dropped to the other side, where the opening yawned before them. They kindled the glow from the medallions dangling over their mail and crept inside.

NINE

Heimdall ate the last bite of his remaining cloudberry and then sucked tart juice from his fingers.

He didn't know precisely how long he and Sif had been in the Realm Below. There was no way to know when there was no day or night, only endless darkness. But, thus far, thirst hadn't proved to be a problem. Periodically the two of them happened upon pools and rivulets whose cold water might taste of iron or sulfur but seemed safe enough to drink. Even if they stopped finding those, there should still be places where dampness oozed from the cavern walls or dripped from the ceiling, the *plop-plop-plop* echoing away down the tunnels.

Hunger, however, could prove to be another matter – one that preyed increasingly on his mind – if they didn't find their way back to the surface soon. He doubted they could eat the mosses and lichens they saw. He'd sooner try his luck with the mushrooms they'd once or twice discovered, but that would indeed be a gamble. He'd heard that many of the varieties that grew in the Realm Below were poisonous, and as he had no firsthand knowledge of them, only experiment would reveal whether a particular type would nourish them or kill them.

Trying not to worry about it, for there was, after all, nothing to be done about it at this moment, he shifted in a vain attempt to become more comfortable. He was stiff and sore from the bruising the trees had given him, and sitting on hard stone in the little natural alcove where he and Sif had stopped to rest wasn't making things any better.

The light of his medallion faded to nothing, like a candle flame guttering out. His sister's light was still shining, but even so, the ambient gloom thickened in a way that made him think of a cat gathering itself to pounce, and with one source of illumination extinguished, new shadows sprang into being.

Alarmed at the prospect of losing the ability to light his way through the blackness, he touched the amulet and willed it to light up again. Nothing happened. He gripped it, squeezed, and thought the silent command more insistently. This time, much to his relief, a silvery glow leaked between his fingers.

"Well," said Sif, "we did buy the medallions cheap from a marketplace conjurer."

"True," Heimdall replied, deciding not to add that if both amulets failed, they were unlikely ever to find their way back aboveground. He was fairly certain the demoralizing thought had already occurred to her, and if not, he saw no reason to make her see their prospects as even bleaker than they might seem already. She deserved a better comrade than that.

After a few more moments, Sif said, “Do you remember when we were children, and a group of us would go camping in the woods?”

“I do,” Heimdall said.

“I loved moving away from the campfire into the trees and the night,” she continued. “It was thrilling. I loved sneaking around playing Seize the Banner or just creeping up behind someone and shouting ‘Boo!’”

“I remember,” he said, smiling at the recollection. “You caught me a time or two.”

“Well, just so you know, I think I may be losing my fondness for the dark.”

He chuckled. Whether it was genuine or a façade, he greatly appreciated her continued display of good humor. It helped him to keep up his own spirits. “I can imagine losing one’s appreciation of trees, too, and the marvels of witchcraft, for that matter.”

Her tone and expression turned serious. “Do you have *any* idea where we are?”

“Not much of one,” he admitted. “Unless they’ve expanded their territory, I don’t think we can be anywhere near the caves of the regular trolls. This is wild troll territory.”

“Is there really a difference?”

“As I understand it, the regular trolls have more laws, organization, and knowledge. The wild trolls are more savage and primitive.”

Sif smiled. “You almost make the regular trolls sound civilized.”

“Well,” he said, “it’s all relative, isn’t it?”

“Not according to our childhood tutors.”

"Who were wise, but perhaps didn't know everything. I don't think any of them had traveled to all the Nine Worlds and observed firsthand how people live."

Sif shrugged. "Maybe not. In any case, it hardly matters at the moment. We need to decide what we're doing next."

He grunted. "You're right, considering that we're lost." He ran his fingers through his hair as he tried to come up with an idea. After several moments, something occurred to him. "You know who does know the way out of here? Trolls. Every cave mouth on the map I studied was indicated because someone spotted trolls venturing out onto the surface or going back in."

Sif frowned. "When we first came down here, we took care to avoid that wild troll village or outpost or whatever it was." Shortly after entering the Realm Below, they'd heard some of the creatures speaking to one another farther down the tunnel, and they'd hurried down a branching passage before the trolls noticed them in turn.

"Because we wanted to pass by without a fight. But we've been thinking we should stay well clear of all trolls since, and maybe that isn't the right course of action. Perhaps it will only take us down tunnels that don't connect to the surface to wander lost until we starve to death."

"Whereas," said Sif, picking up on his train of thought, "if we find a troll village or guard post, we may also find a way up nearby. Failing that, if we spot a troll on his own, we can capture him and force him to tell us the closest way out."

"That's what I'm thinking." He felt encouraged that she seemed to be embracing the idea.

"There's only one problem." Sif touched her glowing

medallion. "How are we going to sneak past or sneak up on trolls when we need these to see?"

The comment brought Heimdall up short, because his sister clearly had identified a weakness in the plan. But it was still the only plan that came to mind. "You're right," he said, "that *is* a problem, and if one of us comes up with a better idea, obviously, we'll use that one. But if neither of us does, maybe we can figure something out."

Sif nodded. "Agreed. If need be, we'll think of something. Shall we go looking for trolls immediately, or should we sleep first?"

Heimdall considered. Once again, the disquieting realization came home to him that he didn't know if it was day or night in the world above. He was gradually losing *any* sense of how long he and Sif had been in the caves. There was a mad tiny voice in the depths of his mind whispering that it might have been weeks and weeks already, that perhaps the disaster they were struggling to avert had already overtaken Asgard.

Maybe the voice was the reason that, though he was tired, he was also too restless to sleep just yet. "Let's move on," he said.

TEN

Every ten paces, Heimdall stopped moving to listen. The glances Sif gave him conveyed her growing impatience with the frequent pauses even though he knew she understood the reason. With their amulets glowing, they had no hope of seeing wild trolls before the creatures spotted them. They might, however, hear them approaching while remaining unheard themselves.

Eventually soft sounds did come echoing down the passage from up ahead. The pad of footfalls on rock. The creak of leather. A few growled words and a grunt in a brief exchange of conversation.

"Back!" Heimdall said, relieved to have finally found trolls and simultaneously keenly aware of the danger the creatures posed. He and Sif mustn't allow them to round the bend in time to see their lights.

The two Asgardians turned and hurried back to a space where the way widened out into a cave full of stalagmites, stalactites, and pillars formed by the fusion of the two.

He crouched behind a waist-high lump of stalagmite, and she, broadsword in hand, took cover behind one of the thicker columns. They then extinguished the glow of their medallions.

After that, there was nothing to do but wait in the impenetrable dark, which he did with his nerves taut with anxiety and the pulse ticking quickly in his neck. Gradually the sounds of the approaching trolls grew louder, and the stink of unwashed bodies supplanted that of stone, until he could tell the creatures were padding down the path that wound through the center of the cave.

Unless, of course, they weren't. *They* could see in the absence of light, and what if brother and sister hadn't hidden as well as they'd intended? Heimdall's anxiety-fueled imagination conjured a grinning war leader commanding his followers with hand signals. What if he was really hearing wild troll warriors creeping up on him and Sif? He wished he'd already drawn his great sword and, aware that it was too late, that at this point any movement might betray him, fought the impulse to do so now.

It was only when the sounds receded that he was certain the trolls hadn't spotted him or Sif. He realized he was holding his breath and let it out slowly. He counted to a hundred in his head to give the trolls ample time to round the next curve in the section of tunnel he and Sif had recently negotiated. He then willed his amulet to resume shedding light. As before, it took repetition and forceful squeezing.

Sif lit her own pendant. "What's next?" she asked. "Do we go where they've been or follow to where the trolls are headed?"

He considered the question. "If we follow," he said at length, "there's less chance of losing the trail, and they're likely to lead us to some sort of village or stronghold eventually."

Sif nodded. "That makes sense. Let's go."

Following the trolls was a nerve-wracking business of constantly guessing how much of a lead the creatures had and how much they ought to have. Heimdall and Sif didn't want to lose the trolls, but they likewise needed to keep at least one bend in the passageway between the underground dwellers and themselves lest the trolls see the light of the amulets.

At one point the single tunnel branched into three, and the wild trolls had for the moment fallen silent. Denied sound to guide them, the two Asgardians scrutinized their surroundings, and Heimdall felt a pang of dismay when he could see nothing to guide them down the proper path. After a few seconds, though, Sif pointed to a scraped bit of lichen on the wall in a passage entrance that a troll might have rubbed brushing by. She and Heimdall took a chance on that passage, and when the sounds resumed – a troll grumbling about an aching tooth – they knew they'd chosen correctly.

A cool breeze wafted down the tunnel. The moving air suggested a change in conditions up ahead, a far more open space, conceivably, and Heimdall felt an upwelling of hope. Perhaps he and Sif had finally had a piece of luck, and the wild trolls ahead were leading the two of them back aboveground.

The tunnel slanted upward. Surely that was a good sign.

He glimpsed the faintest hint of reddish light up ahead and told himself that was a good sign too. He didn't know what was causing it, but any light seemed more likely to originate in the surface world than in the eternally dark maze of passageways that was the Realm Below.

When he and Sif came to the top of the slope, however, he saw how wrong he was, and, for a moment, his spirits fell.

The tunnel came out in the side of one of the walls of a huge subterranean vault. The continuation was a trail that switchbacked down to a length of stone spanning a gulf of prodigious depth. On the other side of the bridge were tiers and tangles of chambers that, by the looks of them, made up a sizable wild troll habitation. Scattered lights shined there in various shades of red, some wavering like firelight, others steady.

Sif extinguished the glow of her amulet and snatched for Heimdall's to kill that light as well. He realized her caution was well taken. The wild trolls they were following were still negotiating the switchbacks. They could have noticed the white light overhead. For that matter, trolls on the far side of the bridge might have done the same. Tense, he held his breath until the lack of any answering commotion indicated that none of them had.

With the magic of the medallions quiescent, he could still make out the points of red light, and they sufficed to vaguely delineate or at least imply the lumpy hodgepodge of shapes that was the wild troll habitation. But the trail down to the bridge and the span itself had vanished completely in the dark.

"Apparently," Sif whispered, "trolls like light some of the time."

As it had before, her matter-of-fact calmness helped to quiet his nerves. He and Sif had wanted the trolls to lead them to one of their habitations, albeit ideally not one this big, and not one where the only past it was right on through. Yet, the creatures had. Now the Asgardians had to determine how to follow through on their plan.

"If they want their food cooked," Heimdall said absently, replying to his sister's remark while starting to turn the real problem of infiltration over in his thoughts, "they need fire, and maybe light reveals details and colors they can't see otherwise."

"My point," she said, in a tone that suggested he was a dunce for not having grasped it already, "is that there may be enough light over there for us to sneak through without shining our amulets."

He smiled. "That's an excellent thought. But first we have to get down the wall and across the bridge and do that without the use of our talismans as well."

Sif made a dismissive spitting sound. "Easy enough for warriors of the Vanir."

They gave the trolls they'd been following ample time to cross the span and proceed deeper into the warren of stone. They then groped their way down the switchbacks. Keenly aware of the possibility of a fall into the depths, Heimdall kept one hand on the wall, stayed well away from the outer edge of the trail, and hoped Sif was doing likewise.

On the ledge at the bottom, he drew his two-handed sword and used it to find the edge without stepping over it. He then felt along and found the protrusion that was presumably the start of the bridge. "It's here," he said.

"Good." It was both reassuring and vaguely unsettling to have Sif speaking right beside him when he couldn't see her at all. "Let's cross."

They went single file. He wanted to be in the absolute center of the bridge, and perhaps Sif felt the same. The span wasn't all that narrow, and he had only to walk a straight line to traverse it safely, but he nonetheless used the great sword to probe for solid footing as he headed across. He touched as lightly as possible to avoid a tapping some troll might hear.

Above his head, something fluttered. "Listen!" he whispered.

"I don't hear anything," Sif replied.

Neither did he, now.

"We should keep moving," his sister said.

Maybe, but Heimdall was still tense with the suspicion that *something* was about to happen. Maybe it was because he'd watched animals in flight, and they didn't beat their wings constantly.

He stood still, listened, and caught a second soft *flap* on his flank. It was lower, as if the creature – assuming there was only one – had circled and was now swooping at them in the middle of the bridge. His imagination suggested a bat-like horror with talons poised and fangs bared to catch and rend its prey.

He swung his sword at the instant when instinct prompted him, and the blade caught some part of his attacker's flesh and tore loose. Something thumped down behind him, and he caught a musky animal smell.

Leather creaked and mail clinked. The sounds suggested Sif had somehow found where the wounded creature had dropped and was likely slashing at it with her broadsword.

Then came a scrabbling, fumbling noise that might be the beast tumbling off the edge of the bridge. A split second later, Sif said, "Falling!" Even now, she kept her voice low, but the urgency was unmistakable.

Desperate with the need to help her, Heimdall dropped the great sword, stretched out his arms and touched her back. He found her shoulders and hauled her backward.

"Thanks," she whispered. "I chased the bat a step too far. I was tottering right on the brink."

"'Easy enough for two warriors of the Vanir?'" he asked.

"We killed it, didn't we?" she replied. "The question is, did the trolls notice us doing so?"

He listened. If trolls were coming, he couldn't hear any sign of it.

"I think we're all right," he said. "The fight was pretty quiet."

"In that case," she said, "keep moving. We're exposed out here on the bridge."

"Just a moment." He squatted, groped, and found the two-handed sword. "Now I'm ready."

At the far end of the bridge there was enough red light that he could at least make out his sister as a shadow in the gloom and discern the start of several pathways leading into the chaotic pile of habitations that was the wild troll settlement. Sif pointed to a trail that climbed up and around to the right. It might, if they were lucky, skirt the perimeter of the village and minimize the chances of detection. He nodded his agreement, and they stalked up the incline. Recognizing the absolute need to go unnoticed, he was intent on moving stealthily, but even so, the curiosity that was so much a part of him made him take in incidental aspects of his surroundings.

He soon decided wild trolls must not care about privacy. Some of the dwellings he and Sif were creeping past appeared to be natural chambers in the rock. Others bore the marks of the tools used to hollow them out. In no case, however, had anyone attempted to cover the openings and shield the spaces and their meager contents from the view of passersby.

Heimdall supposed that was fortunate as it allowed the red light to escape. As he'd surmised, some of the illumination came from fires burning fungus and oils that tinged the air with malodorous eye-stinging smoke. The steadier glow came from chunks of luminous scarlet crystal, a very few of which also had also been set along the twisting, rising and falling paths to serve as streetlamps.

He noticed these details in passing, the bulk of his attention focused on finding the quickest way through the settlement and a path back to the surface and on spotting any wild trolls before they spotted Sif or him. Despite the size of the enclave, for a while he didn't see a single inhabitant. He was glad, but at the same time it seemed strange enough to worry him. If he hadn't known for a fact that a patrol had just marched into the place, he might have thought the trolls had abandoned it, possibly fleeing to escape a curse or plague.

Eventually, though, he and Sif came to a bit of the high path that afforded a clear view down into an open space at the center of the habitation. The biggest piece of luminous crystal he'd seen yet was glowing there, and it revealed scores of wild trolls gathered together.

"They're deliberating about something," murmured Sif. "Lucky for us. Come on. Keep moving." It was no doubt sensible advice, but then Heimdall spotted something that commanded his attention.

"Wait." He pointed. "Look at the one standing in the center of the circle talking to the others. Does *he* look like a wild troll?"

On average, trolls were a bit taller than an Asgardian, although some were bigger than that, while others stood no higher than dwarves. All of them, however, were stocky and gnarled, with thick hair, like fur covering their bodies. The bearded warrior addressing them, though, gesticulating with a great axe for emphasis, more nearly resembled a man of Midgard or a god. His bare limbs weren't hairy, and though the ruddy light made colors uncertain, he didn't appear to be orange like a troll either.

"Is he *blue*?" asked Sif, squinting.

"I think so," Heimdall said. "Making him a frost giant."

"A small one," she said.

"They can be born small and take time to grow huge. What's important is that he's talking to the trolls. Trying to persuade the tribe to ally with Jotunheim would be my guess." If the emissary succeeded, Asgard's military situation would be even more precarious, and Heimdall felt a mix of anger and concern.

Sif frowned. "I never heard of frost giants doing any such thing before."

"We can probably blame the head of Mimir for this too."

"At least the envoy doesn't seem to be getting very far."

Heimdall realized she was right. When the frost giant finished speaking, a troll stepped forth and replied. Distance kept the Asgardian warrior from making out what anyone was saying, but he could tell when the ring of onlookers exploded into laughter, and the emissary scowled. The knot of anger and worry in Heimdall's chest loosened to a degree.

Perhaps, he thought, the lack of progress was only to be expected. Frost giants and trolls alike tended to be arrogant and hostile to other races, and neither quality seemed conducive to diplomacy.

Having gleaned what there was to be gleaned, and knowing they invited discovery every moment they lingered, Heimdall and Sif prowled onward. Near the uppermost reaches of the settlement, they happened upon a cave-like dwelling that wasn't empty. A wild troll slumped on a flattish rock that was evidently deemed comfortable enough to serve as a chair. His expression glum, he seemed too lost in brooding thought to notice the man and woman peeking in the doorway.

Heimdall and Sif exchanged glances, discerned they were of the same mind, and rushed the troll. The creature sprang up and whirled toward the crude war hammer – a flint head lashed to a bone handle – leaning against the wall, but the Asgardians had their blades poised to cut him down before he could pick up his weapon.

"Easy!" said Sif. "You can live through this, but not if you fight us or cry out. Only if you give us what we want."

"I will," the wild troll said. Trembling a little, he eased his hand away from the hammer.

"Why didn't you go to hear the frost giant?" Heimdall asked.

The troll grimaced. "I made fun of Korzar when I thought he couldn't hear. Korzar is big."

Heimdall held back a smile. "Understood. My sister and I don't want to harm you or any of your people, but we need to get back aboveground."

"I can tell you the way. Please, just don't kill me."

"Yes, tell us," Heimdall said. "You're also going to map the route and the tunnels that run off from it. Pick up that rock on the floor, slowly, and scratch the lines on the wall."

The troll did as ordered.

"One more thing," said Sif. "Tell us about the guards stationed near the cave mouth, and *don't* try to tell us there aren't any."

The captive sighed. "There are a couple. Maybe. Not more. The tribe hasn't raided Asgard in a long time, so no one's expecting trouble."

"Certainly not coming up from below," Heimdall said. "But there's one thing I don't understand about your map."

The troll turned back toward the sketch on the wall. Heimdall raised the great sword to clout him in the back of the head and then hesitated to strike the unarmed creature from behind. Memories of trying to knock the warrior standing guard at Odin's vault unconscious and then learning he'd killed the fellow instead came surging back.

But he and Sif couldn't afford to dawdle, they couldn't leave their captive conscious to raise the alarm after they departed, and surely you could depend on a wild troll to have a thick skull. He struck with the flat of the blade, and the troll grunted, jerked, and spilled to the floor.

"Do you think he told us the truth?" Sif asked.

"I hope so," Heimdall said. "He was plainly afraid for his life, and I think that meant he was too afraid to lie. Anyway, I don't think we have much choice but to trust him."

Sif nodded. "There is that. I have an idea about how we can get within sword range of the sentries without taking an arrow or javelin in the guts."

Brother and sister headed up the trail, in due course passing a couple branching passages that seemed to be where their grudging informant had indicated they would be. Once the last trace of red light disappeared behind them, they woke the glow of their amulets. Doing so gave Heimdall a pang of apprehension, but they had no choice if they were to advance with any speed at all.

Eventually they came to a place with a pile of rocks near either wall. According to the wild troll Heimdall and Sif had questioned, these were blinds, and there were likely sentries behind each, alerted by the approaching light of the medallions and ready to attack the bearers as they passed between the mounds.

They might be ready, but since they didn't come pouring out and attack instantly, they were perhaps not certain of the need to. Not if the glow was dazzling them a little. Not if they knew about the frost giant envoy visiting their settlement, who surely needed a light source of his own.

"Good news!" called Sif to the hidden sentries, pitching her voice as deep as she could. "Your people and mine have sealed an alliance. Together we'll grind Asgard into dust for good and all."

Four wild trolls emerged, two from behind each blind, to make a line across the tunnel. Heimdall and Sif kept advancing as though it didn't even occur to them that the sentries might try to deny them passage.

A troll carrying a flail-like weapon made of vertebrae strung together with a lizard-like skull at the end raised one hand to shade his eyes. "Hey!" he growled. "You're not giants!"

Now that the troll recognized Heimdall and Sif for what they were, the time for subterfuge had passed. They charged.

Though their ruse had allowed them to close much of the intervening distance before the fighting started, two of the trolls managed to throw javelins. Sif twisted aside and avoided one of the missiles. Anxiety fell away, displaced by a flash of anger that these creatures were trying to block their path when he and his sister were on the verge of making their escape, Heimdall deflected the other javelin with his great sword.

Another stride brought him into striking distance. The vertebrae clattering, the wild troll with the flail swung his weapon at Heimdall's head. The Asgardian ducked, and the lizard skull flew harmlessly by above him. He cut to the knee, and, howling, the troll fell with a maimed leg, the splash of blood momentarily filling the air with a coppery scent. Heimdall didn't bother following up with a killing stroke. Wild trolls weren't the enemy, not like frost giants were, and there was no need.

Instead, he cast about. Sif had already accounted for

the other three sentries and headed farther up the tunnel, where she was fighting her way through still more trolls that had emerged from somewhere close at hand. The creature the two Asgardians had questioned had apparently underestimated the number of his fellows his captors would encounter here. Maybe the chieftain of the tribe had added more sentries just in case the wild trolls did ally with the frost giants and launch a new war against Asgard.

Fortunately, there were only a few more trolls, and, pivoting to face one foe and then another, Sif was holding her own in a superb display of swordsmanship that made her brother proud, steadily dropping slain or wounded creatures in a ring around her. Heimdall was confident that once he advanced to fight beside her, they'd swiftly win through the final barrier separating them from the world aboveground.

Then, to his dismay, the light of his amulet went out. Sif's medallion was still shining, but with her farther up the passage, turning constantly, and trolls shifting around between her and him, the fight she was fighting became murky confusion, the tunnel itself dark and indistinct. At certain moments, there was scarcely any light reaching him at all.

Heimdall shook off the shock the failure of his talisman had engendered and tried to draw light from it. It still refused to glow. But even so, he told himself, he could catch up to Sif. She was only a few strides away. He started toward her.

A stray troll rushed him with a war club. They traded attacks, neither scoring, and at the end of the first exchange, he took a retreat. His back foot came down on empty air. He'd missed seeing some sort of low place in the floor.

He *might* have managed to heave his weight forward and escape a fall except that at the same instant the troll swung the war club. He reflexively shifted away from the arc of the blow, the sweep of the weapon fanning his face, and the action ended any hope of regaining his balance. He'd roll when he landed on the floor to avoid further bludgeoning blows until he could scramble back onto his feet.

Except that he didn't come down on the floor. As he realized he'd blundered into an actual pit or crevasse, he banged his head on the rim, and, stunned, plunged into *absolute* darkness.

Eleven

When Heimdall woke and opened his eyes, the world was utterly black and utterly silent. If not for the sore spot on the back of his head and the aches elsewhere in his body, he might have imagined himself a ghost condemned to a particularly hellish part of Niffleheim.

Even as it was, the absence of his two primary senses, and the disorientation that came with it, brought a jolt of terror verging on outright panic. Then he remembered falling into the hole, and that limited understanding of what had happened steadied him, at least a little.

Breathing slowly and deeply, striving to control his respiration and so further subdue his fear, he sat up and rubbed the sore spot on the back of his head, registering as he did that his helm was gone. He sought for a better comprehension of his current circumstances and what, if anything, he could do about them.

After some thought, he decided he must have plunged down a sort of chute. A long straight drop might well have killed or crippled him, and though he ached and one impact or another had knocked him unconscious, he didn't seem to have broken bones or to be otherwise incapacitated.

What else could he glean even though he couldn't see? The cut in the back of his head had scabbed over, more blood clotting to crust and mat his hair, indicating that he'd lain here for some time. The silence was grounds for hope that at least no trolls were advancing on him to finish him off.

Reassured that he wouldn't draw an immediate attack, he tried once more to evoke light from his amulet. As he expected, though, the talisman denied him even a glimmer. Disgusted, deciding it truly was useless, he yanked it off and tossed it away.

Having reconstructed what had happened to him and assessed his current condition, perhaps the next step was to search for his missing gear. Rolling onto his hands and knees, he felt around the floor of the space he'd fallen into. He heaved a sigh of relief when he eventually found his great sword. Dire as his situation was, at least he was no longer unarmed.

There was no sign of his helm, though. Either it had hung up somewhere in the hypothetical chute or he was simply missing it.

He supposed he should next learn what he could about his surroundings. With the two-handed sword recovered, he felt confident enough to stand and walk. He could use the weapon to grope his way along as he had on the bridge and so avoid falling down yet another hole. He could feel out other aspects of the lightless space in which he found himself as well.

It took a while, but ultimately he determined he was in a tunnel and not some broader space, but for all his probing of the upper walls and ceiling, he couldn't find the hole he'd presumably fallen out of. Otherwise he might have tried to climb back up the chute. Parts of the ceiling were high enough to be out of reach, and the chute possibly debouched in one of those.

If he couldn't climb back up the way he'd fallen, what could he do? He'd memorized the crude partial map the captive troll had sketched, but that knowledge was currently useless. It hadn't included anything about a chute, let alone where the lower end was, and even if it had, Heimdall wouldn't have known which tunnel direction was which. Not only was he bereft of sight, he was entirely lost. Finding the sword had momentarily bolstered his spirits, exploring the space around him had briefly made him feel he was accomplishing something, but now he had to struggle against a wave of despair.

When he scowled and pushed the feeling down, it occurred to him that he was equally ignorant of Sif's fate. Had she defeated the rest of the trolls? Possibly. If so, he hoped she'd escaped the Realm Below and was continuing the quest to recover the head of Mimir without him.

It was a grim, bitter thing to hope for, but he'd fallen in an instant, and, intent on the trolls she was battling, Sif likely hadn't seen what became of him. She wouldn't have any idea where to begin a search, and he hated the idea of her wandering the maze of caverns at random until she succumbed to one or another of its perils. It would be better if she gave him up for dead and finished their mission.

Hopeless as his situation seemed, however, he refused to give *himself* up for dead. Maybe, somehow, he could find his way to the surface even if, at this moment, it was difficult to imagine how. If not, he could at least die trying as befitted an Asgardian warrior. He'd know he'd perished with honor even if no one else ever would. He chose a direction at random and headed down the passage.

From time to time he caught faint sounds, or maybe he only thought he did. Often, when he stopped to listen, the sounds stopped too, and he suspected he'd only reacted to the echo of his own footfalls or breathing, the beat of his heart thumping in his chest, or else simply imagined the tiny unidentifiable noises. Sometimes, though, the sounds continued, and then, nerves taut with apprehension, he insisted to himself that, faint as they were, they had to come from something too distant or tiny to do him any harm. They *didn't* come from some subterranean predator stealing up behind him.

After what seemed a long while, red light tinged the blackness ahead. At first, he wasn't certain he was really perceiving that either, but as he skulked forward it became clear he hadn't simply succumbed to some version of wishful thinking. Several more wary paces brought him to a spot where the passage widened out and exposed veins of dully glowing crystal running through the walls. There were some stone-headed pickaxes littering the floor near sledges made of sheets of hardened fungus with loose chunks of crystal sitting on top of them. The miners presumably employed the sledges to drag the material they dug to the troll habitation.

Fortunately, the miners weren't here at the moment. Maybe they'd taken time away from their labors to hear the frost giant envoy speak. At any rate, their absence meant Heimdall was free to avail himself of a source of light. He could almost have wept with gratitude.

He entered the mining site and picked up one of the loose crystals. He polished the luminous rock with the scarf he'd hoped would conceal his identity from the poor sentry back in the citadel of Asgard, rubbed away dust and dirt, and got the crystal shining a little brighter.

It was still a dim light but infinitely better than nothing. He started to leave, and then, on impulse, decided to search the area more thoroughly. Toward the back was a place where water trickled from the wall to fill a natural bowl in the rock. Beside that was a ledge with a heap of picked raw mushrooms sitting on top of it.

The sight of the water made Heimdall feel parched, and after he scooped up handfuls and slurped his fill, the sight of the mushrooms made him equally hungry. His stomach rumbled.

He hadn't forgotten that the Realm Below reportedly abounded in poison mushrooms, but he was hungry enough to gamble that if a troll could eat something, he could too. He took one bite of a single mushroom. It tasted much the same as raw mushrooms he'd eaten in Vanaheim and Asgard, pleasant enough in a bland sort of way, and it didn't make him fall over dead or experience any sort of distress. He wolfed down more until he'd eaten his fill.

Refreshed, he pondered what to do next. Reason suggested that if the trolls traveled back and forth between the mine and their habitation, maybe he could identify and follow their trail to the settlement. Now that the creatures knew of the Asgardian intrusion, a second visit was likely to prove even more dangerous than before, but, as he needed to find his bearings, it was still the best course of action he could think of.

How, then, to track the creatures? Could the sledges provide an answer? It seemed to him that such a crude conveyance dragging along the tunnel floor might have left marks of its passage.

He took the opportunity for another drink of water from the bowl where it collected, then departed the mine. Stooping and peering by the light of the crystal in his hand, he found the telltale scratches he'd hoped to find, and in due course they led him to a similar glow. He crept forward and found the source was the vault, when its jumble of natural and artificial caves and its mottling of dots of crimson light came into view. He was simultaneously profoundly relieved to have found it and wary of the danger it represented.

With the lights of the wild troll enclave now shining before him, he stuffed his own crystal in his belt pouch and, heart beating faster, crept forward for a better look. As he neared the closest of the chambers, he could make out the chasm on the far side of the settlement, the natural bridge that spanned it, and the high spot from which the tunnel he and Sif had traversed before ascended to the guard post and then to the surface.

That path was still the most direct route to the world above, but he was leery of taking it a second time when the trolls knew he and his sister had gone that way before. Fortunately, now that he knew where he was, he could finally make use of his memory of the map the captive troll had drawn. He could ascend via secondary tunnels coiling around the primary one for most of the way. Ultimately, he'd have to reenter the main tunnel and pass the sentry post, but he'd deal with it when the time came.

He skulked back part of the way he'd come, took his crystal back out of the pouch, and found the branching passageway he wanted. He hurried around the turn and onward.

One final trek and he'd be… somewhere aboveground. As long as he was under the open sky, he'd be happy. Tired and sore though he was, anticipation made him quicken his pace once more.

A cry echoed from up ahead: "There!"

Startled, Heimdall stopped, peered, and saw nothing. The feeble glow of the crystal didn't reach far enough. But he heard the trolls who'd evidently spotted him or the glowing stone he carried. They'd started running, and by the sound of it there were quite a few of them.

Heimdall turned and fled, his boots pounding on the tunnel floor. Desperate, he told himself that if he could maintain his lead, he should be able to detour to a different passage, circle around behind his pursuers, and reach the sentry post ahead of them. Concealed by the ambient gloom, bumps and low spots in the stone tripped him repeatedly, but he managed to stay on his feet.

For a time, he imagined his plan might work. Then a different band of trolls, this one for some reason bearing a red crystal light of its own, appeared in front of him, and all he could do was turn, run back the way he'd come, and hope to encounter yet another branching tunnel before the first group of warriors caught up to him.

He found one, dashed into it, and raced into a space where the passage broadened out into a chamber. He cast about, found the opening in the far wall, and started toward it. When he was halfway there, voices growled and clamored, and an instant later, troll warriors rushed through. With a pang of dread, he realized he was trapped.

Twelve

After a moment, though, fear, if not retreating utterly, yielded its place to another emotion. It was infuriating to have come so close to escaping only to fail at the end. Heimdall dropped his chunk of crystal and drew his great sword to go down fighting as, he thought grimly, an Asgardian warrior should.

Yet something inside him balked at throwing himself at his foes like some mad berserker because that would in a way be accepting defeat, and even now, if he exercised his wits, there might be *some* way to survive. He tried to think of one in the moment he had left and registered that his wasn't the only glowing crystal in the cave. That one band of trolls had carried theirs in as well.

When he took a closer look at them, he knew why. The frost giant emissary had accompanied the wild troll warriors, and he, like Heimdall, needed light to see.

The Asgardian had previously noticed the blue skin, hairless except for a long beard, hair, and eyebrows the color of turquoise. The burly Jotun still wasn't wearing a shirt, tunic, or similar garment above the waist, but he had donned a helm for the hunt. The helm had a pair of golden or gilded tusks mounted on it in such a way that they curved out in front of his head like the tusks of a wild boar. For a weapon, the frost giant carried the same two-handed axe he'd waved around when addressing the assembly of trolls. The iron head and better workmanship distinguished it from the stone-and-bone weapons borne by the other hunters.

Among his other ornaments, he had several baubles hanging around his neck that looked remarkably like tiny human skulls. Their daintiness was surprising, and so, Heimdall thought, was the attention to realistic detail. A Jotun's adornments were generally both bigger and more stylized. The realization sparked the beginning of a notion in the Asgardian's mind, but with the immediate danger of the frost giant and the trolls to concern him, the thought wouldn't come clear.

The emissary leered at him. "Try to take the Asgardian alive. We want to find out what he knows and who else knows it."

The trolls snarled and edged forward. Trying the one desperate ploy that came to mind, Heimdall forced a laugh, and, surprised, the orange-skinned creatures hesitated.

"Even now!" Heimdall said. "Even now! It's so funny everyone should be laughing."

The trolls stood silent for a heartbeat. Then one of the biggest, possibly a chieftain to judge from the numerous carved rings of bone and polished gemstone knotted in his beard and dangling mustache, asked, "What's funny?"

"Him!" Heimdall said, waving his hand at the Jotun envoy. "The mighty frost giant! He wants you to believe he and his people are fitting allies, but even when the odds are dozens to one, he hangs back and looks to you to do the fighting."

The Jotun opened his mouth to retort.

Heimdall raised his voice and talked over him. "Did he try to tell you frost giants are as strong as, no, I'll wager, *stronger* than trolls, and fearless and skilled at arms to boot? I trust you see the truth is otherwise."

The envoy finally managed to make himself heard. "There's nothing wrong with a war leader ordering his warriors to deal with one lone foe!"

"But they're not *your* warriors," Heimdall said. "You're an outsider here the same as I am." He returned his gaze to the circle of watching trolls. "The Jotun hasn't acted like it, though, has he? From the start, he's talked down to you and treated you like inferiors. He's acted as if he were doing you a favor by proposing an alliance."

Heimdall didn't *know* the emissary had behaved that way, but, given the overweening pride of the frost giants, it seemed likely. Even if the Jotun hadn't, the xenophobia of the trolls and their resentment of the scorn with which other races sometimes regarded them might make it seem as if he had.

The frost giant emissary regarded the circle of trolls. "None of that is true!" But his tone was haughty, not friendly or apologetic, and the underground dwellers simply glowered back without offering any reassurance that they thought Heimdall was talking nonsense. Some of them muttered to one another.

"The truth," the Asgardian said, "is that frost giants are clumsy, helpless oafs. Without that red crystal, he couldn't even find his way around."

"You need one too!" the envoy snarled.

"But at least I'm not some coward down here desperate to gain the help of the trolls yet sneering at them to their faces."

The emissary turned to the big troll with the rings knotted into his whiskers. "This is ridiculous! The Asgardian would say anything to put off the moment when we lay hands on him."

The troll chieftain grunted. "I know. Still, he called you a coward. A warrior has only one way to answer that, especially if he wants others to join his war band."

"Fine," the frost giant said. "If you need me to put on a show, so be it." He hefted his great axe and advanced on Heimdall. The trolls pressed back against the walls of the little cave to give the single combat the maximum amount of room.

It was a single combat that, however it turned out, seemed unlikely to alter Heimdall's ultimate fate. But he was grimly determined to win it anyway, if only to vent his anger and gain himself a few more moments of life.

He studied his opponent as the two of them began to circle. He'd suggested the envoy wasn't a particularly skilled fighter, and in fact that was true of many a frost giant. The average Jotun relied on the advantages afforded by his race's enormous size to win battles.

To his disappointment, though, the emissary appeared to be an exception to the rule. His stance, guard, and the smooth, gliding way he moved, all indicated he was a competent warrior and perhaps a superior one.

"You must know," the envoy said, "that even if you could win, you'd gain nothing. The trolls would swarm you and take you down an instant later."

"So it seems," Heimdall replied. "But if I kill you, I kill the hope of an alliance between Jotunheim and the tribe." He sidestepped, and the frost giant shifted to maintain their relative positions.

"You can't kill me," the frost giant said, and followed that with a shout and a swing of the axe.

Reacting instantly, as his trainers had taught him, Heimdall dodged the chop and cut at the Jotun's outstretched arms. The envoy shifted the heavy two-handed axe as though it were light as a feather and parried the sword stroke. Heimdall's blade clanked against the axe head and struck a shower of sparks.

As the duel continued, he looked for weaknesses he could exploit and found nothing. The axe was heavier than his two-handed sword, but the frost giant swung and shifted it just as quickly. Moreover, the envoy was confident and aggressive, but thus far not reckless or undiscerning enough to fall victim to his adversary's feints and traps.

Hoping to find an attack that would score nonetheless, Heimdall cut at the frost giant's head. The Jotun envoy blocked, and once again metal rang on metal. At once, the emissary swept the great axe down and used the head to hook the Asgardian's front leg between knee and ankle. He yanked the limb out from under Heimdall, who slammed down hard on his back. The watching trolls shouted and hooted in anticipation of the deathblow.

Their excitement, however, was at least premature. Heimdall frantically rolled aside, and the axe crashed down in the spot he'd occupied an instant before, the blow echoing off the walls and tossing up chips of stone. He scrambled to his feet and slashed madly. The cuts didn't land but kept the frost giant from pressing him until he recovered his balance and reestablished his guard.

Breathing hard and striving to control it, Heimdall likewise strained to push down the fear that produced a kind of tunnel vision that in turn made for flailing, heedless, losing swordplay. He sought again for some weakness in the Jotun's guard or stance. He didn't find one, but he once again noticed the dangling skulls, and the vague suspicion he'd had before abruptly became clear and sharp in his mind.

The frost giant was also wearing an octagonal golden medallion with a white phenakite gemstone around his neck. It too seemed, if not dainty, at least to reflect a subtler sensibility than a Jotun's ornaments generally did. Perhaps it even glimmered ever so slightly with its own inner light.

Heimdall cut repeatedly at the gold medallion in an effort to break it or the chain it dangled from. Unfortunately, his focus on his opponent's chest and neck only made him more predictable, and the envoy turned that to his advantage. As one axe chop after another nearly found its mark, the trolls roared encouragement to the guest who, by demonstrating his bravery and prowess, had evidently regained their favor.

The great axe whirled at Heimdall. He sought to parry, and the attack looped into a bind. It captured the blade of the two-handed sword and wrenched it from Heimdall's grasp. The axe came up for a follow-up attack.

Heimdall frantically grabbed the haft of the axe to hold it back, and he and the frost giant struggled for control. He could feel that his foe was stronger.

Still, the Asgardian was strong or maybe desperate enough that the envoy lost his patience with the process. He let go of the weapon, freeing up his hands, seized hold of Heimdall himself, and yanked him into a bear hug.

With the long-handled axe pinned between their bodies, the haft digging into his chest, Heimdall had no hope of wielding it even though the frost giant had more or less relinquished possession. The Jotun's arms crushed the air from his lungs and brought blackness swimming around the periphery of his vision. His ribs ached and were perhaps on the verge of giving way.

Heimdall let go of the axe. Afterward, his arms were still caught between his body and the envoy, but *maybe*, he thought, he could work his hands upward. It was the only thing left to try.

As he struggled doggedly to do so, the frost giant raked at him with the tusks projecting from his helm, and the Asgardian shifted his head from side to side to avoid the points. One attack gashed his cheek, but, full of desperation and battle fury, he felt the strike as pressure but not as pain.

The fingertips of his right hand brushed the bottom of the medallion, and with a flare of hope he realized he only needed to reach a little farther. He jammed his arm higher and hooked his fingertips around the chain.

Discerning his intent, the frost giant shouted and let go of him, likely to push him away. But the envoy was too slow. Heimdall jerked, the chain broke, and, separated from the medallion, the Jotun started growing.

With the axe clanging to the floor between him and his foe, Heimdall stumbled backward. The frost giant lunged after him with his blue hands outstretched. Heimdall dodged, sucked in a breath to fill his air-starved lungs, and threw the medallion. It flew far enough that it was lost to sight in the dim red light and amid the feet of the milling trolls.

Bellowing, the frost giant grabbed for the great axe.

Fortunately, dodging the furious chops became steadily easier as the envoy regained his natural stature. His growth ground him against the ceiling of the cave and then forced him to his knees, and his efforts to keep Heimdall in front of him and to swing his weapon became increasingly awkward.

When Heimdall was sure the frost giant was effectively immobilized, he turned to consider the trolls. The envoy had assured him that even if he won their duel, the creatures would rush in and overwhelm him, but he dared to hope that was no longer the case.

It wasn't. For all the wild trolls knew, the frost giant would grow until he filled the whole chamber, and their concern now was escaping. They were rushing for one or another of the exits.

The Asgardian snatched up his sword, retrieved his piece of luminous crystal, and hurried after the group trying to escape through the nearer opening. With a fresh jolt of fear, he saw they were they clogging the exit and striking and shoving at one another as they struggled to squeeze through.

Meanwhile, growth in a space too cramped to accommodate it had crushed the frost giant into near shapelessness, but as his screams attested he still clung to life. His cries mingled with those of the trolls squashed between his bulk and the cavern walls. An enormous foot at the end of a broken leg slid across the floor toward Heimdall, swelling ever larger as it came.

Then, in a sudden surge of motion, the jam in the opening gave way. Some trolls plunged through, leaving their stunned and trampled fellows on the floor. Heimdall rushed after them only to find that several hadn't gone very far. Spying him, they growled and hefted their spears, war hammers, and axes.

All right, Heimdall thought. If he had to fight again, so be it. He dropped the crystal to grip his sword with both hands, took a deep breath, and started forward.

Then new light, white light, splashed into the tunnel behind the creatures. Sif rushed out of a branching passageway with her amulet shining and her broadsword in hand. She attacked the remaining trolls from her side, Heimdall from his, and together they made short work of them.

"Are you all right?" she asked.

"Yes," he panted.

"Good," she said. "This time, keep up. I don't want you getting lost again."

They fled back up the tunnel from which she'd emerged,

and in due course the way connected to the final ascent to the surface. There were new sentries hiding behind the blinds, but not so many this time, and brother and sister fought their way through without either falling down a hole.

After Heimdall's sojourn in darkness, the light streaming in the cave mouth dazzled him, and he squinted and shielded his eyes. It was only after he'd passed through and his vision adjusted, that he realized the sky was overcast and the branches of the trees before him were blocking a fair amount of light from reaching the ground.

Thirteen

Heimdall and Sif hurried onward for a time, and tiny snowflakes began to fall. Finally, when they were some distance from the cave mouth and were reasonably sure no trolls had pursued them aboveground, they slumped down, sweaty, grimy, and exhausted, he with his back against the trunk of a rowan, she sitting against a birch.

After a while Sif stretched, took a long drink from her leather canteen, and offered it to Heimdall.

"Thanks." He'd lost his own water bottle with the gear on the gray stallion, and the lukewarm iron water eased the raw feeling in his throat.

"Better let me see to that cut." Sif poured water to soak a kerchief and used it to clean the gash on his cheek. Her fingers were calloused from years of swordplay and other martial training, but her touch was careful, and as she tended him it came home to Heimdall just how relieved he was to see her alive and well.

When finished, Sif regarded her handiwork. "It's not

bad," she said. "It should heal up fine. What in Ymir's name happened to you? I turned around and you were gone."

He told her the story.

When he was done, she said, "You told me a young frost giant might be no bigger than a man."

"And by all accounts, that's true. But when I found myself facing the emissary, he didn't look especially young, and it occurred to me, would his king really send a stripling to negotiate an alliance with the trolls? Then there were the skulls hanging around his neck. Delicate and detailed as they were, they didn't look like frost giant carvings. Except for being tiny, they looked real."

"So you put it all together and guessed he'd used magic to shrink down small enough to go into the tunnels."

"Yes, and if I could separate him from the source of the enchantment – which I thought might be the gold medallion – and make him shoot up big again, he might end up too big for the cave, and that might crush and kill him." He repressed a shiver to recall just how close the giant had come to killing him instead. "As it turned out, things worked out even better than I expected. The trolls panicked and ran instead of attacking me en masse. Now it's your turn for a question. How did you show up just in time to help me?"

Sif shrugged. "When I realized you weren't behind me any more, I turned back to look for you."

"In that maze of tunnels," he said. It seemed an all but impossible task, and he marveled that she'd succeeded.

She smiled. "Once in a while, brother – once in a *great* while – you do see something I miss. But you weren't the only one with sense enough to memorize the map that troll scratched on the wall, and the giant and the trolls made plenty of noise to lead me to you. You're welcome, by the way."

He felt contrite. "Thank you. I'm grateful, truly. I'm sorry I didn't say it before."

She grinned. "I was only teasing. You don't have to gush. Naturally I came back."

"I didn't know you would. I wouldn't have blamed you if you hadn't. Recovering the head of Mimir is important, it's the one thing that could restore your honor, and so I thought you might head on to Jotunheim alone."

Her grin became a frown that told him she thought he was talking nonsense. "Yes, I'm a loyal Asgardian, but nothing means more to me than my own family. As for reputation, of course I value it. But it doesn't matter if the world thinks you honorable if inside you feel unworthy and full of regret. Really, I don't know why we're even talking about this. If our positions had been reversed, you would have looked for me."

"Well… yes. Probably."

She snorted. "No *probably* about it."

He realized she was right. His head might have told him it was his duty to press on without her, but in that instance, his heart would have overruled it.

"Anyway," Sif continued, "how could I abandon you when this mad search for Mimir's head is your mad plan, and it's liable to take more of your crazy notions to see it through. At least we've shaken Lady Amora off our trail. I suppose that's progress. Do you have any idea where we came up out of the ground?"

He waved his hand at the tiny drifting snowflakes. They were melting as soon as they reached the ground but were an ominous sign nonetheless. "Closer to Jotunheim, evidently."

"Or else the giants are advancing and bringing winter with them." A likely possibility even if he hated the thought of it. "Suffice it to say, I don't know where we are precisely, but we can take our bearings from the sun to get us headed in the right direction. Or ask somebody."

"I favor asking people. We can ask them to give us some food while we're at it. But if you don't mind, let's do that after we've rested a little longer." She drew her broadsword, inspected the edge, and then removed a whetstone from her belt pouch and started honing the blade.

Heimdall realized his great sword could likely benefit from the same sort of care. He found his own sharpening stone, and the rhythmic whisper of the hones was restful. His eyelids dropped, and he slipped into a doze.

He dreamed that there was indeed a traitor in the court of Asgard, someone he *had* to denounce or the Realm Eternal would surely fall. He couldn't call the name of the traitor to mind but would recognize him as soon as he saw his face. He plunged through the throne room, grabbing couriers by the shoulder and wrenching them around, only to find that none of them had a face.

Sif delivered him from his nightmare by kicking him lightly in the ribs.

"Ouch!" he said. "That's where the frost giant squeezed me."

"And whose fault is that?" she said. Illogically and unfairly, it seemed to him. "Come on. Mimir's head isn't going to steal itself back, and we need to move if we're going to get anywhere before nightfall."

At first, Heimdall felt his nap had done him little good, that it had in fact left him feeling dull-witted and on edge at the same time. Then, however, he and Sif came upon a cold little stream and, stooping, washed their faces. That cleared his head and provided another opportunity to slake his thirst.

He and Sif followed the stream as it murmured on downhill and eventually out of the woods. Up ahead, it wound its way into a peat bog.

Old tumbledown shacks with sod roofs revealed that people periodically worked the marshy ground for bog iron, and sections of peeled-back turf indicated that one such harvest was in progress. Nobody was out on the bog wielding a turf knife now, however. Rather, men and a dwarf were bustling around loading their tools and other portable possessions onto mule carts. They'd dumped the pellets of bog iron the wagons were meant to carry on the ground.

"Now we know the way to the battlefields," Heimdall said.

"The opposite direction from the way they're pointed," Sif replied. "But we still need to catch up with them if we want them to feed us." She ran toward the workers and their carts, and Heimdall dashed after her.

Heimdall and Sif plainly weren't frost giants. Still, when they saw the warriors coming, the workers were jumpy enough to clamor in alarm and seize spears, turf knives, and any other real or makeshift weapon that was ready to hand.

Or maybe it was more than jumpiness. With a twinge of trepidation, it occurred to Heimdall that the crew might recognize the supposed traitors for who they were, but he was willing to gamble that wasn't the case. Surely word of the fugitives hadn't spread everywhere, especially when people had news and rumors of the war to concern them. If Amora had reported that the brother and sister had fled into the Realm Below, in all likelihood to die there, perhaps no one was hunting them any more.

He stopped and raised his empty hands to signal peaceful intentions, and Sif did likewise. "We're friends," he said. "We were running at you because we wanted to talk to you before you moved on."

The dwarf stepped forth. He was only half as tall as Heimdall, but his shoulders were as broad, and his hairy arms knotted with muscle. Long brown whiskers hung down the front of his tunic, and the narrowed eyes under his shaggy brows showed he was still wary if not genuinely suspicious. So did the curve-bladed turf knife he carried, not quite presented in a nakedly threatening fashion but ready for use nonetheless.

"My name is Mudbeard," said the dwarf. "I'm in charge here." Heimdall didn't doubt it. A dwarf with any real mastery of his people's arts would likely work in an underground mine or at the forges, but every dwarf had a natural affinity for metals that would make him a good choice to direct the collection of bog iron. "And who *exactly* are you?"

"I'm Sune," Heimdall said, choosing an alias at random. "My friend is Thyra. We fight in Gudrun's company."

"Then what are you doing here?" Mudbeard asked. "The fighting's to the north."

"Unless it isn't," one of the workmen said. "Maybe the

frost giants are on the move again. It's snowing, isn't it?"

"It is," Mudbeard said, "but if the Jotuns were already here, I think we'd be able to tell. My guess is that these two are deserters."

"Then you're guessing wrong!" Sif snarled. Perhaps the words stung because in a perverse way they were true.

Heimdall spoke quickly to keep the exchange from continuing in the same acrimonious vein. "There was a report that a war party of frost giants had somehow slipped behind our battle lines. Thyra and I were sent to scout and see if it was true. I'm happy to say it's not. On our mission we exhausted our provisions, so as warriors in the service of the crown we need to requisition a little of yours." He gave the dwarf what he hoped was a conciliatory smile. "We hope you're of a mind to share freely, be hospitable, and have a meal with us."

Mudbeard glanced up at the glow of the sun shining through the gray clouds. "It's nowhere near evening," he said, "but we are just about packed up. A meal – a *quick* one – it is, then." He raised his voice, making sure everyone in the crew could hear him. "Eat! We're not stopping once we're on the trail!"

The meal consisted of stale barley flatbread, cheese, and smoked fish. Mudbeard ate his sitting on the driver's bench of one of the carts as though to emphasize that he was eager to be gone. His workers hovered near to their leader, Heimdall, and Sif, no doubt to hear whatever tidings their unexpected visitors had to share.

Heimdall related what war news he had to offer, meanwhile recognizing that it was as stale as the flatbread.

He and Sif naturally hadn't heard anything new during their time in the Realm Below. He still didn't know how long that had been and also didn't know how to go about finding out. *What day is it* might come across as a peculiar, suspicious question.

As he'd halfway expected, when he finished, Mudbeard frowned. "We haven't had a lot of news working here. But we have heard all of that."

Sif swallowed a mouthful of her food. "We told you we've been out scouting and not seeing anyone. Tell us what *you* know. Has the All-Father awakened from the Odinsleep?"

"No," said the dwarf. "Not as far as we know, and if he had, wouldn't it be obvious to everyone?"

Heimdall judged that it probably would. In his wrath, the King of the Gods would unleash forces that shook all Asgard as they smashed the frost giant army.

"Are there any signs," he asked, "of the conjunction of Asgard and Jotunheim coming to an end?" Should that happen, the Jotun army would have to withdraw lest it be stranded when the two worlds separated.

Mudbeard snorted. "What am I, a sorcerer? But again, no, not so far as we've heard."

Heimdall glumly decided that made sense as well. He was no mystic either, to understand how the Nine Worlds were likely to move in relation to one another. But he did know conjunctions had lasted as long as a century. This one was less than a year old.

"Then how is the war itself going?" asked Sif. "There must be *some* good news."

"They say Thor and his followers won a battle or two. But he can't be everywhere at once, can he? And the frost giants are pushing forward everyplace he's not. Looks like you finished eating. We have too, so it's time for us to part company."

"Wait," said Sif. "You said it yourself. If the Jotuns were already here, it would be obvious."

Mudbeard took the reins of his cart in hand. "That doesn't mean they won't be here soon."

"I've seen the smithies of Asgard," Sif told him. "They're working night and day to equip our warriors, and they need every scrap of iron workers like you can provide."

"We can't provide any if we're dead."

Sif gestured to the piles of bog iron pellets littering the ground. "At least load this metal up again and take it with you when you go."

"Iron's heavy," Mudbeard said. "It would slow us down."

"Coward!"

The dwarf glared. "What's Asgard to me? My clan never should have come here from Nidavellir, and when I'm back in the city, I'm going to find a witch to send me home."

Sif raked the assembled workers with her gaze. "What about the rest of you?" she asked. "*You're* Asgardians! Surely you mean to do your duty!"

But Heimdall could tell from the mix of shame and resentment on their faces that they didn't. He put his hand on his sister's arm. "We're guests in this camp," he said, "and the last thing our hosts need from us is a scolding."

"But–"

"Enough. Please."

Sif stiffly inclined her head to Mudbeard. "I apologize for my rudeness, and we thank you for the food."

Mudbeard grunted. "Accepted." He raised his voice. "Time to go!" In another couple minutes, the mule carts were rumbling south, the workers who hadn't found a seat inside one hiking along with the procession.

Sif gave Heimdall a disgusted look. "Why did you stop me?"

"I didn't think you were going to persuade them, and I didn't want you to make us memorable. Someone might recognize us when they told the story. Why were you so insistent anyway? It isn't the task of common folk to stand their ground when an army of frost giants might be drawing near."

Sif sighed. "I suppose it was because all the news was so bad. It made me angry to see people not doing everything they could to turn things around."

"Well," Heimdall said, "I agree, the news is bad. If Odin is still asleep and even Thor isn't stopping the advance of the frost giants, then maybe it all truly does come down to us and our mission, and we haven't even made it out of Asgard yet. We've barely managed to keep ourselves alive."

"Still," said Sif, "we're going ahead."

Heimdall squared his shoulders. "I think we have to."

FOURTEEN

Heimdall and Sif hadn't marched far before the snow started sticking to the ground. Then the drifts grew deeper until they were slogging forward with a frigid wind blowing in their faces. He wound his scarf so that it covered his mouth and chin.

"I remember winter," Sif said. Though it now hailed Odin as its king, Vanaheim didn't have the perpetual summer that had formerly prevailed in much of Asgard. "Skiing. Sledding. Snowmen and snowball fights."

Heimdall smiled. "Something else you're losing your fondness for?"

"You read my mind," she said.

Periodically they met bands of warriors trudging in the opposite direction. The fugitives had their false names and their excuse for traveling apart from a company of their fellow soldiers prepared, but not even the thanes were much inclined to question them. Too many of the fighters were wounded, and even those who weren't seemed demoralized.

It was further evidence that the war was going badly, and though it was convenient that almost no one could muster the will to challenge Sif and him, Heimdall felt dismay to see the wounds and despondency of the retreating Asgardians nonetheless.

Heimdall and Sif also met bands of fleeing farmers carrying bundles on their backs, herding pigs and goats. At night, the pair sheltered in the abandoned farmsteads. With the snowfall blighting the fields and wolves stalking from the forests and ranging down from the mountains to kill the livestock left behind, it felt as if the farmers had left their holdings not just days but months or years before.

Thus, despite Heimdall and Sif's outlaw status, it nonetheless lifted his heart for a moment when, after two days' travel, the ongoing spectacle of misery and desolation gave way to the sight of an army that was still ready to fight. The camp stretched along a ridge. Claiming the high ground was a standard tactic even if of questionable use against creatures as tall as frost giants.

Sif smiled. "I even hear some of them singing."

"So do I," Heimdall replied. His moment of happiness faded as the depressing thought came to him that there was no reason to expect this army to fare any better in the long run than the defending armies the frost giants had already broken. "Of course, you'd expect Asgardian warriors to be full of cheer if they haven't gone into battle yet. If nothing's happened to shake their confidence."

"Audhumia's milk, you're gloomy!" Sif replied. "Maybe they're happy because they fought and won."

"I suppose it's possible, but it doesn't seem likely."

"Anyway, do you think we sneak around or through?"

Heimdall took a moment to consider. It would be a risk to enter the camp, a risk that worried him, but the alternative seemed chancier still. "They must have sentries out on their flanks. If we're spotted trying to go around, we'll almost certainly be taken for deserters or, well, ourselves."

Sif frowned. "Someone could also recognize us if we walk right into the camp. There are hundreds of warriors up there."

"You're right, but it's hundreds who have other things to think about than spotting a pair of fugitives, even assuming they've heard about us in the first place. We'll just be two more faces in the crowd."

"Won't it be suspicious when the two faces say, 'Farewell, we're going to wander off in the direction of the frost giants now, without orders and all by ourselves?'"

"When the time comes, we'll think of something." He hoped.

"Sune and Thyra it is, then." Sif sniffed the air. "Somebody's roasting mutton up there. If anyone denounces us, maybe we'll at least have full stomachs when it happens."

By the time they hiked to the top of the ridge, the sun was setting. As Heimdall had expected, a few other folk had business that took them up or down the slope, and nobody paid any particular attention to their approach. Though still on edge, Heimdall felt somewhat encouraged.

There was a scattering of hide tents tall enough for a man to stand up inside, and brother and sister avoided those. The warlords seemed most likely to be on the lookout for the so-called traitors Heimdall and Sif if anybody was. The common warriors had small low tents or had built lean-tos with fires crackling among them. This time of day they were cook fires, but the heaps of firewood sitting close at hand suggested they burned continually so people could huddle around them to combat the chill of the snow and the icy wind blowing out of the north.

Sif led Heimdall to a circle of warriors eating a stew of chicken, peas, cabbage, and leeks ladled from an iron cauldron. He assumed she chose that group because she was hungry and their evening meal was already cooked. The warriors had rye bread, too, and ale to wash everything down.

"Hello, friends," said Sif. "Is there enough of that to share?" Meanwhile, Heimdall tensed. He'd thought entering the camp was the better option, but now anxiety made him doubt his choice. If anyone in the circle of warriors recognized them, or even simply sensed something suspicious about them, he and Sif were in serious trouble.

But no one seemed to find the newcomers remarkable in any respect, although, sitting on a chunk of wood, a warrior with a forked wheat-colored beard glowered up at Sif. "Eat with your own war band at your own fire."

"Our thane sent us to the woodworkers to find out where the new spear shafts were," Heimdall said, "and when we got back, the cursed gluttons had already eaten all the supper."

An apple-cheeked woman with a battle-axe ready to hand chuckled. "Sit down and eat, then. There's enough." She nodded toward the man with the forked beard. "Knud is just in a foul mood because the chieftains haven't sent us forward to fight."

"Do you blame me?" Knud replied. "We keep hearing of battles lost. But the Thirsty Spears would push the frost giants back!"

Several of his Thirsty Spear comrades voiced their agreement. Meanwhile, Heimdall glanced at Sif with a look intended to convey *I told you they hadn't fought yet.* The sour look she returned bespoke her irritation at being reminded he was right and she was wrong.

"Don't fret," said the woman with the apple cheeks. "We're right on the threshold of Jotunheim. The frost giants are bound to come this way sooner or later. Then there'll be fighting enough to suit you."

And you'll lose, Heimdall thought. He wished them only well, but his desire for their victory didn't influence his grim appraisal of their chances. They'd stand behind the usual shield wall, the frost giants would do something clever, and that would be that. He was starting to feel more and more keenly that the outcome of the war might really come down to the success or failure of his and Sif's self-imposed mission. It seemed preposterous that two common warriors could stumble into roles of such importance, but things were as they were.

It was especially daunting to consider what Sif had called his *mad plan* in its entirety. Most of the time, he found it better to deal with whatever was immediately before him. For the moment, that was eating among a band of warriors and listening to their grousing and their banter.

Actually, despite his edginess, that was pleasant. This moment was a respite between the perils he and Sif had already faced and those that lay before them, and when they finished eating he gave his thanks and rose from the fireside with a twinge of regret.

After that, he and his sister wandered through the camp trying to look like they had some sensible reason to be prowling about until it grew late enough that most of the warriors had retired to their tents and lean-tos. Brother and sister then located several supply tents set up in a row with a guard to watch them. Judging from where he was standing, the sentry reckoned that anyone who did try to steal something would go after the casks of ale just visible in the gloom beyond one of the tent flaps.

Still, the guard might spot Heimdall and Sif if they weren't careful or simply if their luck deserted them. His pulse ticked faster as he and his sister crept around behind the row of tents and used a dagger to cut peepholes, then long vertical gashes to enter if the contents warranted. First, they found tubular backpacks made of woven birch bark and then, in a different tent, oat bread, cheese, dried apples, and hazelnuts to stuff inside.

As they crammed food into the backpacks, leather creaked and mail clinked just outside the tent. Heimdall tensed to realize the sentry wasn't content to constantly stand in front of the ale stores after all. Periodically he must wander up and down the line, and who was to say he hadn't somehow sensed the thieves? Heimdall and Sif froze and remained absolutely silent until they heard the guard move onward.

At that point, Heimdall would have liked to make a quick retreat from the vicinity with what he and his sister had pilfered already, but it seemed to him that they needed to venture into Jotunheim fully equipped. Accordingly, he and Sif found and invaded a third tent, one stocked with yew longbows and quivers of arrows. They were examining the bows as best they could in the dark, each looking for a suitable weapon, when the flap abruptly flew open. The guard stepped through with his spear leveled. Though the intruders had done their best to be quiet, he must have finally heard them nonetheless.

Sif stepped toward the man and gave him a smile as though nothing were amiss. "Hello," she said.

The guard glowered back at her. "Who are you? Put down the bow and–"

Sif had succeeded in drawing the guard's attention, and Heimdall lunged in on the fellow's flank and punched him in the face. The sentry fell.

An instant later, Heimdall was aghast at what instinct had prompted him to do. He dropped to his knees beside the fallen sentry, and the sick, stricken feeling only faded when he found that the man still breathed and his heartbeat was strong.

"Is he out?" Sif whispered.

"Yes," Heimdall replied, "but, thank goodness, nothing more."

"Then hurry and find a bow. We need to go before anybody comes looking for him."

They crept some distance from the supply tents without attracting further notice, but, feeling desperate, Heimdall realized that wasn't going to be enough. When the guard woke, he'd have the whole camp looking for the thieves.

Heimdall hadn't thought of a way to exit the camp in the direction of Jotunheim yet. He'd hoped he and Sif might figure something out after a little sleep in some out-of-the-way corner that was nonetheless warmed by a fire. Now, though, they'd have to improvise. He led his sister to the forward edge of the camp, where a string of sentries stood peering out at the night. With no hope of skulking past them unobserved, the two fugitives simply strode between the nearest, much as they'd calmly advanced on the wild trolls in the tunnel.

"You!" barked the closest guard, a big man with a beak of a nose. "Where do you think you're going?"

"There were wolves," Heimdall said, remembering the ones he'd glimpsed prowling around the abandoned farms. "They upset the horses in the paddock." He hoped there was a paddock somewhere in the camp. With one notable exception, mounted troops didn't play a major role in Asgardian warfare, but the average army included a war band or two.

The guard glanced to the right. "The paddock's way down that way."

"And after someone loosed a couple arrows, the wolves ran this way."

"I didn't see anything."

"But you haven't spent your whole life hunting, have you? That's why the army has people like Thyra and me."

"All right," the guard said, "go. But not too far. There are more dangerous things than wolves out there, and not that far ahead by all accounts."

Heimdall didn't doubt it.

Fifteen

As Heimdall and Sif tramped forward, the snow deepened, the wind blew harder, and the world grew colder. He hoped that when the sun rose, the day would prove warmer than the night, but when it did, hours later the dark clouds shrouding the sky from horizon to horizon were so thick that he could barely even determine the position of the sun. Certainly its warmth didn't reach the ground. The sun did, however, provide sufficient light to illuminate the walls of towering peaks ahead.

Sif frowned at them. "That's not Asgard," she said.

"No," Heimdall said. "If not for the conjunction, it would be the edge of this world. As things are, it's the beginning of Jotunheim." Which was exactly where he'd been trying to go, but the sight made him feel more apprehension than satisfaction. At this moment, it truly did seem mad that he hoped to survive an incursion without an army at his back, and profoundly selfish to draw his sister into his madness. He drew a long breath and reminded himself that the mission was important and that he and Sif had already overcome formidable obstacles to get this far. With luck, courage, and the exercise of their wits, maybe they could overcome those that still lay before them.

"I can't say I particularly like the looks of the place," Sif said. "But at least the wind is covering our tracks."

In fact, it was doing more than that. Whistling and then howling out of the mountains to the north, it eventually blew the snowfall straight into Heimdall's eyes. He had layers of clothing and an Asgardian's natural hardiness to help him withstand the cold but felt the bitter chill anyway and had no doubt Sif was enduring the same. As night fell once again, he looked for another abandoned steading in which he and his sister could shelter for the night.

It came as a relief when he spied a barn and a longhouse in the distance. Warmth and rest, it seemed, were finally at hand. He pointed the buildings out to Sif, and they waded through the snowdrifts in that direction until he noticed a speck flying high in the air.

He doubted it was Lady Amora. It would be insanely bad luck if she'd caught up with the fugitives again. But he felt alarm nonetheless. In these savage, war-ravaged lands, the speck could still be something dangerous. "Get down!" he said.

Sif crouched at once, without asking why, and he knelt beside her. The mote in the air swooped lower, and then he could make it out more clearly. It was a woman in mail with a lance in her hand, a shield on her arm, and long blonde braids and a cloak flying out behind her. She rode a dappled stallion with feathered wings that lashed the air. The horse's legs worked too, just as if the steed were trotting on solid ground.

"A Valkyrie," Heimdall said, chagrinned that, even having come this far, he and Sif hadn't escaped the danger their own people posed after all.

"Bad as the light is," Sif replied, "I'm still surprised she didn't see us."

"My guess," Heimdall said, "is that she's already made a circuit or two looking for trouble. Now she's eager to rejoin her comrades and get out of the cold."

Sif scowled. "There's only one place to do that."

"I know."

The Valkyrie rode the winged stallion down to the patch of ground in front of the barn. When she swung open the door, light spilled out to illuminate the murky forms of a couple other female warriors moving about.

"What are they doing out here?" Sif asked. Her peevish tone implied the Valkyries were sheltering in the farmstead specifically to inconvenience her.

Heimdall shrugged. "Scouting? Returning from a raid on some frost giant position? The warriors back on the ridge told us there were Asgardians fighting farther to the north."

"You know," his sister said, "we spent time back in the camp, and nobody thought anything about it. Well, until we sneaked into the supply tents."

Heimdall could well understand why she'd said that. He too felt tempted by all the comforts the farmstead had to offer. There would likely even be hot food. Nonetheless, he said, "So you're thinking we could safely seek shelter with the Valkyries? I'd be afraid to count on it. This is a different situation. We'd have a harder time justifying our presence, and these are elite troops, more likely than the average warrior to have heard about the fugitives Sif and Heimdall."

Sif sighed. "Why are you never right in a way that makes things look better? But I suppose you are. Come on. We'll find shelter elsewhere, and, if not, we can survive another night in the snow."

They stalked on, giving the farm buildings a wide berth and creeping from one bit of cover to the next. As far as Heimdall could see, there were no more sentries on winged steeds flying around in the sky, and he suspected the Valkyries had decided not to subject their tired mounts to any more of the fierce wind and freezing temperatures. Still, stealth was plainly the prudent course, the more so when he glimpsed something moving off to the right. Alarmed, he raised his hand in warning, and he and Sif crouched low again.

The thing he'd seen was a frost giant, but not striding along in the arrogant manner he associated with Jotuns. Rather, the giant was keeping as low as he could and skulking in much the same manner as the two Asgardians. Beyond him, Heimdall could just make out other frost giants creeping in similar fashion. It looked like they were stealing up on the farmstead while employing a tactic possibly recommended by the head of Mimir.

"Maybe they're *only* scouting," whispered Sif. The grim note in her voice told him she doubted it.

He did too and felt worry on the Valkyries' behalf. "Wait for the giants to pass on by. Then we'll sneak around behind them and count them."

It turned out there were seven frost giants. By the time Heimdall and Sif had crept down the line to determine that, the Jotuns had dropped down on their bellies and were crawling, the longhouse and barn in view beyond them. Heimdall realized that even if the Valkyries were maintaining some sort of watch, in the night and at a distance, the Jotuns, despite their hugeness, might easily be mistaken for hillocks in the ground.

He became more worried still when a frost giant in the middle of the line started chanting a prayer of sorts to the snow and the wind, the rumble of his voice inhumanly deep. The other enormous warriors chorused ritual responses, everyone staring at the barn.

Snow began piling up around the building far faster than it was accumulating anywhere else, half burying it in a matter of moments. A glimmering ran through the pile, and although Heimdall couldn't be certain watching from afar, he suspected it was freezing harder, changing from a covering of snow to a shell of ice.

Now it was plain the frost giants meant to attack and do so with every advantage. The Valkyries were fearsome foes, but they owed many of their victories to their mastery of aerial combat. If the Jotuns denied them access to their flying steeds and then assailed them by surprise, the Asgardian warriors were far less likely to prevail.

Heimdall considered how he and Sif could best intervene. To say the least, it was unlikely they could defeat seven frost giants all by themselves. But if *they* attacked by surprise, maybe they could interrupt the spell casting and provoke the Jotuns into making enough noise to alert the Valkyries.

Hard on conceiving the plan, such as it was, the thought flashed through his mind that he and Sif *could* simply go on their way and abandon the Valkyries to fend for themselves. The importance of their errand might serve as justification. But the thought was merely that, with no power to sway him, discounted the moment it occurred to him. As Sif had suggested, some acts were simply inconceivable.

Besides, he thought with a flicker of humor, even if he were inclined to propose such a thing, she'd never go along with it.

He looked over at her and discerned that she was indeed of the same mind as he was. Indeed, she already had an arrow nocked. He readied one of his own, and, doing their best to compensate for the wind, they loosed together.

He felt a moment of satisfaction when the shafts took the shaman or warlock, the frost giant who'd begun the incantation, in the back. They weren't enough to kill the Jotun, but they did make him break off his chanting and lurch around.

Heimdall and Sif nocked new arrows, drew, and shot again. His shaft plunged into the warlock's naked chest, and hers pierced him just below the eye. One wound or the other made him bellow.

That's right, Heimdall thought, roar your heads off!

The warlock giant jerked the arrow out of his face, and blood splashed from the wound. He then scrambled to his feet, and the other Jotuns did the same. They rushed Heimdall and Sif with spears poised to stab and battle-axes and war hammers raised to swing.

Pausing every few steps to loose another arrow, the two

Asgardians retreated toward a stand of pines. His heart pounding, Heimdall hoped it would hinder pursuit. He shot again, and the shaft drove in far enough – all the way up to the fletchings – to fell the frost giant closest to him. The Jotun toppled in a splash of snow, and his fellows shouted in fury.

The frost giants spread out to encircle the stand of pines, then worked their way inward. Some squeezed between the trees, snapping off limbs and scraping away bark as they forced their way through. Others cleared their paths with crashing sweeps of their axes and hammers, felling trees with just a blow or two.

Feeling more trapped and vulnerable by the moment, Heimdall glanced toward the barn. Valkyries were chipping at the ice encasing the door but had yet to batter their way through. He told himself they'd free their steeds and join the battle soon. They had to. It would be too late for Sif and him if they didn't.

Another pine toppled, this one falling straight at Heimdall. He frantically leaped out of the way and looked up at the bald and beardless frost giant who'd smashed it over. The Jotun wore high black boots, a kilt, and massive rings of silver and ivory down the length of his arms. The mace in his right hand had a round iron head bristling with spikes that made it resemble some ugly mockery of the sun. Several arrows that had manifestly done him little harm jutted and flopped from his skin.

Heimdall dropped his longbow and drew his sword, and the huge mace hurtled down. He rushed forward, and the weapon thumped the ground behind him. He swung the two-handed sword, and, to his startled dismay, the blade jarred against the high boot without penetrating. In the gloom, he hadn't noticed that the leather had squares of black iron bolted on. Which meant the only parts of the Jotun's body he could reach were well protected. But maybe there was a way to change that.

The mace swept down, and Heimdall dodged. When the mace struck beside him, it jolted the ground under his feet and spattered him with snow and chips of wood from shattered branches. He lunged, grabbed with one hand, and caught hold of the haft of the mace just as the frost giant hoisted it again.

Even wearing mail, Heimdall's weight was negligible compared to a Jotun's might. The frost giant heaved the weapon high and only then registered that his foe was clinging to it. Eyes as big as shields and as white as the snowfall goggled in surprise.

The Asgardian heaved himself on top of the round wooden handle. He knew the frost giant need only flick the mace to fling him off, but the startled Jotun didn't do it quickly enough. Heimdall raised the great sword in both hands, bellowed a war cry, and leaped into space. As he started to drop, the two-handed sword caught the Jotun just beneath the hairline and slashed a bloody furrow down the forehead, across the eye, and then on down the cheek to the lips before ripping free.

Heimdall plummeted. The frost giant reeled backward with one hand clapped to the gash.

Heimdall landed in a snowdrift, and either that or Asgardian resilience kept the drop from doing him any harm. Now that it was over, the sheer reckless insanity of what he'd just done came home to him, but there was no time to marvel at his luck. The sheltering pines were all but swept away.

At least his sister was still alive, still fighting, slashing and thrusting at the feet of another frost giant wearing iron-plated boots. The Jotun was hobbling and leaving bloody prints in the snow, proof that she'd figured out how to strike past the armor, and after a second Heimdall saw her dart under an upraised foot and stab. She'd discovered that the boots didn't have plating on the soles.

After that, Heimdall had no more time to keep track of her. Two more frost giants were closing in on him, one from either side. Telling himself to stay calm, stay calm, he wondered how he could contend with two at once.

He felt a surge of relief when it didn't come to that. A woman on a winged horse swooped down at the nearer Jotun and shot arrow after arrow into his head. Distracted, the frost giant took a lurching step after her and stabbed with his spear, but with a beat of his wings the flying stallion rose higher and dodged the thrust.

Heimdall saw that the other Valkyries were attacking the remaining frost giants with bows, lances, and javelins. Some hadn't taken the time to saddle their mounts, but riding bareback didn't appear to hinder them.

Emboldened by their arrival, he rushed the frost giant with the spear and, now that he'd seen his sister demonstrate the trick of it, slashed the soles of the Jotuns' feet. For a moment, he felt a savage joy to think that he and his newfound allies might fell the creature without paying with their own lives.

Then, however, the Jotun's huge spear leaped at a Valkyrie hurling javelins at him. Her black steed swooped lower, but not quickly enough. Heimdall cried out to see the spear thrust strike home and knock her from the equine's back. Her body tumbled earthward. Enraged, he charged the frost giant and cut deep into one of his feet.

The Jotun warrior stumbled backward, tripped over one of the toppled trees, and fell on his back. The steed of the slain Valkyrie lit on top of his face and battered his eyes with his hooves, then took flight again before the frost giant could swat or grab him.

Meanwhile the surviving Valkyries drove weapons into the giant's torso. The Jotun shuddered, the blue hands flopped down into the snow, and the creature didn't move thereafter.

A Valkyrie on a white steed swooped low enough for a good look at Heimdall. She wore a winged helm like Sif's except that it, like the rest of her armor, was black. So too were her braids. She carried a broadsword in her hand, and some enchantment sheathed the blade in rippling yellow flame, the firelight glinting on the dark mail. She gave Heimdall a nod and flew on in search of the next foe.

He looked around for Sif and discovered to his relief that she was still on her feet and likewise fighting in concert with several flying allies. He took a deep breath and ran to join her, but she and the Valkyries felled their adversary before he could enter the fray.

In fact, it turned out there was little more for him or Sif to do. The other frost giants were either down or on the verge of it. He and his sister aided in the fight against one more of the Jotuns, and then the battle was over.

Afterward, the Valkyrie with the flaming sword and several of her comrades landed their steeds in front of Heimdall and Sif. To his relief, there was nothing of suspicion or hostility in the Valkyries' manner. He hadn't really expected such, but life as a fugitive was teaching him to take nothing for granted.

"I'm Uschi," said the one in black, who possessed, Heimdall now observed, a lean, long-legged frame and a long, dark-eyed, serious face to go with it. "I'm the thane of this company."

"I'm Sune," Heimdall replied, hoping the lie would pass muster one more time, "and my friend is Thyra."

"Welcome to you both," Uschi said, "and thank you. The frost giants would likely have slaughtered us all if not for you. Please, share our camp and the supper we were about to prepare."

"Gladly," Heimdall said, "it will be our pleasure."

It was not, however, time to retreat indoors just yet. Four Valkyries and two of the winged stallions had perished during the fighting. The surviving members of the company first searched the bodies, scavenging any gear deemed useful and any items that kin or friends might want for keepsakes. They then built funeral pyres from the wood of the fallen pines and laid dead warriors and dead horses alike on top of them. Uschi set the piles alight with her burning sword, the surviving Asgardians sang a song of mourning, and the remaining winged stallions looked gravely on with eyes that seemed full of an almost human intelligence.

When the funeral observances were through, Heimdall and Sif were finally able to go inside the longhouse with its wattle and daub walls, floor of pounded earth, and thatched roof. Supper was leeks, cheese, rye flatbread, and dried eel. With their stomachs full, their bodies warmed by the fire and exhausted from marching through the snow all day, the two siblings fell asleep soon after on two of the built-in benches lining the walls.

When Heimdall woke sometime later, it was to discover that the Valkyries had gathered around him and Sif with weapons in hand and their expressions somber. Alarmed, he reached for the hilt of his great sword and found that the blade was no longer beside him.

Sif woke an instant later, saw the armed women clustered around her and Heimdall, and snatched for her broadsword. The Valkyries had taken this as well.

"What is this?" she demanded.

"A problem," Uschi said. "I don't like it, but apparently the two of you are not who you claim to be."

SIXTEEN

"I don't understand," Heimdall said. It was a lie. As his anxiety attested, he understood all too well, the *what* if not the *how* of it.

Uschi gestured toward one of the other Valkyries, and Heimdall realized he hadn't seen this one before. She was still in full armor and cloaked and hooded against the frigid winter weather outside.

"This is Quy," Uschi said. "She carries messages to and from various warlords, thanes, and companies, and she's just arrived with one about the two of you."

Heimdall could readily imagine what the message said. No doubt Sif could as well, but evidently she still had hope of brazening the situation out. "That seems unlikely," she said.

Quy pushed back her hood. She had a stern oval face with narrow green eyes and tousled auburn curls. "It's a message from Queen Frigga herself," she said, "about the traitors and murderers Sif and Heimdall."

"Then you have the wrong people," Sif replied. "I'm Thyra and he's Sune. We serve under Captain Gudrun but were separated from our patrol when frost giants attacked it." She looked to Uschi. "We already explained all this."

"And apparently you were convincing," Quy replied. "But unfortunately for you, the queen didn't just send word of your crimes. She sent these."

The messenger reached into the pouch hanging from her shoulder and brought out a parchment. Unrolled, it displayed two well-rendered sketches, one of Sif and one of Heimdall. Some talented artist must have drawn the originals, after which a sorcerer duplicated the images to put them into general circulation.

None of the other Valkyries looked at the parchment closely, no doubt because they'd already done so while the two Vanir were sleeping. Heimdall, however, stared at it in shock and with a sick feeling in the pit of his stomach. He no longer saw *any* hope of claiming that Sune and Thyra simply bore unfortunate chance resemblances to the fugitives. The likenesses were too exact. Which meant that only the truth offered any hope of saving him and Sif.

His sister began a protestation of innocence, and he talked over her. "Yes," he said, "I admit, it's us. We're the ones Frigga is looking for."

Sif shot him a startled if not disgusted look.

"But I beg you to listen to the whole story," he continued. "Yes, to my shame, I killed a guard, and I'll answer for it when the time comes, but it was an accident. Yes, Sif and I intruded on the vault where the All-Father sleeps the Odinsleep–"

"You mean you tried," said Quy.

"No," Heimdall said. "I understand why it seems that way, but we did get in, although the door locked after we came out again and created the appearance that we didn't. We intruded because we feared some enemy had put Odin under a spell, and that was why the sleep has lasted so long just when his people need him most. We understood it wasn't our place to go, but no one else would heed our fears."

Quy made a spitting sound. "Save your lies and excuses for the tribunal that will judge you."

"It's all right," Uschi said. "It does no harm to let them speak." She looked at Heimdall. "*Did* you find proof that Odin has fallen prey to sorcery?"

"No," Heimdall said, "but we did find proof that another intruder had entered the vault before us. Possibly even a traitor still going undetected and just waiting for the chance to do further harm. Someone *must* have entered the chamber because one of the king's treasures was missing. Someone stole the head of Mimir."

"If you know anything about it," said Sif, "you know it's a source of great wisdom, and now the frost giants fight with a cunning they never displayed before. Clearly, they have the head, and my brother and I intend to get it back."

Quy sneered. "How noble of you. And here I thought you were simply running in the direction of Jotunheim to escape punishment for your treachery."

"That's not so," Heimdall replied. "Dangerous as Asgard has become for us, we wouldn't run to a place more dangerous still." He gave Uschi a pleading look. "Captain, I realize you only just met us, but you've seen enough to form an opinion. We helped you and your company against the frost giants when we could have simply sneaked on by and left you to your fate."

Some of the Valkyries looked uncomfortable if not actually guilty that they'd turned on the people who'd fought to save them. Uschi turned to Quy. "You have no way of knowing this," said the commander in black, "but he's telling the truth. I think we all would have died if not for his sister and him."

"And therefore what?" Quy replied. "Queen Frigga commands that the fugitives be apprehended and returned to the citadel for judgment. If you and your company don't obey, you'll stand condemned as traitors too."

Uschi grimaced. "I know."

At the show of acquiescence, Quy's manner became less truculent. "I know you don't like it – I wouldn't either in your place – but we can't know what game Heimdall and Sif are playing, or why they truly chose to help your company. Let the wise ones back at court sort it all out. The prisoners will have their chance to speak."

Uschi gave Heimdall a regretful look. "We have no choice but to obey the queen." She turned to Quy. "After the fight, my warriors and our steeds are exhausted. I imagine you and your horse are tired too. We can take the prisoners back in the morning."

"Of course," said Quy. "The journey will be less dangerous in the light of day."

"Then it just remains to secure the prisoners." Uschi turned back to Heimdall and Sif. "We need to tie you up now. I ask you not to resist."

Heimdall thought grimly that it was an unnecessary request. Surrounded by Valkyries with weapons in hand, he saw no hope of resisting successfully, and, scowling, Sif had evidently arrived at the same conclusion. She too suffered one of her captors to bind her hands behind her and her ankles together and then lay her back on the bench.

"Tying them's not enough," said Quy. "Someone needs to watch them."

"I'm well aware," Uschi said, a sardonic note in her voice. "I *have* commanded this company for a while. In fact, unless I'm mistaken, I outrank you, courier."

Quy blinked. "Yes, Captain. I didn't mean–"

"I'll take first watch myself," said Uschi, cutting her off. "The rest of you, get some sleep. We have a long flight ahead of us in the morning."

The other Valkyries sought their own benches and bedrolls. Once everyone was lying down, the buzzes and snorts of snoring arising here and there, Heimdall started tugging at the coarse rope around his wrists, trying to loosen his bonds and slip his hands free. His struggles, however, served only to scrape his wrists raw. He had an Asgardian's strength, but so too was this rope Asgardian, tied by someone who knew how to secure prisoners.

And what good, he thought, not far from despair, would it do him even if he did succeed in loosening his bonds? Uschi was sitting right across from him with a trestle table between them. If he jumped up, her cry would rouse the other Valkyries in an instant.

He hated the thought that this was how it was all going to end. Even now, he couldn't find it in himself to be sorry he'd helped the Valkyries, but he bitterly regretted that it had been necessary. It was probably going to cost Sif and him their lives.

He felt a twinge of surprise and anxiety when Uschi stood up and came around the table. He wondered if she was coming to check his bonds and if she'd see he'd been pulling at them. If so, she was likely to have him restrained even more securely. But she passed on by without so much as a glance.

Uschi walked to the spot where the Valkyries had stowed their shared provisions, found the white cheese that had been part of supper, drew a dagger from her belt, and cut off a fresh slice. Munching it, she headed back in Heimdall and Sif's direction. Still without acknowledging the prisoners in any way, she put the dagger on the trestle table. The knife was only a few steps from the benches on which they lay. She then returned to her bench.

At first what had happened seemed too fortunate to be true. Heimdall almost felt he didn't dare believe it, as if embracing hope would somehow turn it false. Surely Uschi had set down the dagger absentmindedly, by accident. Surely she'd notice the lapse at any moment, rise, and retrieve it.

That wasn't what happened, though. Instead she slumped and eventually let out a soft snore, either truly asleep or more likely feigning it, and the knife remained where she'd set it.

Heimdall heaved a shivering sigh of relief. Now it seemed plain that, reluctant either to openly defy Frigga's express command or to repay benefactors with captivity and the likelihood of execution, Uschi had opted to steer a middle course and give Sif and him a chance.

It was *only* a chance, however. Now it was up to him to take advantage of it. He swung his legs off his bench and stood up. One of the Valkyries had covered him with his cloak when he lay down, and the garment spilled down around his feet.

The cloak nearly tripped him when he started hopping. He felt a jolt of alarm, and Sif gave a tiny involuntary hiss of dismay. Recovering his balance, he headed on toward the dagger. Tense as he was, it seemed to him that each little jump thumped the earthen floor like a drumbeat, and he feared each would rouse his captors. But none of the Valkyries stirred, and in due course he reached the trestle table. Facing away from it, he groped for the dagger, put the blade to the bonds securing his hands, and sawed.

It was awkward work and seemed to take forever. Once, he fumbled his grip, the dagger fell back on the tabletop with a clink, and he flinched. It hadn't fallen far, though, and no one roused at the sound either. His heart thumping, trying not to let nervousness make him clumsy, he took a long breath, expelled it slowly, and picked up the knife again.

Finally, one of the loops securing his hands parted, a second did the same, and then he was able to shake off the rest of them. He freed his feet, then tiptoed back to Sif and relieved her of her bonds.

They found their armor, backpacks, and the weapons the Valkyries had taken from them but didn't immediately put them on. They begrudged the time the process would take and the noise it might make. They slipped outside into the cold and donned their gear in the wind and the snow.

As the two Vanir readied themselves, Sif said, "I should have gone after Uschi's dagger. You were lurching around like a three-legged cow."

Heimdall chuckled. "You can do it next time." He buckled his baldric and then adjusted it, making sure he could draw the two-handed sword hanging down his back without difficulty.

"Let's hope there won't be a next time." Sif frowned at her quiver, or rather, her brother suspected, at the fact that after the fight with the frost giants there were only a few arrows remaining. "Are you ready to run?"

"I don't think we should try it on foot. Uschi gave us our chance, but come morning, the Valkyries will hunt us. Frigga's command doesn't leave them any choice. They'll catch us, too, if we're on the ground."

"Wait," she said. "Are you saying we should steal two of the winged stallions?"

"That was my thought. If you noticed, two survived the fight with the Jotuns when their riders didn't."

"That may be," Sif said, frowning dubiously, "but there are stories about the mystic bond between the Valkyries and their steeds. Supposedly the horses won't carry anyone else."

"We can hope," Heimdall said, "they're *only* stories."

"Even if they are, nobody ever taught either of us to ride a flying horse. Wait, don't tell me. We'll figure it out." Sif grinned, her doubts abruptly giving way to boldness in the way they often did. "And maybe we will. I know I've always *wanted* to ride a Valkyrie's steed across the sky ever since I was a little girl."

"On to the barn, then."

They crept to the adjacent structure, where, as warriors obeying the exigencies of war, the Valkyries had turned out the abandoned cattle in the stalls to fend for themselves before putting their mounts in their places. As the door creaked open, Heimdall tensed and held his breath at the thought that the equines might raise an immediate commotion that would bring Quy and the other Valkyries. That didn't happen, though. The moonlight shining through the door revealed the horses standing placidly, majestic magical creatures incongruous in such mundane surroundings.

Brother and sister moved down the central aisle of the barn, and Heimdall found a roan steed with feathered wings sunset red and another horse that was black except for golden eyes and a golden mane.

"These are the two that lost their riders," he said. He saw no reason to affront one of the surviving Valkyries by taking her particular mount.

"Are you sure?" asked Sif.

"Fairly."

"Let's get to it, then." Sif eased toward the roan and swung open the stall door. "Hello, beautiful boy."

Heimdall did his best to approach the golden-eyed horse with the same gentleness. "Hello, my friend." Nonetheless, the winged stallion whinnied and reared as soon as he entered the stall. Startled and dismayed, recalling how the steed had hammered the face of the downed frost giant with his hooves after the Jotun killed his rider, the Asgardian made a hasty retreat.

Sif shot him an irritated look. The Valkyries had left the horses' accouterments hanging on the wooden sides of the stalls, and she already had the roan's bridle on. "What are you doing?"

"He doesn't seem to like me," Heimdall said. "I don't know why. I generally get along with animals."

Sif frowned. "The stories that only a Valkyrie can ride a Valkyrie horse may be false – let's hope – but I doubt a male has ever tried to ride him before, and after losing his rightful owner, he's not having it. Let's see how he responds to me." She scratched the roan's withers with her fingertips. "Wait for me, beautiful boy. I'll be right back."

With that, she entered the black steed's stall humming a Vanir lullaby about a little girl and the pony that carried her to the Moon and under the sea before the two decided the meadows of home were best. The stallion snorted and permitted her to stroke his nose.

"I know," she crooned, "I know. My brother is an ugly, stupid man. But he has a kind heart, and he'll treat you well." She looked back at Heimdall. "Shall I saddle him for you?"

"No," Heimdall said. "If I can't even get him ready to ride, I'll never manage him well enough to get far from here before the Valkyries start hunting us. Just keep him calm for another moment." He cautiously eased back into the stall and stood beside his sister. This time, the black stallion allowed him to approach. As he looked into the animal's golden eyes, he fancied he once again saw understanding surpassing the comprehension of ordinary horses.

"You just lost the rider you loved," he said, "and I'm not what you're used to. For all I know, someone taught you never to let someone like me on your back. But I promise you, your rider wanted the same thing Sif and I want: to protect Asgard, home to all of us, from its foes. If you'll carry me, we'll honor your rider by accomplishing her purpose. We'll avenge her too, along the way." He glanced at his sister. "Let me pet him."

Sif pulled her hand back.

Heimdall stroked the black steed's nose as she'd been doing, and the winged horse didn't shy or try to bite. Instead, he nickered. "I think it will be all right now."

"Maybe so." Sif returned to the roan.

Heimdall found the black stallion's saddle blanket and laid it across his back. The winged horse allowed it. "My name is Heimdall," he said, crooning as Sif had done. "My people the Vanir will tell you I have nine mothers, but really there's just the one mother who bore me and eight godmothers. It's a silly way of speaking, isn't it? I wish I knew the name your Valkyrie gave you, but since I don't, I'm going to call you Golden Mane. I hope that's all right."

The steed tossed his head in a way that might have been intended for a nod.

When the winged stallions were ready with the two Asgardians' packs, quivers, and bows secured to the saddles, they led the animals out of the barn, closed the door behind them, and mounted up. "Let's ride them on the ground a little way," Heimdall said. "Get used to them and get them used to us. Then we'll figure out how to manage them in the air."

That, however, was not the way it worked out. He and Sif rode the horses away from the barn at a walk. Slightly in the lead, she then urged her steed into a canter, and he did likewise.

The roan stallion's wings beat, and he and his startled rider rose into the air. A moment later, Golden Mane and Heimdall ascended too. Apparently, the steeds' nature and training were such that it never occurred to them that their new riders might want to remain on solid earth.

Heimdall's saddle and stirrups were essentially the same as those of any ordinary mount and suddenly seemed very inadequate contrivances to keep a rider from falling off. Pushing fear away, he told himself that if the Valkyries kept their seats, he could too, and forced himself to keep his head upright, his back straight, his weight evenly distributed on both seat bones, and *not* grip with his knees, all as his boyhood riding tutor had instructed. After a few moments, he felt somewhat more confident.

Up ahead, the roan accelerated, and Golden Mane's wings, like those of a raven grown to enormous size, lashed faster to keep up. Heimdall allowed the stallion to fly as he would, and they pulled up even with the red horse and Sif.

His sister was grinning. "This is fun!" she called.

Heimdall smiled back. "You know, it is, once you stop worrying about falling to your death."

"Do you think we're far enough from the farmstead to study how to guide the horses?"

"Yes, and we'd better. I don't want to go riding into Jotunheim on a mount I'm not sure I can control."

He found that the familiar commands delivered via tugs

on the reins and nudging heels worked well for telling Golden Mane to go right or left or faster and slower. The trick was communicating to the stallion that he wanted to ascend or descend. There was no way to discover how to do that except pure experimentation.

At one point the black horse seemed to fall like a piece of stone. Some frantic pulling on the reins made Golden Mane level out, and in the aftermath, panting, sweating despite the ambient chill, Heimdall decided he hadn't really inadvertently given a command that would prompt the steed to smash himself and his rider to bits on the ground far below. Rather, he'd stumbled on the way to tell Golden Mane to furl his wings and dive at a foe like a hawk plunging at a hare.

Gradually he worked out what he needed to know. Where up and down were concerned, the black horse responded to light little flicks of the reins, the number of flicks conveying exactly what his rider intended him to do. Heimdall rode close enough to call to Sif across the intervening distance, told her what he'd learned, and she found that the roan responded to the same commands.

With that, they flew north, still experimenting, but now to make the new commands second nature to themselves, and, if Heimdall was being honest, because flying and maneuvering in flight were truly exhilarating. The steeds performed what must have seemed to them all the unnecessary swooping and climbing obediently although Heimdall could imagine the moment would come when they'd exchange some sardonic comments in the language of their kind.

"We made it this far!" Sif called to him. "Which means no more misguided Asgardians trying to take us prisoner. There's nothing ahead but enemies!"

She sounded happy about it, and Heimdall supposed it might indeed make life simpler. But it plainly wouldn't make it any less dangerous.

SEVENTEEN

Enfeebled by the cloud cover though it was, the light of dawn sufficed to clearly reveal the border mountains of Jotunheim, jagged snowy crags like swords up and up and up where, a year ago, a person would have reached the edge of Asgard and, had they been bold enough to stand at the very brink, peered over and gazed into the infinite gulf below. Now, thanks to the conjunction that was a recurring natural phenomenon of the cosmos, the Realm Eternal and Jotunheim sat fused together as seamlessly as adjacent lands on the same continent.

Initially Heimdall had thought to fly so far above the snow-covered peaks that no frost giant lurking on them would even notice him and Sif, but it proved impossible to go that high. The cold was too bitter and the air too thin. It quickly became plain that the altitude was likely to kill both the winged horses and their riders.

Accordingly, Heimdall and Sif had no choice but to fly through one of the mountain passes with walls of gray rock, white snow, and glittering ice to either side. He warily scanned the steep slopes and narrow, crumbling ledges and thus far had seen no signs of trouble. Maybe, he thought, with the frost giants on the offensive, pushing across Asgard and driving its defenders before them, the creatures had neglected to guard the ways into their own country. Given that the Jotuns had Mimir's head to advise them it seemed unlikely, but anything was possible.

"Now that we're in Jotunheim," Sif called, "I trust you know the way to the fortress of the frost giant king?"

"I think so," he replied, drawing on the reins to steer Golden Mane closer to the center of the pass. "Jotunheim's not like the Realm Below. There are maps. Crude ones, but still."

"Then I'm glad you've looked at them," she said.

He smiled. "Someone had to give our childhood tutors something to do while you were skipping lessons to roam the fields and woods and practice swordplay."

"I did what a warrior in training… what's *that*?"

Heimdall looked where she was looking. A figure was peering at them from the shadow of an overhanging jut of stone with icicles dangling underneath.

The creature was as big as a frost giant, but the skin wasn't blue, and his proportions were less manlike, lending him a brutish, uncouth appearance to Heimdall's eyes. His hide was a blotchy, ruddy pink, and he had two stubby little horns spouting from his bald head and only four fingers on each hand. He was wearing a brass-studded leather tunic, more clothing than many of the Jotuns Heimdall had seen, but appeared equally indifferent to the cold. He glared at the travelers with rage on his ugly, twitching face.

If Heimdall wasn't mistaken, the watcher was a storm giant. The chronicles his boyhood curiosity had led him to read both described the creatures and said they'd once dwelled in Asgard alongside the Aesir. Eventually, however, there was a war, and the storm giants lost their lands and relocated to Jotunheim. Not willingly, though. Their enduring hatred of Asgardians was notorious.

This particular storm giant didn't appear to have a bow, spear, or any weapons for that matter. Relieved by that at least, Heimdall kicked Golden Mane into what, for a common earthbound horse, would be a gallop. He hoped he and Sif could race on by before it occurred to the massive creature to throw stones.

The storm giant shook his fist at them, and a frigid, howling wind sprang up to blow straight in the Asgardians' faces. Golden Mane whinnied, and his wing muscles bunched as, to Heimdall's dismay, the black steed suddenly had to struggle to make forward progress. Hoping to escape the effect, he sent the stallion swooping lower, but it didn't help. The wind was blowing just as hard at that altitude, the force increasing every second.

Sif snarled an obscenity, unlimbered her bow, and started loosing her few remaining arrows at the storm giant. Heimdall urged Golden Mane higher again and did the same. The attacks didn't help. The screaming gale tumbled every shaft off target.

The storm giant laughed a rumbling laugh and shook his fist again. Hail pummeled down with stinging force, the white stones the size of a child's fist and growing larger by the moment.

Grimly aware that he and Sif couldn't withstand the painful battering for long, Heimdall drew his great sword and rode Golden Mane straight at the storm giant. Sif readied her broadsword and followed.

The horned creature shook his fist a third time. Bolts of lightning blazed down from the clouds above to the snow-choked floor of the pass far below.

For a terrifying second, Heimdall felt as if one of the thunderbolts had struck him and his steed. Then he realized his senses had simply been overwhelmed. The constant flashes were blinding, and the booming thunder was deafening. It started avalanches pouring down the mountainsides, and the rumble and crash added to the cacophony.

Dazzled though he was, Heimdall *thought* he could still see where the storm giant was standing beyond the searing, stabbing brightness. Desperate, he kept charging – if Golden Mane's struggling progress could be called a charge – toward the foe.

The icy screaming wind blew harder still, so hard that Golden Mane strained in vain to stay on course. Then, suddenly, the black steed wasn't flying any more. Screaming, he was tumbling like a gale-blown leaf.

As the horse flipped upside down, Heimdall felt his feet slipping from the stirrups and his body starting to drop out of the saddle. Frantic, he kicked his feet forward, bent forward too, and flung an arm around Golden Mane's neck. Thus anchored, he stayed with the winged steed through the next terrifying, nauseating spin and the one after that.

Golden Mane lashed his wings. The moment was too

chaotic and Heimdall's sight too crippled for him to perceive how the black horse managed it, but suddenly he and his rider were upright again and stayed that way. He realized Golden Mane was flying before the wind, racing back down the pass the way they'd come, and he gave the stallion his head.

Heimdall's vision was a cloud of afterimages from the lightning strikes, and he didn't see how Golden Mane's could be any better. Periodically he spotted a vertical gray escarpment before him only when he and his mount were a scant instant away from crashing into it, and he desperately hauled on the reins to turn the stallion in time. At other moments, Golden Mane veered to avoid perils the warrior astride him only discerned afterward.

As his eyesight gradually improved, Heimdall cast about for Sif and felt a jolt of fear when he saw no trace of her. Then she called, "Here!" She was overhead and behind him, and he'd simply missed her. His shoulders slumped, and he heaved a sigh of relief.

They set their weary, trembling mounts down in the foothills that were the borderland of Asgard and ran up to the mountains. They gentled and praised the animals, and then, just as spent and frazzled themselves, sat down on the leeward side of a ridge that provided cover against the wind and any frost giants who might come marching out of the pass.

"Thank the Fates you made it," Heimdall said.

"It was all thanks to Bloodspiller," Sif replied. "He's a good horse."

Shaken though he was, for a moment, the name roused

Heimdall's sense of humor. "That's what you called him?"

"He's red, and he's a *war*horse. It's a better name than Golden Mane." Sif removed her water bottle from her belt, took a drink and then passed it over to him. The contents were nearly as cold as if he'd scooped up a handful of snow and put that in his mouth. There were flecks of soft mushy ice floating in the liquid.

As he passed the bottle back, his sister said, "So. That could have gone better."

Heimdall grunted. "I think that's a fair statement." Thanks to the trials of the journey thus far, he'd been gaining confidence in his martial prowess. The prospect of fighting frost giants no longer seemed as daunting as it had before. But the encounter with the storm giant had been different. He and Sif hadn't landed a single attack, and it was only luck that had allowed them to escape with their lives. He held in a shiver that had nothing to do with the cold.

He suspected Sif was still as rattled as he was, but, as usual she was doing a good job of masking any such feelings. "I wonder why the frost giant king is holding the storm giants back," she said.

"We can only guess," Heimdall replied, trying to match her calm, practical demeanor, "but he hasn't needed them to win battles so far. So why not use them to prevent incursions into Jotunheim and otherwise keep them in reserve? I imagine they'll turn up as an unpleasant surprise if the giants lay siege to the city of Asgard itself."

"Someone," said Sif, "should warn the queen what's coming."

"I agree. But even assuming Frigga would listen to us

traitors, we can either turn around and tell her what we've learned, or we can press on and recover Mimir's head. We can't do both at once."

"Assuming we can even get into Jotunheim," Sif replied. "Does every storm giant have the magic we were just facing?"

"I think probably just the sorcerers and witches. But I don't know how many of those there are. For all we know, enough to protect every path into Jotunheim."

"Even if there aren't," Sif said, "we have no way of knowing which passes they're watching and which they aren't. Or what defenses are waiting in any passes the weather workers aren't protecting. Something nasty, I imagine."

Heimdall hated the thought of his sister daring one of the passes again. "It occurs to me that maybe we *can* handle both tasks at once. You can turn back and find a way to convey what we've learned to Frigga. I can keep trying–"

Sif scowled and answered as he'd expected. "Don't be stupid. We already had this conversation. I'm sticking with you, and that's that. We just have to find a way in."

They sat in silence for a time, while the wind – not the raging, freezing gale the storm giant had conjured, thank goodness, but cold nonetheless – whispered out of the north. Heimdall strained to find a stratagem but could think of nothing. The intent, sour look on Sif's face revealed she was trying too and not faring any better.

After a time, she said, "Thor would smash that storm giant magic like it was nothing."

Heimdall didn't doubt it. Thor was the God of Thunder, after all, the supreme master of the powers of the storm. But what did it matter? "Thor isn't here," he said.

"I know that. I'm just saying." She paused for a beat. "Here's a thought. The storm giant spotted us when we flew in. What if we ride in at ground level?"

Heimdall shook his head. "I don't think that would help. Most Asgardian warriors travel on the ground. The storm giants are surely watching the floors of the passes as attentively as they're watching for flyers."

Sif sighed. "I suppose so. Do *you* have an idea?"

"No." He was chagrined to admit it. Sif might tease him about his bookishness and his musings over things no one else considered worth pondering, but he knew that, deep down, she thought him clever if eccentric, and now it hurt to feel he was letting her down. "Except choose a different pass and hope we can contend with whatever's waiting for us there."

His sister snorted. "I could have come up with that. But all right. Let's rest a while longer and then have at it."

EIGHTEEN

Eventually Sif gave Heimdall a questioning look. He nodded, and they rose, stretched, and shifted their limbs to shed the stiffness that had come from sitting on the cold ground.

As they moved to Bloodspiller and Golden Mane, Heimdall tried to summon up the dauntless attitude of a proper Asgardian warrior, the confidence that his prowess would see him through any fight, and that if it didn't, that simply meant fate had chosen to favor the other side and it was time to die bravely if need be.

But he couldn't feel that way, not when failure would likely mean defeat for Asgard and the loss of his sister's life as well as his own. He was no seer to glimpse the future, but at that moment he had a premonition nonetheless, a certainty that if he and Sif couldn't come up with a better plan, they were surely riding to their doom. Perhaps, he thought, he was fey. That was what the skalds called it when, at the end of a saga, the hero was stubbornly embarked on the course of action that would spell his doom.

Well, he thought defiantly, he didn't *want* to be fey, and perhaps it was the trapped, desperate feeling he was experiencing that finally made an idea pop into his head.

"Wait," he said.

Sif had already mounted the roan and looked down at him from the saddle. "What is it?" she asked.

"Maybe I have an idea after all. We've been thinking of the Valkyries as Odin's flying warriors."

His sister shrugged, making the pauldrons of her red and white armor clink. "That's what they are."

"In times of war, yes. But they're more than that. They're the choosers of the slain. The All-Father sends them flying over the battlefields of Midgard to collect the souls of fallen warriors to live new lives in Valhalla. To do that, they have to cross between worlds, and apparently they can do it because their steeds can do it."

"Apparently," Sif repeated. From the skeptical tone of her voice, she understood what he was suggesting but had considerable misgivings.

"That's what the stories say."

"You're still putting an inordinate amount of faith in the stories."

"For want of anything better."

"Well," said Sif, "I haven't heard any tales of Valkyries crossing from Asgard into Jotunheim, only into Midgard. Even if it's possible, we don't know how to tell Golden Mane and Bloodspiller to do it. It was difficult enough just figuring out how to manage them in the air."

"But we worked it out," Heimdall said, "and if we open a magical way into Jotunheim, we avoid the mountain passes."

Sif suddenly flashed a grin. "Well, no one can say life isn't interesting following you around. All right, then. Mount up, and we'll see what we can do."

They flew the winged stallions into the air, where they tried to discover a new combination of rein flicks that would send their mounts flying out of one world and into another. The only results were pointless veerings, swoops, and ascensions that, Heimdall sensed, were making the steeds increasingly annoyed. In his imagination, Golden Mane asked, "Didn't you already put me through all of this?"

Heimdall called to Sif. "Anything?"

"I'm still here, aren't I?"

"I'm going to try voice commands!" He leaned close to Golden Mane's ears. "Take me to Jotunheim, boy! Jotunheim!"

The black steed just kept gliding beneath the heavy lead-colored clouds that covered the sky where Asgard and the land of the frost giants met. Maybe that was the problem. Golden Mane judged they were already in Jotunheim.

"Midgard!" Heimdall said. "Let's go to Midgard!" If he could get the black steed to cross into any other world, that would at least be a start.

Once again, their surroundings didn't change.

"From time to time," Heimdall said in frustration, "I thought you more intelligent than an earthbound horse. You're not showing it at the moment." He sighed. "But no, forgive me, that's not fair. I'm the stupid one for not knowing what the Valkyries taught you."

He tried to imagine what it must be like to pass between worlds when they weren't in conjunction and no sorcerer's incantation was whisking you from one to the other. Perhaps, in those circumstances, you didn't simply step or blink to your destination. Maybe there was a kind of limbo you had to cross.

"Take me to the place between worlds!" he told Golden Mane. That didn't work. "Take me to the void!" That didn't work, either. "Take me to the gulf!" Nothing. "Take me outside!" Still nothing. "Show me Yggdrasil!"

A luminous circle, a sort of doorway or tunnel, he couldn't tell which, irised open in the air before him, its coruscating, shifting rainbow colors a contrast to the gray and white sky and landscape. He twisted in the saddle to shout to Sif and tell her what he'd said, but the circle of light engulfed him and his steed before he could get the words out, and an instant later, he and Golden Mane were somewhere else.

Feathered wings beating slowly, Golden Mane was cantering through a space illuminated by stars and phosphorescent nebulae on every side, and in the center of that seemingly limitless void stood – or floated – Yggdrasil the World Tree, its topmost reaches a leafy crown and its bottom roots that twisted away and dwindled to points without ever anchoring in solid earth like those of a common tree.

The Nine Worlds perched along Yggdrasil's length. Poised on three of the upper branches were Asgard, loftiest of all, then Vanaheim, and next Alfheim, home of the bright elves who existed on friendly terms with the Aesir and Vanir. Midway down, encircling the trunk like a ring on a finger, was Midgard, home of mortal men, and below that, likewise circular but bigger, surrounding Yggdrasil like a hoop, was Jotunheim. At the bottom, poised on one or another root, were Nidavellir, the land of dwarves like Mudbeard; Muspelheim, home to the fire giants and fire demons; Svartalfheim, the realm of the malevolent dark elves; and Niffleheim, where the goddess Hela ruled over a kingdom of the dead.

Frozen, his eyes wide, Heimdall stared at the sight in amazement, in part because surely no one could regard it without awe and in part, he realized now, because until this moment he'd shared Sif's doubts that his idea could actually work.

Having thought of Sif, he looked around and realized with a pang of dismay that she wasn't with him. But as he wondered how to return to his former location and fetch her, another prismatic circle opened near him, and she and Bloodspiller flew through, after which the ground shrank out of existence.

He gave her time to gawk at the spectacle before them. He was sure she needed it. When he judged that if her astonishment hadn't passed – for how could it ever truly pass? – it at least wasn't stupefying her any more, he called, "How did you know how to follow me?"

"I didn't," Sif replied. "But when you and Golden Mane vanished, Bloodspiller followed of his own accord. This… this is unbelievable."

"It's what sages and philosophers said it would be, but I know what you mean, and I agree. The sight is overwhelming."

Sif took a deep breath. "It is. But we can't afford to be overwhelmed. We have to figure out the next step. You're seeing what you expected to see, but do you understand it?"

"Not really," Heimdall said. "I don't know how we're not dying of the cold and lack of air out here when we couldn't even survive a flight high over the border mountains of Jotunheim. For that matter, how can we make out the Tree so clearly with only starlight to reveal it?"

The consideration of all the things he didn't understand gave him a pang of trepidation. How could he hope to accomplish his goal when he knew so little about this uncanny place? But now that he and Sif were here, he had to try.

His sister made a spitting sound. "All of that just is what it is. We can simply be glad of it and move on. I meant, do you understand what matters to us? Why aren't Asgard and Jotunheim touching? Does that mean the conjunction is over?"

"Wouldn't that be nice? But my guess is no. The mystics say Yggdrasil gives a different view of reality. Higher. Eternal. Likely unchanging no matter how the various worlds move in and out of alignment."

"In that case," said Sif, "here's the most important question. By the looks of it, we're thousands and thousands of leagues from any of the Nine Worlds. How do we ride to where we're going without it taking us years?"

"It doesn't take the Valkyries years," Heimdall replied. "Maybe distance is different here, or the magic of the horses overcomes it. There's one way to find out."

"Fair enough." Sif nudged Bloodspiller with her heels. The roan's wings beat faster, and his legs galloped. "Come on, beautiful boy! We're going to Jotunheim!"

Heimdall urged Golden Mane to go faster and keep up. He thought that after the black stallion reached full speed, another shimmering circle might open in front of them, but if that was going to happen, it wasn't happening yet. He pushed away the dismal thought that perhaps it wouldn't happen at all because he and Sif would never figure out how to give the proper command.

Meanwhile, though the two Asgardians had yet to ride appreciably closer, Yggdrasil and the worlds it contained somehow seemed to loom even vaster than before. Merely by being what they were, they inspired the terrifying feeling that they were on the verge of crushing an ephemeral mite like himself into nonexistence.

The silence of the void reinforced the burgeoning fear as if it was another aspect of the dreadful spectacle before him, the totality that finite beings looked upon at risk of madness or perhaps even annihilation. He heard the tiny clinks of his armor, the creaks of his saddle, the rustle of Golden Mane's lashing wings, but nothing else. He wanted to call out to Sif just to make more noise but could think of nothing to say.

Gradually he came to feel as though all thought, all memory, all purpose was abandoning him, as if the erasing of his consciousness and perhaps his very being had already commenced. He wanted to keep his steed pointed toward his destination, less now to fulfill his mission than simply to escape the obliterating pressure of the void, but he'd forgotten what his destination was.

For a time, numbness and dread smothered him, and then Golden Mane slowed from an aerial gallop to a canter. The shifting attendant upon the altered gait roused Heimdall, and with a flash of terror, he felt he'd been on the verge of losing himself completely and forever.

He looked over at Sif. To his horror, she was slumped and lolling in the saddle, her features vacant. She was clearly in the same perilous condition he'd still be in himself if Golden Mane, apparently feeling his rider's slackening grip on the reins and no longer certain of his intent, hadn't slowed down.

At that, Heimdall was afraid he'd only delayed the inevitable. He could already feel the ghastly majesty of the sight before him threatening to grind him beyond insignificance into nothingness. "Please," he said to Golden Mane, "I know I don't know what I'm doing, but you do. Get us out of here! If you don't, Sif and I are going to die!"

The black steed tossed his head and resumed his gallop. To Heimdall's relief, Bloodspiller accelerated to keep up with his stablemate.

But, Heimdall wondered, were the horses actually racing through the void to any purpose? He feared not, but with his thoughts crumbling once again, there was nothing to do but trust them.

After an excruciating time, another glittering portal opened. Heimdall had just enough of his faculties left to be glad. Golden Mane flew through, Bloodspiller followed, and the Asgardian's thoughts jolted back into focus. For an instant he rejoiced, then realized that just because he'd emerged from the ordeal alive and sane didn't mean his sister had. Tense with dread at what he might discover, he looked over at her and called, "Are you all right?"

"More or less," she answered, a tremor in her voice. For a

heartbeat, he closed his eyes in relief. "How do the Valkyries endure that?"

"Training, I imagine," he replied, "or some initiation into the sisterhood that grants them immunity."

"Well," she said, "however they manage it, they're welcome to it. Are we where we're supposed to be?"

He realized it was a good question. It didn't matter how shaken the void had left him. There were practical matters to attend to. "Let's look around and find out."

For a little while, as they soared over glaciers white as salt, Heimdall dared to hope this might indeed be Jotunheim. But in time, the glaciers gave way to evergreen forests. When he and Sif passed over a village in which the folk were no bigger than they were, had pink skin rather than blue, and cried out in wonder instead of shouting an alarm and raising weapons, the truth was undeniable.

"We're in Midgard," said Sif, frustration in her voice.

"Yes," Heimdall said. He shared her disappointment. "I suppose that when we became incapable of riding in the proper direction, the horses came to the world they're accustomed to visiting."

"I'm grateful they brought us anywhere that isn't that emptiness. But we still need to get to Jotunheim."

"I know."

"They must have sorcerers on Midgard. Someone who can shift us to where we want to go."

Heimdall frowned, considering the idea and then reluctantly deciding that – much as he dreaded returning to the void where Yggdrasil stood – it wouldn't serve. "Maybe, but by all accounts, true, powerful wizardry is even rarer here than in Asgard. How long would it take to find a warlock with the proper skills? Does Asgard have that kind of time?"

"Curse you, your knowledge, and your logic! But all right. If we have to go look at the Tree again, I suppose we have to."

"Let's take a rest first, and when we do go back we can talk to one another throughout the ride. The conversation will fill our minds and distract us from the void."

"That makes sense." Sif pointed. "I see a stream down there."

Hissing over mossy stones, the water was bracingly cold. Kneeling beside the stream, Heimdall drank his fill of it and scrubbed his face with more. Afterwards, he and Sif ate some of the pilfered food from their backpacks while the horses grazed. The two Asgardians then sat in companionable silence and he sought to think of things they might talk about when they returned to the void.

He also found himself thinking of how difficult and dangerous it had been just to get this far. It was likely to be more difficult and dangerous still to deal with the perils of the void, Jotunheim, and ultimately stealing Mimir's head from the stronghold of the frost giant king himself. Seeking to bolster his resolve, he told himself he and Sif had overcome daunting perils already and honed their skills in the doing of it. Surely they were ready for what would come next.

Finally, her voice steady, Sif asked, "Ready?"

"Yes," he said, doing his best to hide his anxiety as, he suspected, she was hiding hers. They mounted their steeds, and, splashing up water, the stallions galloped down the stream where there were no branches overhead to hinder their ascent and after a few strides lashed their wings and rose into the air. When they'd climbed above the trees, Heimdall said, "Take me to Yggdrasil!" A round luminous portal opened before him.

The spectacle of the colossal Tree was as awe-inspiring as before but more frightening because now he knew how quickly its transcendent immensity would start eroding his mind. He made sure Sif had emerged safely into the void and then, determined to exit the gulf as quickly as possible, turned Golden Mane toward Jotunheim.

"Do you think," Sif called, "that when we return Mimir's head to Asgard, that will truly be enough to absolve us of blame?"

You, anyway, he thought. You're not the fool who killed that poor guard. "I do," he said aloud. "There has to be some limit to everyone's blind adherence to tradition and Odin's decrees."

"I have to point out that if *you'd* blindly adhered to tradition and the All-Father's decrees, we wouldn't be here looking at this wretched Tree. I can feel the weight of it pushing down on me already."

"Don't think about it," he replied. "Concentrate on what we're saying to one another and on keeping Bloodspiller – I still say that's a name for a sword, not a horse – pointed in the right direction." He strained to think of what to say next. Yggdrasil's terrible magnificence was making it difficult to recall any of the topics he'd hit on while sitting beside the stream. Eventually, however, he remembered one. It was a good one, too. Teasing and thus annoying Sif might help her keep her thoughts sharp. "You made a point of saying

Thor's power was more than a match for any storm giant's."

"Well, isn't it?"

"Almost certainly," Heimdall said, "but since he isn't with us, I wonder what brought him to mind. You fancy him, don't you?" Sif and Thor had played together as children when Odin was paying a state visit to Vanaheim or her parents had taken the family to visit Asgard and had occasionally seen one another since.

"If I did," Sif said, plainly annoyed by the question, "it would be no business of yours."

Heimdall grinned. "That's not a denial. If Thor returns your feelings, maybe you should talk to our parents. Odin might look with favor on a union between his house and a noble family of the Vanir."

"I said leave it alone. When I marry, *if* I marry, it will be without any prompting from you. What do you know about courting anyway? I don't see women lining up for you. Well, except for Myrgiol back home, but she had a nose like a woodpecker and a laugh to match."

"That," Heimdall said, "is a filthy slander."

They continued to tease one another as the horses winged their way toward Yggdrasil. For a time it was enough, but all the while Heimdall felt the inimical hugeness of the World Tree and the gulf gnawing at him. It became steadily harder to think of what to say next or remember why he should say anything, and the lengthening pauses before his sister's replies and even in the midst of them showed she was succumbing to the same mind-devouring power.

"Do you remember… Odger?" Sif asked. "He used… to go ice skating with us."

Heimdall struggled to dredge up an appropriate reply. "Yes. I remember him. Why?"

"Just... I remember too..." Her voice trailed off as if the surrounding silence had encroached on it and smothered it.

For a while, his thoughts fading and blurring into blankness, Heimdall didn't care that his sister wasn't talking, but then a flicker of alarm reminded him he should. "Sif!" he shouted. "Sif!"

She didn't answer. Insensible, she was swaying in the saddle as if she were a scarecrow, and he was sure it was only due to the instincts and training of their two steeds that they were still riding along side by side and not lost to one another in the vastness of the gulf.

He cast about. Just as it was difficult to think, so too was it difficult to perceive and understand what he beheld. But there was a world spread out before him, undeniably larger to the eye and therefore nearer than any of the Nine had been before. He frantically urged Golden Mane toward it, and another round gate opened before them. They flew through, and Sif and the roan emerged from their own portal a moment later.

For a moment, his mind filled only with the relief that came from escaping the void, he closed his eyes and slumped in the saddle. Then it came to him that the air was smoky and hot, so hot that sweat was already pouring from his body.

He regarded the land spread out below him. It was a barren expanse in which nothing grew but heat and fire. Lava flowed from erupting volcanoes in the distance, and flame leaped from huge pits in the ground. Awful as the vista was, he was still grateful to have escaped the void but likewise alarmed to have blundered into a world as hostile as Jotunheim and frustrated that he and Sif had failed again to reach their destination.

To judge from her reaction, Sif primarily felt the frustration, for she snarled a string of obscenities. "This has to be Muspelheim! In our daze, we flew too low on the Tree."

Heimdall struggled to find something good to say about that. "At least now we know the horses can reach any of the Nine Worlds, not just Asgard and Midgard."

"Yes," Sif said grimly, "and I suppose it's time to try again."

Despite their inhospitable surroundings, Heimdall felt a pang of trepidation. "You don't think we should rest again first?"

"Where?" she asked. "Do you see somewhere cool and comfortable that I'm missing?"

"No."

"Then, horrible as the emptiness outside is, we need to go. We're going to cook if we stay here."

"You're right." Heimdall addressed himself to Golden Mane. "Take me back to Yggdrasil!" Their fiery surroundings persisted. "Come on, my friend! Yggdrasil!" As before, they remained in Muspelheim. He looked around. Sif and Bloodspiller were still flying along beside him.

"What's wrong?" she called.

"I don't know," he said. "Maybe we've pushed the steeds too hard."

Sif frowned. "They don't seem tired. They're flying as fast as before."

“Maybe the power to cross between worlds is different. Separate from their physical stamina.”

“So what do we do?”

“Wait a while. Give them a chance to recover their magic.”

“I hope we have a while.” Sif pointed.

Heimdall looked at the place she was indicating. Their progress had brought them near a kind of encampment. He would gladly have given it a wide berth, but columns and drifting veils of smoke and the glare of magma and leaping flame had concealed it hitherto.

The tents and lean-tos glowed red, seemingly built of lava that had hardened but retained its heat, or even some sort of solidified flame. Their forms gaunt and angular, sheathed in fire or made of it entirely, the fire demon inhabitants were agitated at the sight of the Asgardians and winged steeds above them. They clamored to one another in their hissing, crackling language and rushed about grabbing javelins and bows.

“Yggdrasil!” Heimdall cried. Sif shouted the same. But neither Golden Mane nor Bloodspiller opened a gateway.

Well, in that case, Heimdall thought, maybe the horses could climb higher than a fire demon could throw a spear or loose an arrow. He urged the black steed to ascend, Sif followed, and the first blazing missiles dropped back down short of reaching their marks.

With every wing beat, the Asgardians were leaving the fire demon tribe behind. Relieved, reasonably certain he and Sif were now safe, Heimdall took a cautious look backward.

The spirits of flame had formed a circle around one of their number who was brandishing a staff and probably chanting an incantation although Heimdall couldn't make out the recitation at such a distance with columns of flame roaring and erupting volcanoes booming all around. The spell brought forth new fire leaping from the earth in discrete lines that drew a jagged arcane figure around the tribal warriors. When the drawing was complete, the fire demons hurtled up into the air. The enchantment had evidently given them the ability to fly.

"Watch out!" Heimdall called. "They're coming after us!"

Sif looked back and cursed. "Some of them still have bows! Don't let them hit you!"

They guided the horses, veering back and forth and bobbing up and down to throw off the fire demons' aim. Shafts of flame shot past them and arced downward. Despite Heimdall's attempts at evasion, one missile pounded him in the back but failed to penetrate his armor. Golden Mane whinnied as the burning arrow tumbled down his flank and away.

"You see?" Heimdall gritted. "Yggdrasil would be a very good idea."

Golden Mane neighed again. The Asgardian hoped that meant the horse was trying.

He glimpsed red and yellow brightness from the corner of his eye. Somehow flying faster than his fellows, a fire demon with a blazing lance was closing in on him. Heimdall let go of the reins and, now guiding the stallion with his knees, readied the two-handed sword.

The fire demon turned in flight to come in straight behind him. Twisting at the waist, Heimdall parried a lance thrust and cut at one of the hands gripping the weapon. He half severed the extremity, and the demon shrieked, dropped the spear, and abandoned the chase.

When Heimdall looked forward again, to his relief, a sparkling circle, the glimmering pastel colors a contrast to the glaring brightness of Muspelheim, was opening before him. He and Golden Mane plunged through, and Sif and Bloodspiller followed a second later.

"It looks different!" Sif called.

She was right. They were flying not far above a gnarled, colossal tubular growth. Well, *not far above* relatively speaking. They didn't have a clear view of the World Tree in its entirety, although if he tried, he could make out the trunk rising and rising to inconceivable heights above him.

"I think that before," he said, "the horses took us to a point from which all Nine Worlds were readily accessible."

"Readily accessible," Sif repeated sardonically.

"Well, if we were Valkyries who weren't bothered by the void and knew what we were doing. This time, though, maybe the steeds only had strength for a short jump. My guess is that we're flying above a length of the same root that Muspelheim perches on. Or anyway, one of the roots at the base of the Tree."

"Then what do we do now?" she asked.

He frowned, pondering. "I doubt the horses have the strength for another try at Jotunheim. Even if they do, I don't know if we could bear it. This time around, we've only been here a minute, and I already feel stupor or insanity nibbling at my mind."

It was so. He might have hoped that with repeated exposures he'd build up a tolerance to viewing the universe in its entirely, a view that apparently only special individuals with extraordinary gifts were ever meant to see. Or that his current vantage point, from which the whole of Yggdrasil was less clearly in sight, would prove easier to bear. But to his dismay, neither was proving to be the case. He struggled against the ghastly feeling that he'd landed Sif and himself in a deadly puzzle they couldn't solve. What if they never made it to Jotunheim? What if they couldn't even find their way back to Asgard or Midgard again?

Scowling, Sif said, "So trying for Jotunheim is what we *don't* do. What we don't do isn't a plan."

Trying to emulate her stalwart, practical example, he pushed aside his fears and then realized there was at least one more thing to try. "Follow me." He sent Golden Mane swooping toward the colossal tree root.

As he and Sif descended, he waited for the two steeds to open new portals, but they didn't, and apparently they didn't need to. To his burgeoning relief, the root expanded in his sight, seemingly shedding its cylindrical nature to become a more or less flat expanse of land, a gray-brown territory mottled with patches of dull green moss that hadn't been visible from higher up. The approach relieved him of the cosmic perspective a pair of common Asgardian warriors simply couldn't tolerate for long.

Brother and sister set their steeds down on what now appeared to be a tableland with hillocks and declivities discernible in the distance. They dismounted, praised and stroked the winged horses, and then, exhausted, slumped to the ground to rest.

NINETEEN

"Well," said Sif after they'd been resting for a while, "since I started following your lead, I've been outlawed, hunted, had to fight my fellow Asgardian warriors, trolls, frost giants, and storm giants, and now I suppose you could say I've lost my very existence in Odin's world. Or any of the Nine Worlds, for that matter."

Heimdall felt relief at the wry comment. It showed Sif was still in her right mind and her morale remained strong. He supposed there was reason for that. Whatever dangers awaited them here on the surface of the root, at least they couldn't see the whole of Yggdrasil clearly and thus didn't suffer the debilitating effects of that terrible spectacle.

He smiled a crooked smile. "I didn't know you were keeping score."

She grinned back. "I just want you to realize how many favors you're going to owe me when we finally get out of all this."

"Believe me, I know." The glum thought occurred to

him that he might never be able to give them when he was called to account for killing the guard, and he pushed the reflection aside. There were far more immediate things to worry about. "Is this the moment when you ask me what the new plan is?"

"I was actually going to let you rest for a few more minutes, but if you're up to it, feel free to dazzle me with your cleverness."

Frowning, he sought to recall everything he'd ever heard about Yggdrasil itself as opposed the various worlds it supported. Eventually he said, "I don't know that we should try again to reach Jotunheim in the same way we did before. Unless we're simply lucky, I don't see why we'd fare any better than we did previously."

Sif nodded. "I agree. That's the last resort. What do we do instead?"

"Supposedly," he said, "there are three wells to be found down here among the roots. One is Udarbrunnr, the Well of Fate, which the Norns tend to make sure the World Tree continues to flourish."

Sif's blue eyes narrowed. "The Three Sisters live up in Asgard, in Nornheim. Everybody knows that."

"Exactly," Heimdall said. "So they must have some quick way of getting back and forth. Perhaps it would serve to take us to Jotunheim as well. If we can catch them at the Well of Fate, we can ask them."

Sif grunted. "If we'd known we were going to end up here, we could have asked them in Asgard."

"Or, we could have stolen Skidbladnir from Odin's vault and sailed comfortably between worlds. But we couldn't know, and now we have to contend with our situation as it is."

"Go on contending, then. Are the Norns our only chance, other than riding back out into the emptiness and hoping our luck will turn?"

"No," he said. "Another of the wells is Mimisbrunnr. Mimir's Well. Legend has it there's a path to Jotunheim somewhere in the vicinity."

Sif brushed back a stray lock of her black hair. "That doesn't make a lot of sense. Mimir wasn't a Jotun. He was of the Aesir."

"I know. But he was also one of the ancient ones like Odin, and, like the All-Father, may have had secret dealings with the people of any number of the Nine Worlds back at the dawn of time."

"More to the point," said Sif, "we're at the bottom of the tree with Jotunheim high above us. How could one of the roots connect to it?"

"That puzzles me too. All I can think of is this is a different reality than the one we're used to. The rules are different and likely to work in defiance of common sense."

Sif frowned skeptically. "It's *possible,* I suppose. Are we likely to find anything useful at the third well?"

"No. My other idea is that we fly straight up Yggdrasil's trunk, still too close to see the whole of the Tree at once, until we come to a branch that extends out to Jotunheim and then venture along it."

"Like ants climbing the trunk of a common tree. Could that work?"

Heimdall shrugged. "If the tales are true, there's a sort of squirrel called Ratatoskr, another primordial being, that scampers up and down the length of Yggdrasil. If a squirrel can do it, why shouldn't we?"

"A squirrel?"

"So the mystics say. According to the stories, she carries slander and cruel gossip among other creatures who live up and down Yggdrasil, apparently just because it amuses her to stir up trouble."

"Like if Loki was a squirrel?"

Heimdall smiled. "More or less."

"We'll hope to avoid her, then. I get my fill of Loki back in Asgard."

"Better get used to him," he said. "If you marry Thor, Loki will be your brother-in-law."

Sif glowered. "I told you to shut up about Thor and me. Anyway, if we don't run out of water or food, one of your notions should work. Finally. Let's mount up and find ourselves a well."

The winged stallions flew along the root, and Heimdall occasionally caught sight of other roots sprouting from it along the way. Given the frequency with which he spotted them, he inferred that distance worked differently here, and Golden Mane and Bloodspiller were traveling faster than would have been possible inside one of the Nine Worlds.

Even so, their speed wasn't so fast that water and food weren't matters of concern. Sif had been entirely right in that regard. Heimdall and his sister shared the very last of the contents of her water bottle, and sometime after that, he grew thirsty once again. He suspected the horses, despite their extraordinary hardiness, must be thirsty as well. He pinched the skin near the point of Golden Mane's shoulder, and to his dismay, when he let go, it took a moment for it to snap back, confirmation that the black steed too was in need of a drink.

A band of dull green appeared up ahead and to the right. Hoping it could provide the answer to the food and water problem, Heimdall led Sif toward it, and as they approached it visibly became a mass of the moss he'd spotted when flying higher up. Down here, it was a veritable range of hills made of moss, the individual strands as thick as his leg.

He landed, dismounted, and took up a hatchet Golden Mane carried among his previous rider's gear, a tool intended for chopping firewood and similar chores. Going down on one knee, he attacked the surface of the root. To his relief, despite Yggdrasil being, in effect, the structure supporting the entire universe, the wood broke like any other, and eventually, when he cleared away the scraps and chips, he had a basin.

He then chopped strands of moss, and they too yielded to his efforts. When he squeezed them over the basin, water trickled out. It had a brackish taste and grit suspended in it, but he, Sif, and the horses all found it potable.

That, however, was as far as his luck extended. To his disappointment, when he chopped up some of the moss to use as feed, Golden Mane and Bloodspiller spurned it, and he assumed that if they couldn't eat it, he and his sister couldn't either. The scraps of tough fiber seemed as if they'd be indigestible even if pounded and thoroughly cooked.

Having determined that, he and Sif brought out the last of the cheese, oat bread, dried apples, and hazelnuts they'd pilfered from the supply tent in the Asgardian military camp. They kept the cheese for themselves and gave the rest to the horses. The equines munched the meager meal down eagerly and then regarded the Asgardians with a questioning and ultimately dissatisfied demeanor as though asking, "Is that all?"

"Sorry," Heimdall said, "but yes, it is." He and Sif climbed up onto the stallions and flew on.

Heimdall thought that by rights, slaking his thirst and putting food in his belly should have eased his anxiety for a while, but in fact it was working the other way. Knowing the very last of the provisions was gone made him feel the need to find a way off the root and into Jotunheim all the more acutely.

Each diverging root he and Sif rode by tormented him with the knowledge that they might be leaving behind the very path to one or another of the places they were seeking. Yet there was no sign to hint that any of those ways truly was the right way, and what if he and his sister abandoned the path they were on when it was the one that actually did lead to the Well of Fate or Mimir's Well?

Perhaps, he thought, he should fly up high enough that Yggdrasil's trunk came into view again. Inwardly, he winced at the mental punishment that would involve, but maybe he could weather it, and maybe it would help him get his bearings. He drew breath to tell Sif what he intended, and then she called to him. "What's that?"

She was peering at the next diverging root, and he looked in the same direction. Down that path were a vague arch of color and a faint, sustained roar. He thought of the rainbows he'd sometimes seen in the mist at the foot of a waterfall and the steady rumble of the river streaming over the edge.

"A well?" Sif asked, her voice hopeful.

"Possibly," Heimdall replied. He wanted to share her hope but had his doubts that it was warranted. "It sounds like more than a well, but everything's huge here. Who's to say what the word *well* actually signifies? But one of the three wells is Hvergelmir. The Roaring Kettle."

"The one we don't want."

"Yes."

"And whatever's that way," said Sif, "sounds like it deserves the name. But you said it yourself. We don't know what the wells truly are. Maybe they all roar, and Hvergelmir is just the one that roars the loudest."

Heimdall frowned. "You're right. We have to check. But carefully."

They flew down the gnarled secondary root, past others that branched off from it, and as it narrowed, while the part of it directly beneath the horses still seemed more or less flat, the curvature where it rolled out of sight at the edges became more apparent. At the same time, the Asgardians came upon enormous raw pits and gouges in the surface of the root itself. They looked somewhat like the damage Heimdall had inflicted with the hatchet, but he would have required the relative stature of a person attacking a normal-sized tree to be responsible. They heightened his sense that he and Sif might be in danger, but he still agreed with her that they needed to see what lay ahead.

Squinting, trying to spot whatever actually was to blame for the gouges, he peered ahead. There was nothing to see but the rainbow, clearer now, just as the roaring was louder, and it seemed unlikely that anything huge could escape his notice. Still wary but somewhat reassured, he flew onward, and Sif did the same.

Eventually they came to a point where the root, now no more than a long bowshot wide, twisted downward and disappeared into a huge pool – a lake, really – of foaming, churning water contained by nothing whatsoever as far as he could see, its limits set solely by the invisible play of whatever forces governed reality here. It was just as impossible to see where or how new water entered the pool, although the agitation and now-prodigious roar attested to the fact that it was rushing in from somewhere.

He and Sif glided out over the pool, and the haze dampened and cooled his face. Below him, he spied motion of a different sort than the churning of the water, and after another moment identified the source. A huge green serpent, long as a frost giant was tall, was swimming in the lake.

Was that reptile the only one? Now that he was looking straight down into the water, Heimdall spied a dozen snakes swimming to and fro, and several more coiled around the root that plunged into the depths. The enormous reptiles were gnawing on it, chewing pits in the wood that, while smaller, were otherwise much like the scars he and Sif had seen proceeding down this particular system of roots.

Plainly, this seething cauldron was indeed Hvergelmir, the Roaring Kettle, where serpents eternally attacked the substance of Yggdrasil, and he felt foolish for imagining it could have been anything else. He told himself he should have trusted his instincts. As it was, he and Sif had wasted precious time coming here and possibly put themselves in danger.

At least the source of the danger wasn't actually present at the moment. He and his sister needed to get away before it returned. He wheeled Golden Mane, Sif and Bloodspiller followed, and they all flew back the way they'd come. Then, to his horror, he spied Nidhogg, lord and perhaps progenitor of the serpents of Hvergelmir, crawling up a branching root ahead.

Nidhogg was a dragon so huge the serpents in the Roaring Kettle seemed tadpoles by comparison, a creature big enough to have bitten and clawed the pits and gorges in the roots that Heimdall and Sif had flown over previously. He had splinters long as trees still caught between his fangs from the last such repast. His scales gleamed a dull green in the light of the stars and nebulae, but his eyes glowed crimson.

Heimdall struggled to shake off the terror Nidhogg inspired and think. He and Sif were still on the final section of the root they were traversing. If they turned around, the way led nowhere but back to the Roaring Kettle. Thus, if they retreated down it and the wyrm took the same path, as it seemed likely he would since that's where his progeny were, they'd be trapped.

"Come on!" cried Sif. "Let's try to get past him!"

Heimdall realized it was a good idea. Maybe the dragon's very size could work in the Asgardians' favor. Perhaps, if they made haste, Heimdall and Sif could streak on past the wyrm before he reached the root that terminated at the Roaring Kettle and blocked the way without the creature even noticing, just as a person wouldn't notice mosquitos flitting in the distance.

Sif and Bloodspiller raced onward. Heimdall urged Golden Mane forward, and though he was certain the winged stallion was no more eager to go closer to Nidhogg than he was himself, the black steed too put on a burst of speed.

Unfortunately, Sif lost her gamble. Manifestly spotting the flyers, Nidhogg scuttled and lunged onto the root they were traversing. He reared and spread his bat-like wings to block the way even more thoroughly than he had done before.

Still, Heimdall thought desperately, perhaps people on flying horses could evade the dragon if they left the root system entirely. He dreaded the prospect of seeing the whole of Yggdrasil once again, but maybe both he and Sif could bear it for a little while. He turned Golden Mane to the side, and his sister followed his lead.

Nidhogg flapped his wings and raised a blast of wind that struck with stunning force. Heimdall blacked out, and when he woke, he and his mount were falling.

A gargantuan clawed extremity – not really a hand but not quite a normal reptilian appendage either – caught him and Golden Mane in its upturned palm, shifted, and caught Sif and Bloodspiller as well. Terrified, Heimdall fully expected the extremity to close and crush riders and horses together into one dead mass of pulped, bloody flesh and broken bones. Instead, it then descended nearly to the surface of the root and turned over to dump them out.

The Asgardians and their horses clambered to their feet,

none apparently injured. At least not yet. Sif reached for the hilt of her broadsword, and Heimdall reflexively caught her wrist to stop her. Nidhogg was so colossal that blades were manifestly useless, and maybe, *maybe* there was a better option than going down fighting. The fact that the dragon hadn't killed them instantly at least suggested the possibility.

Nidhogg regarded them with his crested head tilted downward. Up close, it was impossible to take in all of him at once. A person could focus on an immense talon-bearing forefoot, a leathery wing, the burning red eyes, but not all of them. Which reinforced Heimdall's grim certainty that the dragon was simply too gigantic for swords and fighting prowess to be of any use.

"Who–" Nidhogg began. His snarl of a voice was so loud that Heimdall and Sif clapped their hands over their ears, and the winged horses cringed.

The wyrm snorted and shrank, for some reason changing color from deep green to a greenish-yellow as he did so. Afterward, the wedge-shaped head at the end of the long serpentine neck still loomed high over the Asgardians, but facing Nidhogg wasn't like standing at the foot of a mountain any more. A watchtower, perhaps.

"I have heard," Nidhogg said, the volume now bearable, "of warriors slaying dragons of this runty size. Don't be deceived. I am as strong as I was before. Try me if you doubt it."

Heimdall didn't. His heart pounding, still profoundly frightened but trying to appear calm – his instincts told him that acting like prey might provoke an immediate and fatal attack – he said, "That won't be necessary."

The scraps of wood had shrunk with the jaws that held

them. Nidhogg's forked tongue licked one loose from between two fangs, and he swallowed it. "Who are you?" He sniffed. "Vanir, by the smell of you."

Sif stepped up beside Heimdall, trying also to appear calm and composed. "That's right," she said, her voice steady. "I'm Sif, and this is my brother Heimdall. We're warriors in service to Odin, and we ask a favor."

"A favor?" Nidhogg asked, amusement in his voice.

"Please, point us to the Well of Fate," said Sif, "and Mimir's Well while you're at it."

"Why, tiny Asgardian, would I do any such thing?"

"Because," Heimdall said, "as Sif told you, we serve Odin. We're on a mission for him." It was, he thought, more or less true even if the sleeping god didn't know it. "And if you help us, the All-Father will owe you a favor in return."

"*All-Father*, you say. He's not *my* father, and there's nothing I need from him, ruling over his speck of a kingdom high up in the Tree. No, you two have strayed where you don't belong, and now you must pay the price. I've not tasted Vanir in a long time."

"Why bother tasting it at all?" Heimdall asked. "Isn't it the wood of Yggdrasil that sustains you?"

"Yes," the dragon said, "but over time, it grows monotonous. Every few centuries, I like a change."

At the periphery of Heimdall's vision, Sif was easing her hand toward her sword again. He shot her a warning glance, and she forbore with a scowl.

"But there's so little of us," he called up to Nidhogg, "it scarce seems worth your while. We'll make a mouthful at most."

The dragon cocked his head and considered his prisoners anew. "No," he said at length, "now that I've shrunk, two Asgardians and two Valkyrie horses should make a decent snack. Maybe I'll even save a little for my spawn back in the Kettle to fight over. They like a change too."

Heimdall could feel he was sweating and struggled again to appear unconcerned. "It still seems a waste," he said. "After all, curiosity is a kind of hunger, too. Don't you want to hear what Sif and I are doing here?"

"Not particularly," Nidhogg said. "The doings of the Nine Worlds are no concern of mine."

"Well…" Heimdall strained to think of something else that might divert the wyrm from his sanguinary intent. "You spoke of the monotony of your diet. Living here as you have for ages, nothing ever changing, you must suffer other kinds of boredom, too, boredom that a mouthful or two of Vanir flesh and horsemeat will only relieve for a moment. Why not let me entertain you?"

Nidhogg grunted. "How could a flea like you possibly do that?"

How indeed, when neither he nor Sif were any sort of skald? Heimdall blurted out the first thing that popped into his mind. "Do you know hnefatafl?"

Hnefatafl was a board game in which the two players controlled differing numbers of pieces and had opposing objectives. The smaller side represented a defending army, all but one of the pieces were warriors seeking to protect their king as he made his way to safety at the edge of the board. The larger side was the warriors of the attacking army striving to capture the fleeing monarch.

Now that it was too late to take back the suggestion in any case, Heimdall thought hnefatafl might actually be a sound idea. He was good at it and generally won. Just as importantly, hnefatafl was an ancient game played in several of the Nine Worlds, which increased the likelihood that Nidhogg knew it and conceivably even had an interest.

Or perhaps it wasn't such a shrewd suggestion. "I have lived since the beginning of all things," Nidhogg said. "My intellect and experience are immeasurably greater than yours. How could your footling efforts provide a challenge?"

"They might," Heimdall said, "if the stakes inspire me to do my very best."

"The stakes?" the dragon rumbled.

"If I win, you give us the directions we need and let us go our way in peace."

"And if I win, I eat you, your sister, and the horses?"

"If you insist."

Nidhogg laughed. "I do. Hnefatafl it is, then. Give me a moment, and I'll produce what we need." The scarlet eyes narrowed, and he whispered a sibilant incantation.

Sif stepped closer to her brother. "Are you certain this is a wise idea?"

"No," he answered. "But it's a better idea than being chewed to bits and dead inside Nidhogg's belly. Which is what and where we would otherwise be already."

"There is that," his sister said. "Good luck, then."

The patch of root between the Asgardians and the dragon cracked and churned as Nidhogg's sorcery took hold of it. Playing pieces rose, took shape, and separated themselves from the underlying wood, those of the attacking army turning green and those of the defending force darkening to black. When fully formed, they were about half as tall as Heimdall, big enough for Nidhogg to pick up and move without fumbling yet small enough for his opponent to shift if he walked out on the game board.

Once Nidhogg finished making the pieces, said game board shaped itself beneath them, eleven squares by eleven squares. The defending king stood at the center surrounded by his twelve warriors. The twenty-four attacking warriors stood at the edges of the board, six to a side.

"You are trying to save the king," Nidhogg said.

Heimdall wasn't surprised. Though he generally subsisted on a diet of wood, the wyrm seemed a predator through and through. It made sense that he preferred the aggressor role.

The Asgardian, however, didn't mind being the defender with a smaller number of pieces to control. The king was more difficult to capture than a warrior, and that combined with the differing goals of the two sides made hnefatafl an even contest.

Heimdall walked to the center of the board and, with Nidhogg towering over him, shifted a warrior in what was his favorite opening. The dragon immediately picked up a green game piece between two talons and set it down beside the black one, establishing half of the sandwiching that would remove it from the board, and the game was on.

After the first few moves, play slowed considerably as complexities presented themselves and man and dragon took time to ponder their options and consider what their opponents might be up to. It appeared to Heimdall that Nidhogg was following the common strategy of forming a ring around the defending pieces. Once it was in place, the dragon would tighten the circle, capturing warriors and finally the king.

Happily, an attacking player couldn't form such a blockade all at once, only gradually, a move at a time. That gave the defender the chance to make sure there were gaps in it and to slide warriors all the way to the peripheries of the board, where they helped to establish the king's escape route and threatened enemy pieces from the rear.

Heimdall pursued such a defense and for a time felt he was holding his own. Then Nidhogg laughed a hissing laugh, shifted a piece, and the Asgardian saw the move had created a fork. Two of his warriors were under threat, and his next move could only save one of them. He considered and then shifted the one he thought it more important to preserve. The dragon moved his piece again, catching Heimdall's doomed warrior between that token and one already in juxtaposition with it, and so drew first blood.

Heimdall thought he'd been playing carefully hitherto, but he took an even longer time studying the board before he made his next move. That forking move had seemed to come out of nowhere, and now, to his dismay, he belatedly recognized a deeper level to the positioning of Nidhogg's pieces. What had seemed a fairly standard arrangement was in reality something subtler, a design containing several traps the dragon was waiting to spring.

Heimdall's confidence – to the extent that he'd had any – shaken, the Asgardian resolved that he wouldn't fall into any more traps, and yet, a few moves later, it happened anyway, and he lost another of his warriors. He then captured the attacking piece in its turn, but with fewer warriors at his disposal it was a losing strategy to trade man for man, especially as he had as yet made little progress establishing a safe path for his king to exit the board.

It was coming home to him that when claiming to be the superior player, the wyrm had spoken only the truth, and for a moment he hated himself for imagining he could outthink and outplay an intellect that had existed since the beginning of time. The knowledge that it was the only ploy that had occurred to him, and that it had at least extended his life and Sif's by a few more minutes, was scant comfort.

He wondered if he could surreptitiously signal to Sif to slip away while Nidhogg was intent on the game, but even in the unlikely event that she could do so successfully, he knew his sister wouldn't abandon him. Which meant he *had* to win, but how?

He'd always approached hnefatafl as an exercise in pure reason. It was why he enjoyed it. But he wasn't going to defeat Nidhogg if his play remained solely on that level, and in fact, a player's state of mind entered into hnefatafl no less than into a contest of arms. Which was to say, if Heimdall could upset or irritate Nidhogg and make the wyrm lose focus, he might yet defeat the gigantic reptile just as a mediocre swordsman could occasionally best a good one if the latter was distracted.

"Hurry up and move," Nidhogg said. "I'm getting bored. And peckish."

Heimdall glanced up at the dragon. "You're still certain you're going to win, aren't you? The Norns said you were arrogant."

Nidhogg cocked his head. "The Norns? I thought you didn't know the way to Udarbrunnr."

"We don't. The squirrel told us when we ran into her."

"Ratatoskr?"

"Is that her name?" Heimdall shifted his king.

Nidhogg said nothing more for the next two moves, long enough for the Asgardian to fear that the dragon wasn't going to take the bait. Finally, however, his clawed extremity hovering over the board but not yet touching a piece, the creature asked, "Did Ratatoskr tell you anything else?"

Hiding a surge of excitement, Heimdall hesitated. "I probably shouldn't say. I probably shouldn't have said anything in the first place. Let's just concentrate on the game."

"Tell me, mite! I want to hear."

"Well… apparently the Norns are tired of you. So tired they're looking into ways to get rid of you."

"Ridiculous!" Nidhogg said. "Ratatoskr is a liar. Everyone knows it."

Heimdall shrugged. "If you say so."

According to all accounts, Ratatoskr *was* a liar, and Nidhogg likely had ample reason to know it firsthand. But perhaps, like Loki, the squirrel also occasionally told the truth, truth his hearers would have learned nowhere else, for the legends also said they continued to heed him. At any rate, Heimdall hoped the dragon, possessing what appeared to be a suspicious nature, wasn't truly ready to dismiss tidings that supposedly came from Ratatoskr out of hand.

After another exchange of pieces, that proved to be the case. "The Norns have no reason to wish to be rid of me,"

Nidhogg said. "They nourish Yggdrasil, and I eat of its substance. Everything is in balance."

"I don't know anything about it," Heimdall said. "But in Asgard, we don't say the Three Sisters' duty is to keep any sort of balance. We say they want the World Tree to flourish, and how abundantly might it flourish if you weren't around to gnaw at it?"

"Absurd! As you say, you know nothing about it." Nidhogg chose a piece and shifted it.

Play continued, and in due course Heimdall captured a green warrior without losing one of his own in the doing of it. It was a small victory that by no means changed the overall complexion of the game, but it provided the first tangible cause for hope that perhaps the tide was starting to turn.

Minutes later, Nidhogg growled, "Even if the Norns wanted to be rid of me, they couldn't do it. You've seen how strong I am."

"Of course," Heimdall said. "I'm sure you'd have nothing to worry about. Although ..."

"Although what?"

"Sorcery is mighty too. The Norns are three of the mightiest mages in Asgard, and if they have an ally's strength to add to their own–"

"What ally?"

"In Asgard, wise folk say an eagle lives near the top of Yggdrasil. Is that true?"

"It is."

"Well," Heimdall said, "I assume that to perch on one of the branches, he must be as big as you. As strong as you and with an equally prodigious hunger. If he and the Sisters joined forces, he could make a meal of your carcass, a feast more sumptuous than any he's known before."

"The eagle would never dare! Nor would the Norns!"

"I'm sure you're right," Heimdall said. "As you told me, Ratatoskr's a liar. It's your move, by the way."

They played on with the endgame now in sight or at least a possibility. Eventually, with an upwelling of elation he once again sought to conceal, Heimdall discerned a genuine weakness in Nidhogg's position that, assuming the wyrm didn't make the appropriate countermoves, offered his king a path to safety.

Or maybe it did. After the moment of delight came doubt. Perhaps, Heimdall fretted, the dragon had known all along what his talk of Ratatoskr and his gossip was meant to accomplish and had simply been pretending otherwise for his amusement. Maybe Nidhogg's play was every bit as cunning as it had been at the beginning, and there was a final snare waiting to enclose the king and give the wyrm the victory.

Maybe, Heimdall thought grimly. But having come this far, there was nothing for him to do but play on to the best of his own ability. He moved a warrior.

After lengthy consideration, Nidhogg responded with a move his opponent hadn't foreseen. Unless there was something Heimdall was missing, it wasn't the best possible move, but he tensed to recognize it still might close his own path to victory. It depended on what he did next and on how the dragon followed up.

As he pondered, Nidhogg snarled, "It wouldn't matter if

the Norns did make common cause with the eagle. I have allies of my own."

Though it seemed like an opening to nettle the wyrm yet again, Heimdall couldn't see how to exploit it. To his dismay, he was out of ideas, or maybe the anxiety of the moment was preventing them coming to mind.

Sif, however, had evidently understood what he was attempting and stepped in to continue the strategy. She looked up at Nidhogg and asked, "Do you mean your spawn? The serpents swimming in the Roaring Kettle? How sure of their loyalty are you?"

"Completely sure!" the dragon snapped.

"Then no doubt everything's fine," said Sif. "I just wondered, how old are they, and none of them grown to be a mighty wyrm like you? Is it your magic that keeps them from maturing into proper drakes? Your will that keeps them nibbling on that one root while you roam all around the foot of the Tree eating as much as you want? Because you don't want full-grown rivals to contend with? If that was true, I could imagine them betraying you just at the moment you need them."

"Nonsense!"

Heimdall carried one of his warriors across the oversized board. "There. It's your move."

Nidhogg's wedge-shaped head snapped down to regard the board as if, for a moment, he'd forgotten all about the game. He only briefly considered the positioning of the pieces and then shifted one of his own warriors.

Heimdall felt like letting out a cheer. This was it! Masterful player though he was, Nidhogg had made a fatal mistake.

Or so it appeared. Heimdall pushed eagerness aside and forced himself to study the board anew. Only when he was satisfied he hadn't missed something critical did he shift his king.

"I win on the next move," he said. "There's no move you can make to prevent it."

Nidhogg peered at the board for a few moments, then swept his forefoot in a backhand blow that knocked pieces tumbling and clattering away. It would have pulped Heimdall's body as well if he hadn't jumped backward in time.

Absorbed in the game, Heimdall had assumed victory mattered. Now, though, it came home to him with a flash of self-disgust that he'd really had no reason to assume Nidhogg would abide by the terms of their wager. In light of the dragon's reaction to losing, it seemed that Nidhogg regarded any promise given to insignificant creatures like common Asgardian warriors as meaningless, and Sif had been right from the start. There was nothing to do but go down fighting.

Heimdall and his sister reached for the hilts of their swords. Golden Mane and Bloodspiller neighed and spread their wings. But after that one instant of naked anger, Nidhogg contained himself.

"Two out of three," the dragon said.

Heimdall nearly laughed in mingled surprise, relief, and genuine humor but repressed the impulse. Nidhogg might take a show of mirth as disrespectful and yet decide to eat a bite or two of Vanir.

"I'm sorry," Heimdall replied. "I would, truly, but time

presses. Can you please go ahead and tell us how to get to Udarbrunnr and Mimisbrunnr?"

"If you insist," Nidhogg grumbled. "But I advise you not to cross paths with me again. Looking at the two of you, I really do find myself craving a taste of Vanir." Using one of his claws, he started scratching a crude map on the surface of the hnefatafl board.

Twenty

It was difficult to measure the passage of time in the realm of Yggdrasil, where there was no day or night. But Heimdall judged that, since leaving Nidhogg, he and Sif had been riding for several hours when the winged stallions came to the divergence of two particular roots. If the dragon could be trusted, the greater led to Mimir's Well, the lesser – small and seemingly insignificant in relation to the immensity of the other – was the path to Jotunheim. After some discussion, Heimdall and Sif had agreed they should seek the direct path to Jotunheim in preference to the Well of Fate because this route to the world of the frost giants was supposedly always here and open to all. Whereas the Asgardian warriors might need to wait for the Norns to pay a visit to their well. With their food supply exhausted, that could well turn out to be a wait they couldn't afford. Moreover, even when the Three Sisters did appear, they'd still have to convince them to help alleged traitors avail themselves of their magical means of travel.

Heimdall turned to Sif. "As long as we're here, why don't we pay a visit to Mimir's hut?"

"Why?" she asked. "Why detour when our errand is urgent?"

He realized it was a good question, but thought he had a reasonable answer. "The whole errand is about Mimir. So maybe it would be a good idea to learn all we can about him."

She snorted. "I think you're just curious."

He didn't think he was *only* curious, but perhaps after all that was the greater part of it. "If you believe it's best," he said, "maybe we should press on to Jotunheim."

To his surprise, though, Sif said, "No, it's all right, provided it isn't far and we don't dawdle when we get there." Having gotten him to admit she might be right, she now seemed willing to let him have his way, albeit within limits.

"I promise," Heimdall said, grateful for her indulgence, "if it's far, we'll turn around, and I only want to look around for a moment.". He tugged on the reins to point Golden Mane down the larger root, and she followed.

In fact, it wasn't far at all. They soon came within sight of Mimisbrunnr and the habitation Mimir had raised beside it.

As was the case with the Roaring Kettle, the root they were following made nearly a right-angle bend to extend down into a lake suspended like a bubble in the void, with no ground or other visible barriers to set its limits but confined to a certain area nonetheless. There were no serpents in evidence, however, and no prodigious gushing noise, although, Heimdall reflected, if the root drew water from it, some unseen source must likewise be replenishing Mimir's Well.

Just at the point where the root twisted downward was a bump, and Golden Mane winged his way closer. Smiling at the prospect of satisfying his curiosity, Heimdall made out irregularly shaped openings that might have served for a doorway and windows. It appeared to him that Mimir had used magic comparable to the spell that created the hnefatafl pieces and board to raise a modest dwelling from the substance of Yggdrasil, a dwelling as much like a little cave as a common hut.

Heimdall and Sif set the steeds down on the surface of the root, and the stallions' hooves clicked and clopped on the wood. The two Asgardians dismounted and entered Mimir's retreat through the doorway. The opening was higher on one side than the other and rounded overall.

It was gloomy inside, although the openings admitted enough of the light of the stars and nebulae that the darkness wasn't absolute. Heimdall could make out rumpled blankets on the floor that had apparently served Mimir as a sleeping pallet. Other than that, the space was empty.

Sif peered about. "Well," she said, "this isn't much of anything. It doesn't look like Mimir even cooked or lit a fire to warm himself when he stayed here. Can we go now?"

Heimdall had to admit it seemed as though they might as well. Still, curiosity bolstered by stubbornness wouldn't let him leave quite yet. Mimir was a figure out of legend, not as awesome as Odin, but mythic in his own right nonetheless. It ought to be possible to discover *something* here.

"Just one more moment," Heimdall said. Small as the hut was, it should take no longer than that to thoroughly search the interior.

He paced around the limits of the wooden cave – ducking when the downward-sloping ceiling made it necessary – and, with a thrill of excitement, found a hollow in one wall where the dimness and the many bulges and depressions in the wood had masked the nook hitherto. Inside reposed a writing tablet and the iron stylus used to inscribe the runes marked on its surface of blackened wax.

Heimdall picked up the tablet and squinted to make out the runes and whatever secret lore they might have to impart. The ancient wood crumbled to scraps and dust in his hands, destroying the inscription as it disintegrated.

Sif laughed at her brother's dismay. For a moment that annoyed him, and then he too saw the humor and ended up laughing along with her.

"Now can we go?" she asked.

"Yes," he said, but just as he was turning to do so, he spied an object sitting even farther back in the darkness of the nook. He pulled it out and, with a surge of amazement, found it was a long curving ox horn with a wide brass fitting around the wide end, a stopper of the same metal in the pointed end, and a leather cord that would allow someone to hang it around his or her body.

"What is it," asked Sif, "a salt horn?"

"I don't think so," Heimdall answered. "If it was, the big end would have a cover. I think it's a drinking horn."

"If it was a drinking horn, you wouldn't want to plug the hole in the little end."

"Ordinarily, no. But I still think this is the Gjallarhorn. The vessel from which Mimir drank the waters of his well every day he spent here, and from which Odin drank after he traded Mimir his eye for a secret source of wisdom. Waiting here, in this place, it almost has to be."

Sif frowned. "That would mean it's a sacred, magical thing. Maybe you should put it back."

He thought she might be right. But, on the other hand, Mimir was dead even if his head could still whisper wisdom on command, so it wasn't as if taking the Gjallarhorn would be robbing him, and perhaps there was good reason to take it.

"Asgard's in trouble," he said. "Perhaps Frigga or one of the royal mages could turn a lost magical treasure to good use. If so, it would be feckless to leave it behind."

Sif frowned, "I'm still leery of it. But I admit you're already touching it and it hasn't turned you to stone or anything. Bring it, then."

Heimdall slung the Gjallarhorn over his shoulder, and he and Sif exited the hut. Then, as they were walking toward the horses, an idea struck him. If simply taking the horn had been presumptuous, surely the action he was now contemplating was considerably more so, but now that it had occurred to him, he found he couldn't dismiss it out of hand.

Sif noticed he'd halted. "What is it now?" she asked.

"I said we should take the Gjallarhorn in the hope it would prove useful in the defense of Asgard. But what if we're overlooking the obvious? Odin and Mimir used the horn *here,* in *this* place. The All-Father traded his eye to Mimir for wisdom, and in exchange Mimir used the horn to give him a drink from his well. So it occurs to me, what if one of us used the horn to drink from it? Maybe we'd acquire wisdom that would help us complete our mission. The wisdom to unmask the traitor in Asgard, if there is one."

Sif shook her head. "*No*. I agreed to you taking the horn, but this is surely overstepping. We're warriors, not mystics, certainly not gods in any true sense. These mysteries are beyond us."

For a moment, it seemed to him that she must be correct, that what she was saying was only common sense, but then something inside him, the part of him that had always prized independent thought and chafed under the assumption that tradition and obedience to authority were always the proper course, rebelled.

"You could be right," he said. "But we weren't supposed to go into the vault of the Odinsleep, either, and yet when we did, we learned something important. On our journey, I've had other ideas, notions that seemed unlikely, and while they didn't all work out as planned, they got us this far. And now my idea is that I should drink. I think it's worth the risk."

Sif scowled. "You just prize cleverness so highly that you're willing to chance anything to sharpen your wits."

"I admit, that might be a little of it too. But I swear, it isn't the greater part."

Sif strode to Bloodspiller and swung herself into the saddle. "All right. If I can't talk you out of this stupidity, let's get it done."

Her grudging acquiescence gave him a twinge of guilt. "If you don't agree with what I'm doing, you don't have to be a part of it."

"Of course I do," Sif said. "We didn't see any serpents in

this well, but that doesn't mean there aren't any. If you fly too low, something might rise to the surface to gobble you up, and then you'll need me."

Heimdall mounted up, and then brother and sister sent the winged stallions flying out over the well. As they swooped downward, Heimdall, mindful of Sif's concern, studied the surface of the pool but saw nothing rising from the clear quiet depths to menace him.

When Golden Mane was low enough that his hoofs were splashing up water, Heimdall leaned sideways out of the saddle and held the Gjallarhorn beneath the surface. He scooped up enough water to fill the vessel nearly to the brim, then righted himself and sent the black horse climbing upward. They landed back in front of Mimir's hermitage, and, with a final flutter of ruddy pinions, Sif set Bloodspiller down beside them.

Heimdall smiled at her. "No serpents."

She didn't smile back. "Serpents were never the truest danger. The water is, and you haven't drunk it yet."

Perhaps it was the dour warning that gave him a pang of uncertainty. Pushing the feeling away, he tilted back his head and drank deeply from the horn. The water was cold and tasted of nothing in particular. Drinking it was like quaffing water from any mundane well, spring, or river.

Still, he thought, surely it would grant him some profound understanding of which he'd been incapable before. He spent the next several seconds contemplating the course of his thoughts, the inner workings of his mind, only to find that no matter how intently he scrutinized them, nothing had changed. The realization arrived with a crushing feeling of anticlimax. He told himself that at least nothing terrible had happened as a result of drinking the water, but the reflection did little to ease his disappointment.

"Anything?" asked Sif.

He sighed. "Nothing at all. Maybe you have to make a sacrifice to activate the magic."

Sif glowered. "You are *not* going to pluck out an eye like Odin did. I'll beat you senseless, throw you over Golden Mane's back and haul you away from here if that's what it takes to stop you."

Her truculence made him smile and feel a little better. "You won't have to. I'm not *that* eager to sharpen my wits. But there's still some water left. Maybe the magic will work for you." He proffered the Gjallarhorn.

"No," she said. "I already have enough wisdom to swing a sword and loose an arrow. How much more do I need? Why would I risk changing the insides of my head and maybe not being the same person any more?"

Heimdall studied her. "Is that the real reason you didn't want me to drink? You were worried *I* wouldn't still be the same person?"

Sif shrugged. "Maybe. A little."

He felt a surge of affection. "There's nothing that could ever stop me being your brother."

She smiled. "Yes, that's my burden to bear. Come on. Jotunheim awaits."

He tossed out what was left of the water and hung the drinking horn back over his shoulder. The vessel hadn't helped him, but he hadn't given up hope that Frigga or some Asgardian sorcerer could still put it to good use. He and Sif then flew back to the secondary root that was supposedly the way to the world of the frost giants.

The root twisted and narrowed as they flew along it. Eventually it was no wider than the battlements atop the wall of Asgard, and not long after that, it tapered to a rounded terminus no bigger than a person's finger sticking out into empty space. Heimdall and Sif flew past the end of it, and nothing changed. They were still soaring over Yggdrasil's root system.

Sif cursed obscenely. "The story lied! Or Nidhogg lied when he drew his map!"

Heimdall feared she was right, but wasn't ready to accept that conclusion yet. He pondered, and after a moment a thought came to him. "I never heard that Mimir had a winged steed or any other means of flying. Is it possible the secret path only works if you walk it?"

"Who knows what's possible in this place?" Sif replied. "Let's give it a try."

They wheeled their mounts and set them down near the end of the root, Heimdall in the lead and Sif behind. Then they walked the horses forward.

Heimdall could see nothing ahead that hadn't been there before, and Golden Mane tossed his head in displeasure. If the black steed was going to venture out into the void, he plainly wanted to do it flying, not falling off the end of a root. The Asgardian kept him walking, though, and after another moment, cold air gusted at them from somewhere they couldn't see. Golden Mane stepped out into empty space and suddenly they were on a snowy peak with dark gray storm clouds overhead. A howling wind chilled Heimdall's face, and, excited and wary in equal measure at the sudden arrival, he made haste to wrap his scarf around his mouth and nose. As he fumbled with it, Sif and Bloodspiller appeared beside him.

"Welcome to Jotunheim," he said. "At last."

Sif tugged her cloak tighter around her body. "Suddenly Yggdrasil doesn't seem so bad."

Twenty-One

Asgardian warriors were hardy, Valkyrie steeds were more than a match for them in that regard, and the snow provided water. Still, after two days of traveling across the country of the frost giants, Heimdall's belly was growling – he actually felt faint at moments – and though Golden Mane and Bloodspiller were still willing, it was plain their strength was dwindling as they fought Jotunheim's frequent gales.

Heimdall pushed away the dispiriting thought that if things continued as they were, he and Sif might never reach Utgard, the Jotun capital, where they were guessing Mimir's head resided in the citadel of King Skrymir. He told himself firmly that hunger, both that of the horses and of their riders, was simply another problem to be solved as he and Sif had already solved others.

She called across the space separating the two horses. "How much farther?"

"A ways, I think," Heimdall answered. Jotunheim was

the largest of the Nine Worlds, and as best he could judge from the recognizable landmarks in this frozen landscape, Mimir's path hadn't opened particularly close to the stronghold of the frost giant king.

"The horses need food!" Sif called.

"I know. We'll just have to keep looking for it."

Inhospitable as the mountains and valleys of Jotunheim seemed, they harbored animal life, much of it on a scale with the frost giants and their ilk. The huge wolves, bears, and saber-toothed tigers hunted the deer, elk, and wooly mammoths that, Heimdall assumed, must eat something in their turn.

Heimdall kept an eye out and eventually spied a herd of elk heading down a pass. Elk, he thought, ate plants, and in all likelihood what they ate the winged stallions could eat too. He and Sif followed the herd from on high until they came to a place where long blades of grass poked up out of the snowfall. There, the animals began to graze.

Heimdall cautiously set Golden Mane down at some distance from the herd but at a point where the grass still grew. Sif followed him to the ground. The towering animals turned their antlered heads to regard the newcomers, then, apparently deciding the small, unfamiliar creatures posed no threat, returned to their feeding.

But Golden Mane and Bloodspiller had scarcely begun to munch the lengths of grass, broad as sword blades to Heimdall's eyes, when the elk abruptly raised their heads and all peered in the same direction. They then bounded in the opposite direction, which by ill fortune was straight at the Asgardians.

Heimdall felt a jolt of alarm. With no time to mount their steeds and fly or to seek any sort of cover, he and Sif could only crouch and hope not to be trampled. The enormous animals thundered by them, over them, casting up showers of snow, and then they were gone, leaving both riders and steeds unscathed. Unfortunately, he barely had time to breathe a sigh of relief before a far greater danger arrived.

Amber eyes burning, white gray-striped fur making it hard to see despite its size, one of the gigantic saber-toothed tigers charged down the pass. Arriving too late to kill an elk, it turned its gaze on the little creatures still within its reach.

Sif dashed to Bloodspiller and swung herself into the saddle. Heimdall ran to Golden Mane. As he leaped onto the black stallion, the saber-toothed tiger charged. Galloping away from the cat and lashing their feathery wings, the Valkyrie horses ascended into the air and put themselves and their riders above the saber-tooth's reach. Thwarted, the huge tiger glared up after them.

"Curse it!" said Sif, sounding as frustrated as the cat. "The horses didn't have time to eat enough!"

"They still might get their chance," Heimdall replied. "The elk are gone. The tiger can't get us while we're this high. Maybe it will just go away."

That didn't happen, though. Heimdall and Sif circled the spot where the grass grew out of the snow, and perhaps deciding they were unwilling to abandon the place, the saber-tooth didn't either. Rather, the cat stalked back and forth beneath them.

As Heimdall looked down, studying the beast as it was glaring up at Sif and him, he realized something that surprised him. He wasn't especially afraid of it. Wary of it, certainly, respectful of its strength and ferocity, but not truly afraid.

He could attribute part of that to presently being where the saber-tooth couldn't get at him, but that wasn't the whole of it. After successfully battling frost giants and trolls, he'd come to feel more confident in his ability to contend with even enormous foes and in his fighting prowess in general. As a result, he could contemplate a threat like the tiger with a cooler head.

"The cat's not going away!" Sif shouted.

"You're right," Heimdall answered.

"I don't want to go away, either. Who knows long it would take to find other forage for the horses? I'd rather fight. Kill the cat or chase it off."

"I agree. That's the better option." Heimdall had never expected to fight a battle over blades of grass, but so be it. He took a deep, steadying breath and drew his two-handed sword from its scabbard.

Sif swooped downward. The saber-tooth reared and clawed at her, and Heimdall felt an instant of dread on her behalf. Bloodspiller, however, lashed his pinions and dipped below the attack. Cloak streaming out behind her, shouting "Vanaheim," Sif slashed at the dark pads on the underside of the tiger's paw. The broadsword came away bloody, and the cat snarled.

While she had the saber-tooth distracted, Heimdall urged Golden Mane into a dive. The winged stallion hurtled along above the saber-tooth's back. Heimdall leaned sideways out of the saddle and stabbed down repeatedly.

Snarling, the tiger whirled in a blur of white and gray. The beast's jaws gaped, and Golden Mane veered in flight to avoid the bite. A long tooth flashed down just shy of his wing.

Heart thumping, Heimdall sent Golden Mane climbing and then he and Sif hurtled down again. The saber-tooth pivoted toward his sister, and he thought he had an opening. Then the cat spun back toward him, reared, and bashed him and his steed.

Time skipped. When Heimdall came to his senses, his head was ringing and he was lying half buried in a snowdrift. For an instant he was dazed, and then a jolt of alarm cut through the fog. Yellow eyes blazing, the tiger was gathering itself to pounce at him. Wheeling above the cat, not yet in position for another attack, Sif shouted taunts and obscenities at the top of her lungs in a vain effort to distract the animal.

Heimdall cast frantically about. To his relief, the two-handed sword had fallen within easy reach. He grabbed it and scrambled to his feet just as the tiger lunged.

He dodged a raking paw, and then the fanged jaws were opening right in front of him. He dived under the tiger's head, rolled onto his back, and slashed at its throat with all his strength.

Red blood gushed to spatter his face, arms, and chest. The saber-tooth shuddered and collapsed. He scuttled out from under just in time to keep the beast from thudding down on top of him.

Breathing heavily, his body trembling in reaction to what had just happened, he warily watched the saber-tooth to make sure it was truly dead. Meanwhile, Bloodspiller and Golden Mane descended to earth. "Are you all right?" asked Sif.

Only then did he realize with a pang of alarm that he might not be, because the paw had struck him and Golden Mane. He hastily checked himself and the stallion too, now standing in the snow and shaking out his wings. Neither of them bore any grievous wounds. He surmised that while the saber-tooth's paw had struck them, the claws hadn't.

Relieved, he rubbed the horse's shoulder. "I hope you appreciate all the trouble I went to just to get you something to eat."

Golden Mane tossed his head as if to say that so far as he was concerned, he was owed that service and more.

"The horses can eat," said Sif. "That leaves the two of us."

"We shouldn't overlook the obvious." Heimdall returned to the saber-tooth's carcass and hacked into it with his sword. He cut loose a scrap of flesh. "We should be able to make some excuse for a fire by burning blades of this grass. Then we can eat the meat."

His sister grimaced. "I imagine it will be awful."

"Almost certainly," he replied. "But it *is* meat, and we *can* eat it. I think we're all going to make it to Utgard alive, us and the horses both."

"And afterwards," Sif said with a wry smile, "we'll only have surviving the citadel of the frost giant king to worry about. You're covered in cat blood, by the way."

"At least for a moment I was warm." Heimdall picked up a handful of frigid snow and used it to scour his face.

Twenty-Two

Shortly after the encounter with the saber-tooth, Heimdall spied three towering volcanos in the distance, each putting forth a plume of smoke in seeming defiance of Jotunheim's generally frigid aspect. The smoking peaks were one of this world's most prominent and unmistakable landmarks, and, along with his memory of the maps he'd seen, they enabled him to take his bearings. After two more days of travel, he and Sif reached Utgard, the capital city of the frost giants.

He and his sister landed on a mountain ledge at what they hoped was a safe distance to view the city and the royal citadel rising in the center of it. Utgard was of a piece with the desolate landscape on which it sat, a jumble of gray stone spikes, the conical roofs of the towers encrusted with snow. Like Asgard, it was a walled city, with blue-skinned frost giant warriors patrolling the lofty battlements.

"Do you think we can fly in unnoticed?" asked Sif.

"In time of war?" Heimdall replied. "I wouldn't count on it even if we wait until after dark. Nor could we be certain of finding a safe place to leave Golden Mane and Bloodspiller while we searched the citadel."

"That's what I think too." Sif frowned. "How, then, do we get inside?"

"That way, perhaps." He pointed.

Beyond the city, the mountains sloped down to a sea with icebergs floating in the distance and a strip of harbor running alongside it. Sailors had moored ships at the docks, some of the vessels seemingly carved from icebergs. A bit inland were wrecked ships and fishing boats made of wood, some small enough that they appeared to have been plundered from other peoples inhabiting other worlds. Such shanties, Heimdall had heard, were the common habitations of the brine giants who apparently worked the docks.

Sif grunted. "The harbor is outside the city walls."

"But that works to our advantage," he said. "We can get to it without having to scale a wall or slip through a gate, and then, as there's trade, there must be cartloads of goods going up into the city and probably even the citadel itself. We can sneak onto one of those."

"All right, that might work." It was Sif's turn to point. "Let's come in from that direction. It doesn't look like there's much of anything or anyone atop those crags. We can hide the horses there where nobody will find them, and they'll be close – well, relatively speaking – if we need to leave Utgard in a hurry."

It pleased Heimdall to discover there was more of the long, coarse grass growing on one of the peaks. There was also an overhang of rock that might provide at least a modicum of shelter when Jotunheim's blizzards were blowing, so they flew to that.

Heimdall and Sif removed the horses' tack and stowed it

under the overhang. He then stroked Golden Mane's face. "Wait for us," he said, feeling an upwelling of fondness for the steed that had borne him valiantly thus far, "and don't let anybody see you."

Sif grinned. "I wonder how much of what we say the horses truly understand."

"Well, they are Valkyrie horses."

"That's true." She rubbed Bloodspiller's flank. "You heard what my brother said. Take care of yourselves, and we'll be back soon."

The roan steed nickered.

Sif turned back to Heimdall. "All right," she said, "*how* do we get through the harbor?"

He realized it was an excellent question. They had cloaks and hoods in which to muffle themselves, and as he'd observed in his various encounters with them, some frost giants were bigger than others. But all those in view were at least three times as tall as an Asgardian. That suggested this wasn't like back in the troll tunnel. Disguises wouldn't serve. But perhaps the intruders could exploit their relative smallness to their advantage.

"Maybe," he said, "we just sneak. We're small as mice to the giants. For the most part, they won't be looking down. If we're careful, they might not notice us."

Sif grinned. "That's just mad enough to work."

With that, brother and sister began the clamber down the escarpment. It was grueling work made harder by cold gusts of wind and slick ice, and when they finally happened upon a steep switchback trail, the two Asgardians exchanged glances, saw they were in agreement, and descended it thereafter. In the unlikely event that a frost giant came along, they'd conceal themselves somehow.

In fact, there was no need. They met no one on the trail, and in due course the harbor stretched out not far below. Looking down from above, where the differences in scale were less glaring, it was a strange mix of familiar and odd. Cranes creaked as they swung back and forth loading or unloading nets full of cargo or fish. Wagons rumbled, the shaggy oxen drawing them grunted and lowed, and sailors and stevedores shouted and cursed to one another. The cold air smelled of salt water. All of that was much like ports Heimdall had visited in Vanaheim and Asgard.

But there was also the blue skin of the frost giants and the gray-green skin of the brine giants, some of whom likewise sported patches of scales, webbed fingers and toes, or gill slits opening and closing in the sides of their necks. There were the ice ships and the wrecked ships converted into shacks, and a strange beast somewhat like a hut-sized dragon but with a blunter head and long white fur standing guard like a watchdog over what was presumably an especially valuable wagonload of crates.

Moreover, with every step the Asgardians took, the hugeness of everything before them became more apparent. His heart beating faster, Heimdall found the sight daunting. Thanks to the fights he'd already won, he'd largely shed his fear of individual frost giants, but creeping into a whole city of them was still an intimidating prospect.

He glanced at his sister stalking along beside him. If she felt at all intimidated, as usual he couldn't tell it. In fact, she was half smiling, as if slipping through the giants would be an amusing game. Resolving to emulate her example, he drew a long, steadying breath.

Once he and Sif reached the harbor, they sought cover and crouched low whenever a giant tramped near. At one of those moments, it occurred to Heimdall to be glad that neither his sister's armor and other trappings nor his shined brightly any more. The journey had dulled and dirtied them. Dried to a rusty brown, the saber-tooth tiger's blood had added a final layer of dinge to his own appearance.

In time, brother and sister came to a wrecked ship shanty where a frost giant sold ale through the window someone had cut in the hull. Chains attached the drinking horns to the counter to ensure customers didn't walk away with them.

Three of those customers, a trio of brine giants, stood outside. Two were drinking. The third was tossing a dagger into the air and catching the spinning blade again. Either it was a game, and his companions would take their turns in due course, or he was simply showing off his dexterity.

Whatever exactly was happening, his attention was on the blade, and the other giants' attention was on him. Heimdall thought he and Sif would have no trouble slipping by.

Then, however, the brine giant who'd been playing with the dagger cried out. Heimdall looked up, and the weapon spun earthward to land in a mound of dirty slush. Snarling curses, the wounded giant clutched the gashed fingers from which blood now dripped. The others laughed at his discomfiture.

In a moment, though, the brine giants were going to look down to retrieve the fallen knife, and when they did, they were going to spot the Asgardians creeping along nearby. Heimdall frantically cast about and spied a ragged hole in the base of the shanty. He lunged through, and Sif scurried after him.

A shaft of Jotunheim's wan light shined through the opening to illuminate floating particles of dust, but there was gloom beyond together with the smell of damp, rotting wood and a ceiling scarcely higher than Heimdall was tall. That, he supposed, was preferable to being in the same space as the giant selling ale. He and Sif were inside the wrecked ship's enclosed bilge with the ale vendor presumably standing on the deck above their heads. When Heimdall peered, he could make out some of the ballast stones that had steadied the vessel at sea.

Hunched forms scuttled from behind the stones. Sif said, "Watch out!" and snatched for her sword. With the ceiling so low, he had to crouch to draw his own blade over his shoulder. He barely had time to do that, straighten up, and assume a proper fighting stance before the giant rats were on them, creatures of gnashing chisel teeth and coarse bristling fur as big as the Asgardians were themselves.

Heimdall slashed again and again, eliciting squeals of pain, and beside him Sif did likewise. At one point, a rat lunged and caught her by the leg, but before it could bite through her armor or yank her off her feet, she thrust her broadsword into its neck. A moment later, the surviving rodents retreated into the darkness leaving the carcasses of half a dozen of their pack behind.

So far, so good, but, Heimdall realized with a twinge of alarm, one of the brine giants outside might have heard the frenzied squealing and wonder what the commotion was about. He looked back at the opening, and an enormous gray-green leg was bending as a giant lowered himself to one knee. In a moment, the creature was going to peer inside the rat hole.

"Get out from in front of the opening!" Heimdall said. He and Sif took up positions on either side of it with their backs pressed against the wall. The light spilling through the rat hole dimmed as the brine giant's head presumably blocked a goodly portion of it.

"See anything?" one of his companions asked.

"Just a pile of dead rats," said the giant who was looking.

"Then get up. Unless you're hungry."

The remark sparked another round of rumbling laughter from all the giants except the butt of the joke, who growled an obscenity in response.

New scuttling, the click of claws faint on spongy decaying wood, sounded in the dark. Heimdall wondered if he and Sif would have to fight a second wave of rats. He didn't relish the prospect, but he and his sister nonetheless stayed where they were to give the brine giants a chance to walk away.

The rodents *didn't* try again, and when he judged enough time had passed, he peeked outside. The giants had indeed gone on their way leaving behind only footprints and drops of blood from the knife juggler's cut hand in the slush. He nodded to Sif, and they exited the rat hole and prowled onward.

"For a moment there," he said, keeping his voice low, "when the rat took you by the leg, I was worried."

"My saga might have ended with me slain by Nidhogg.

Or even the giant tiger. It won't end with me losing a fight to vermin."

"You think you'll have a saga, do you?"

"If we steal back Mimir's head, I expect so."

"Is it going to mention me?"

"I'll ask the skald to work in a line or two." Sif's tone turned serious. "Being small and inconspicuous is all very well, but as we just saw, we're still in danger every moment we're out in the open. Maybe we should hop on any cart we can. At least get ourselves up into the city and past the first set of walls."

"Maybe," he said, and then, up ahead, a cluster of brine giants broke apart as the green-skinned creatures went their separate ways. Their dispersal revealed the ox-drawn wagon loading on the other side. "On the other hand, take a look at that."

The wagon was big, and heaped with sacks. Painted yellow crowns adorned the sides of the conveyance.

"I see it," said Sif. "Also, the driver loitering beside it."

"But he's looking down the dock yonder," Heimdall replied, "impatient for the rest of the king's goods to come off that ice ship, not paying attention to what's already in his wagon. If we're careful, he won't notice us jumping in."

"Let's do it, then." The Asgardians crept forward.

There was one bad moment when a fishwife pushing a barrow full of the day's catch unexpectedly looked down, and Heimdall was all but certain she was peering directly at him. Then, however, she simply wheeled the barrow on her way, and as she did, he noticed the milky cataracts clouding her sight.

A few seconds after that, he and Sif reached the back of the wagon. They jumped, caught hold of the edge of the cargo bay, and heaved themselves aboard. They then squirmed into the tight spaces among the sacks, concealing themselves. Up close, the bags smelled of the plums the frost giants evidently obtained somehow despite their frigid climate. Heimdall's mouth watered at the temptation of something other than coarse, foul-tasting tiger meat, but he told himself the prudent course was to leave the bags alone.

Stevedores loaded in more sacks. Ensconced in his hiding place, Heimdall couldn't see it happening, but he heard the soft thumps and felt the bags around him shift as new ones pushed up against them.

A few moments after that, the wagon lurched into motion, and the rumbling, shaking ride commenced. To Heimdall, it seemed to last a long time, time that gnawed at his nerves. He could think of no reason the driver would stop in the middle of the city, go rummaging among the sacks, and discover him and Sif, but he found himself imagining it anyway.

Mere fanciful trepidation gave way to a sense of genuine urgency when the wagon came to a halt. That was because he suspected he and Sif had only moments to escape the conveyance before giants came and started unloading it, an event that would almost certainly lead to them discovering the stowaways. He squirmed out of the mound of sacks, and Sif burst out beside him.

Scrambling out of the back of the wagon, they found themselves in a courtyard with frost giants towering on every side and tramping back and forth. Heimdall judged that the wise course was to get out from among the Jotuns as soon as possible. Not caring where it led, he bolted toward the nearest open archway, and Sif dashed after him.

When they were halfway there, she grabbed him by the shoulder and jerked him to a stop. He realized that in his haste he'd somehow missed a frost giant warrior striding at right angles to their own path, and if his sister hadn't brought him to a halt, the Jotun's enormous foot would have kicked him or come down on top of him. As soon as the danger was past, Sif shoved him into motion again.

They ran through the arch and on into a shadowed passageway that evidently saw less traffic than the courtyard. At the moment, there were no giants in it at all. At their backs, a Jotun apparently spotted them scurrying into the gloom, but all he said was, "Cursed rats!"

Twenty-Three

Hours after sneaking into King Skrymir's citadel, well after night had fallen, Heimdall and Sif stood at the base of a tall spire, pentagonal in cross section, that was windowless for much of the way to the top. After getting inside the castle, they'd spent considerable time spying and eavesdropping and had gleaned that the common run of citadel retainers didn't even know the head of Mimir existed. That suggested it wasn't in his throne room or his royal apartments either.

However, sorcerer that he was, the frost giant king also spent considerable time in this tower in the center of the castle where he practiced the mystic arts and which others were forbidden to enter on pain of death. The spire seemed an eminently likely repository for a magical artifact like the head, and the Asgardians had resolved to search it.

No Jotun was in the small graveled yard surrounding the tower. Perhaps the lateness of the hour accounted for some of that, but not, Heimdall suspected, all. His hunch was that most of the frost giants avoided the area altogether. Who knew what uncanny things one might encounter near a mage's sanctum?

Sif glowered at the flight of stairs rising into the structure's interior. "Are chambers devoted to sorcery always either underground or at the top of towers? Give me a warlock with a bad leg who works on the ground floor."

Heimdall smiled. "That would have been preferable. But it's our bad luck that Skrymir's hale and hardy."

"So up we go," his sister replied. "You'll notice there's no sentry at the foot of the steps to prevent us, or even a door."

"I did," he said. "Skrymir's chambers may have magical defenses like the vault where Odin sleeps."

"Well, we managed before." Sif took a running start and sprang onto the first stair step, a riser nearly as high as she was tall. Heimdall followed.

They'd stolen water and scraps of pork – roasted with a strange blue fire then burned without heat but somehow cooked food nonetheless – during the hours they'd spent in the castle, and Asgardian vigor saw them to the top of the long staircase. They scrambled over the last step, and then, before Heimdall could form more than the most rudimentary impression of the space before him, it was as if he blinked although he was sure he hadn't actually closed his eyes. An instant later, when the *blink* ended, he and Sif were standing at the foot of the stairs once more.

He felt an upwelling of astonished disbelief, and then that feeling gave way to frustration and slight irritation at his own initial reaction. By now, such marvels shouldn't amaze him. If this mission had shown him anything, it was that magic could accomplish anything, especially if it was inconvenient.

Sif cursed. "We're back where we started!"

"I noticed," Heimdall said. "Maybe a person needs to speak a password or make a magical gesture to open the way."

"We're not going to hear a password or see a gesture from way down here at the bottom of the steps, and there's nowhere to hide at the top."

"I noticed that, too."

"Well," she said, "we're still tiny compared to frost giants. Maybe, when he climbs the stairs, Skrymir will miss us anyway. If he doesn't, we fight. Killing him might be another way to turn the war around." She started forward and, with a jolt of alarm, Heimdall remembered that Skrymir was supposedly adept at creating illusions, and that recollection prompted him to fear what might be about to happen. It was his turn to grab Sif by the shoulder and hold her back.

"What's wrong?" she asked.

"The thought just struck me: Are we sure we're seeing what's really before us? The tales say Skrymir can make you see what he wants you to see."

Sif's eyes narrowed. "Then you think we really are at the top of the steps and just can't tell it?"

"I think it's possible." Heimdall drew his great sword and edged forward using the weapon to feel along the floor as he'd felt his way in the Realm Below. The tip found emptiness. "There's a hole." With Sif following, he worked his way along it until the illusion faded away, revealing the hole and likewise the cavernous room beyond, the chamber he'd glimpsed for an instant before the magic altered his perceptions.

Sif looked down the shaft. "A hole wide enough for a frost giant to fall into and a drop all the way back down to the bottom of the tower."

"And if the illusion fooled a thief, and he turned around and tried to walk away, he might tumble down the stairs and break his neck."

Beyond the pit, readily avoided if a person knew it was there, was a spacious, high-ceilinged chamber. Heimdall's father had a sorcerer among his retainers, and he'd occasionally visited that warlock's quarters. He'd also carried a few messages to wizards affiliated with the Asgardian army. In short, he'd seen enough mages' laboratories to know he was looking at another such. There were, however, differences from those he'd seen before. The magic circles on the floor were made of ice, not chalk or pigment, and there was no hearth or other means of providing the fire often employed in Asgardian wizardry. Bluish phosphorescent crystals mounted in wall sconces provided the ambient light.

"Well, it's definitely a warlock's workroom," said Sif, looking this way and that. "But I don't see the head."

Heimdall likewise peered about at the icy sigils on the floor, the freestanding bookcases full of tomes, scrolls, clay jars, and other items, the racks of ritual staves and swords, a couple long worktables, and all the furniture looming high above him. "I don't either," he said. "But if it's on top of one of these tables we wouldn't see it, not from down here."

Sif nodded. "True. We need to get on top of them. You take the one on the left, and I'll take the right."

The table legs were smooth and rounded, but by dint

of pure strength, clutching with hands and thighs, brother and sister scaled them. The near end of Heimdall's table contained a mortar and pestle that, except for their size, many an Asgardian witch, warlock, or healer might have employed for crushing and compounding ingredients for a potion or spell. Several more of the clay jars reposed in a tabletop rack, perhaps because they contained materials Skrymir used frequently.

Heimdall still didn't see the head of Mimir, however, and after a moment Sif called across the gap between the tables to report she hadn't found it either. He then looked around the room, at the upper reaches of the floor-to-ceiling shelves in particular, hoping his higher vantage point would enable him to spot something he hadn't been able to see from the floor.

It didn't. But while he was trying, a faint sound, part hiss and part scrape, came from farther along the table on which he stood.

The head of Mimir spoke when Odin questioned it. Did it, then, ever shift and make noise of its own accord? Heimdall had never been close to the necromantic artifact and had no idea, but perhaps it did. Or maybe he was hearing something dangerous. Hopeful and wary in equal measure, he readied his two-handed sword and stalked in the direction of the sound.

In the center of the table sat a round, shallow iron basin, flat on the bottom so that, except for the lack of a handle, it reminded him of an oversized frying pan. Contained within was another design made of ice, perforce smaller than the ones on the floor, but just as intricate and infinitely more active because it was busy elaborating on itself. As though laid down by an invisible pen or brush, a thin, continuous line of rime added detail after detail to the drawing. The process was fascinating to watch.

"Heimdall?" Sif called.

He knew he should answer. But it occurred to him to wonder how the design could perpetually add to itself without eventually becoming a solid sheet of ice, and he felt that if he studied it for another heartbeat or two, he'd discover the answer. Then, his curiosity satisfied, there would be time enough to reply to his sister and get back to searching for Mimir's head.

"Heimdall!"

He scowled to have her distracting him, but despite the clamor he spied the solution to the riddle. The design was all one continuous line, and as the head of it defined new angles and curves, the back of it disappeared, possibly melting to provide fresh water for the front end to freeze in place. At the moment, the effect was of an inward spiral that drew a person's gaze toward the center of the figure.

"Heimdall!"

The alarm in his sister's voice finally cut through Heimdall's daze, and he tore his gaze away. Focused solely on the center of the design, he'd missed seeing the outer edge put forth an arm like a bramble with points of ice for thorns. The tendril reared up out of the iron container to slam those spikes down into his body.

He swung the two-handed sword and caught the ice bramble halfway up its jagged length. The tendril broke apart at the point of impact, and the end section shattered into three smaller pieces when it cracked down on the tabletop.

He looked around for other threats. The design had put forth two more arms, but these had snaked past him to snag one of the oversized clay jars on the table rack. They then jerked it over with sufficient force to knock off the lid. The silvery powder inside billowed forth as though borne by a wind, or as if it was a living creature in search of prey. Heimdall just had time to hold his breath, and then the cloud engulfed him.

The glittering powder was stinging cold on his face, and for a moment he wondered if that was the point of the attack, to freeze him and stop his heart where he stood. But in fact the dust wasn't cold enough for that, and after a moment his vision dimmed, and the shapes before him blurred, stretched, or flattened. At the same time, the intensity he ordinarily felt when fighting for his life was warping into screaming, flailing terror.

He struggled against the fear and, when he succeeded in pushing it down, had a moment of relative clarity. The powder was some manner of drug that was affecting both his sight and his emotions.

He mustn't let himself succumb. He hadn't overcome so many previous dangers, honed his courage, his wits, and his swordplay, only to die like this. Not when his sister needed him. He struggled against the unnatural panic that had taken hold of him, and meanwhile the arcane symbol in the basin put forth more thorny arms to strike at him. He pivoted, spun, and cut.

Sif called, "I'm coming!", and he caught a glimpse of

her as he turned to shatter an ice bramble curling around to rip at him from behind. Broadsword in hand, she took a running start, leaped across the space between the tables, and dashed on in his direction.

After that, he had to turn back toward the iron basin and the ice brambles spouting over the rim. He smashed three of them, and then running footsteps thumped behind him. He whirled, cut, belatedly saw that the approaching figure was Sif, and stopped the attack just short of her head. With his mind faltering, he'd forgotten all about her rushing to help.

By the Tree! It was terrible enough that he'd accidentally killed the guard back in the citadel of Asgard. If he'd murdered his own sister –

"Fight!" she bellowed. Heimdall realized she was slashing furiously to protect both of them while he stood appalled and paralyzed at what he'd nearly done.

He smashed the ice bramble that had been about to claw at his head. "Back to back!" he said.

"Yes." She positioned herself behind him. "That way, you won't kill me."

"Sorry," he said, shattering another thorny arm. "It was the dust. It's a drug."

"If you say so. How many of these arm things do we have to break?"

It was a good question because there was seemingly no end to them. For every one the Asgardians shattered, the thing in the basin simply put forth more. Maybe the magical symbol was vulnerable at its core, but a hedge of glinting, clinking, waving ice brambles now rose high above the rim of the container, preventing any attack on what was inside.

Unless…

"I have an idea," he gritted, "but the state I'm in, I don't trust it."

"I trust *you*," she said. "What do we do?"

"You hold here." He chopped a bramble in two. "Keep the thing occupied as much as you can."

"Right. Go!" She attacked savagely to give him the opportunity to withdraw without being clawed down from behind. He ran and jumped into space.

The leap was supposed to carry him to one of the tall bookcases facing the worktable, but it was farther away than it appeared and he fell short. He landed with jarring force but without injury. The latter was fortunate considering that he would now have to climb all the way from the floor to the top of the bookcase.

It wasn't difficult to scramble onto the bottom shelf, but after that he had to stand at the very edges facing inward – his raw nerves and pounding heart making him painfully conscious of the drop at his back – jump, catch hold of the shelf above him, and haul himself up. The ascent took him past enormous pottery jars, moldering books, rolled parchments, a frost giant skull with a sword or axe cut in its frontal bone, and pieces of ivory and ice either etched with runes or carved into squat figurines.

Some of the books and scrolls hissed like snakes as though to warn him not to peruse their contents. Others whispered invitations to do precisely that. Both the forbiddings and the attempted seductions rattled him and fed the fear the frigid powder had induced.

Repeated cracking noises from the tabletop revealed that

Sif was still fighting, still smashing the living sigil's icy arms. He kept imagining the moment when she'd scream, and then the sounds of battle would stop. It was a fear keener than any he felt on his own behalf, and it kept him springing, clutching, and climbing despite his newfound fear of falling.

As he stood on the brink of a shelf and flexed his legs for another jump, phosphorescence glimmered in the eyes of an ivory figure with the body of a frost giant and the tusked head of a wooly mammoth. The statuette rushed him with the daggers in its fists upraised.

Heimdall dived forward onto his hands and knees. The animated statuette tripped over him, pitched forward, and landed at the edge of the drop-off. Heimdall kicked it over and flinched to hear it smash on the floor far below. He tried not to think about how close he'd come to being the one knocked off the shelf.

He ascended two more levels to the top of the bookcase. The tall piece of furniture wasn't quite flush with the wall. There was space enough for someone the size of an Asgardian to brace his back against the stone and push with his legs and feet provided he was willing to brave the inevitable drop when the shelf tilted outward. Heimdall had been afraid of falling as he climbed to the top, and now he strained once again to put that dread out of his mind.

He got himself into position and shoved. The heavily laden shelf didn't move, but he refused to accept that it wouldn't. He had the strength of an Asgardian warrior and was applying it where it should topple the bookcase most easily. Teeth gritted, snarling with effort, he kept pushing and finally felt the shelf starting to go over. He shouted,

"Watch out!" and then, just as he'd foreseen, with the piece of furniture falling outward, there was no longer anything to hold him in place, and he dropped, scraping and bumping down the wall.

He slammed down feet first and rolled forward onto his shoulder. It was still a brutal jolt, but maybe that helped to clear his head. As he sprang to his feet, he was no longer in fear for his own life. He was, however, in fear for Sif's.

Dropping behind the bookcase, he hadn't been able to see what was happening in front of it, but his imagination painted gruesome pictures. Sif hadn't registered his shout of warning or, pressed hard by the ice brambles, had been unable to heed it. A giant book or some other massive item had plummeted on top of her, either killing her outright or pinning her long enough for the thing in the basin to tear her apart. Or else the bookshelf itself had crashed down, caught her, and crushed her.

When Heimdall rounded the fallen shelf, what he saw did nothing to quell his fear. The shelf had smashed the worktable into two pieces, and books, scrolls, and pieces of shattered figurines and jars littered the floor. So too did scraps of ice. No new frozen tendrils were sprouting and coiling about, evidence that he'd succeeded in obliterating the vulnerable heart of the living sigil. But, sprawled in a pile of reddish powder next to the broken vessel that had spilled it out, Sif wasn't moving either.

Horrified, Heimdall ran to her and dropped to his knees beside her. "Sif! Sif!"

Her blues eyes fluttered open, and she sat up. "Next time," she groaned, "I want to hear the *whole* plan."

"Are you all right?"

"More or less, if I can find my sword." She looked around. The blade was several paces away sticking up from an enormous book that had opened as it fell. The broadsword had come down point first atop the right-hand pages and impaled them, with the result that the tome was flopping feebly, like a dying fish at the bottom of a boat, and the pierced spot was bleeding ink or some dark ichor. Seemingly unbothered by the peculiar sight, Sif rose, walked to the book, and yanked her weapon free. Only then did she set about dusting the crimson powder from her person.

"I'm sorry," Heimdall said. "It was the only tactic I could think of."

"It was a good one," she replied, albeit in a grudging tone. "I'm still in one piece, and the thing from the bowl isn't. What do you think it was?"

He shrugged. "A spirit Skrymir bound into his service? Something he brought to life with magic? Truly, I have no idea."

"Then here's a more practical question. Do you think anyone heard the crash when the bookshelf fell?"

He listened for hurrying footsteps thumping up the stairs. "I don't hear anybody coming."

"Nor do I. So I guess we keep looking for the head. If there's anywhere else *to* look."

That, he realized, was the question. They'd already inspected the tabletops and shelves. It didn't appear there was anywhere left.

"It could be," he said, "that while the chamber is generally what it appears to be, Mimir's head, being the treasure that it is, *is* here but concealed in an illusion that makes it look like something else."

Sif scowled. "There are books, trinkets, and whatnot on every one of these shelves. Do we climb up on each in turn, lay hands on every object, and hope touch will reveal what sight doesn't? I'm game, but it's going to take a while."

"To say the least. But before we climb any more furniture, let's start with what's fallen on the floor."

Sadly, as best they could determine, Mimir's head wasn't there, and in due course, pointing, Sif said, "You take the shelves along that wall. I'll finish the other worktable and then search the ones over here."

"Right." Heimdall surveyed the bookcases anew in the forlorn hope of spotting some hint as to which tome, scroll, or figurine might actually be Mimir's head, some clue that would spare Sif and him the necessity of clambering to and examining every single item in its turn. The hour was late, but Skrymir still might walk in on them while they were about it.

He didn't find any telltale imperfections in any object's appearance or any odd blurring or flicker to suggest magic was at work. But just as he was about to abandon the effort, he noticed that one bookshelf stood a bit farther away from the wall than the others. "Hold on," he said.

Sif stuck her head over the edge of the surviving worktable. "What?"

He walked to the shelf he'd spotted, peered around the back of it, and felt a surge of excitement. "Come look at this."

Sif sprang off the table – now that he was in his right mind again, Heimdall could see it wasn't *that* far for a Vanir or Aesir to drop – and hurried to his side. She sucked in a breath at the sight of the little door – which was to say, an Asgardian-sized door – set in the wall. The shelving stood a couple paces out from the wall to provide easy access to people of their stature.

"It makes sense," Heimdall said. "Magic shrank the frost giant I fought in the Realm Below. Skrymir likely supplied the talisman and can shrink himself as well."

"But it wouldn't occur to many of his subjects that their proud king would ever deign to reduce himself to our size," Sif said, "and even if it did, a common Jotun thief couldn't steal what's beyond the door because he couldn't fit through." She clasped Heimdall's shoulder and gave him a grin. "Brother! You did it!"

He grinned back. "*We* did it. *Maybe.* We can't be sure until we look inside. So, shall we?"

The wooden door was arched at the top and had a keyhole in the center. He tried the handle and found the door was locked.

For all he knew, it might have more than the usual bolt securing it. Trying to force it might trigger a burst of destructive magic or wake another guardian like the ice-thing in the basin. But, his pulse ticking faster with eagerness, he told himself that he and Sif had come too far to hesitate now. He booted the door, and it broke away from both the bolt and its hinges to bang down on the floor.

Beyond the doorway, they found luxurious apartments. One room contained high-backed leather-cushioned chairs and other furniture and had embroidered tapestries adorning the walls. A bedchamber contained an enormous bed heaped with pillows and covered in furs. A music room contained several flutes and lyres.

As Heimdall and Sif explored, the spaces felt familiar and strange at the same time. They were finally back in a place made for people their size, but after a sojourn in the hugeness of Jotunheim, what should have been natural took some getting used to.

Once Heimdall adjusted to that, he noticed another peculiarity. As he and Sif had had ample opportunity to observe, while items the frost giants fashioned weren't necessarily ill made per se, they were often utilitarian and graceless, and when the Jotuns did strive for ornamentation, the adornments like pendants, arm bands, and engravings on axe heads tended to be simple if not actually crude.

In contrast, the furnishings in these chambers – the tapestries, the intricately carved furniture, finely crafted golden goblets – reflected a subtler taste and might well be plunder from Asgard, Vanaheim, or Alfheim. Perhaps, Heimdall thought with a twinge of humor, Skrymir had another reason for hiding these rooms away. If his warriors discovered his tastes ran to such elegance, they might deem him too effete to wear the crown.

He forgot all about such musings, however, when he and Sif passed through yet another door. The object of their long search was waiting on the other side.

They were standing in another large conjuration chamber rather like the one they'd come from, had the former been scaled to Asgardian size. The mystical designs, however, were inlaid in the floor in black amber and red carnelian, and, like the furnishings in the adjacent rooms, the ritual staves and swords in the wall rack exhibited more refined workmanship than the ones Heimdall and Sif had seen hitherto.

He barely noticed these details, however, because he couldn't look away from Mimir's head. Leathery and sunken-eyed, the brown flesh shriveled tight to the skull beneath, it reposed on a stand in the center of the room. It didn't move or speak when the intruders entered and in general looked as dead as – if not deader than – any other severed head.

For a second, Heimdall stood frozen. After he and Sif had struggled so long and overcome so many obstacles to arrive here, the moment felt unreal. Dreamlike. But then a surge of joy shattered his incredulity, and he rushed to the head with Sif striding along beside him. She was grinning like a fool, and he imagined he was too.

He wanted to bask in their triumph but told himself that would be premature to say the least. They still had to get the head out of Skrymir's castle and all the way back to the citadel of Asgard. But maybe the relic itself could help with that.

He felt an instant of reluctance to try invoking power, the reluctance stemming from worry he'd be meddling in matters that were beyond him. But he'd dared far too much already for the feeling to make him hesitate for more than an instant. "Speak," he said.

To his disappointment, the head remained silent.

"You're not a sorcerer," said Sif, her impatient tone making it clear that she too had refocused her thoughts on practicalities. "So it won't talk to you. Just take the thing."

"Maybe you have to be touching it," Heimdall said.

He rested the palm of his hand on top of the head's few remaining wisps of dry hair and the withered scalp beneath. "Mimir, wake!"

The dull, yellowed eyes rolled sluggishly back and forth in their sockets. "I am here," croaked the head. The jaw barely moved, the teeth scarcely separated, but the sepulchral words were discernible nonetheless.

Pushing awe aside, Heimdall said, "We need guidance to escape Utgard. Can you help us?"

"Ask," said Mimir's head, "and I will answer."

Sif frowned. "We just did ask."

It took the head a moment to respond, perhaps because she wasn't the one touching it. "Ask as you go along the way."

"Fine." Sif looked to Heimdall. "Let's go."

"Just one moment more." Now that Heimdall was finally in a position to have his curiosity satisfied, his suspicions confirmed or disconfirmed, he discovered there was an urgency to doing so as compelling as the need to escape. "Mimir, did a sorcerer cast a spell to prolong the Odinsleep? And then steal you?"

"Yes," groaned the head.

"Was it a traitor inside the royal court?"

"Yes."

"Who?"

Before Mimir's head could answer, a dulcet soprano voice spoke behind Heimdall and Sif to do it for him.

"That's an easy one. It was me."

Twenty-Four

Heimdall and Sif spun around. Clad in green as usual, her three-pointed headdress confining her golden hair and framing her face, and her tight boots rising above her knees, Lady Amora stood in the doorway leading to the apartments beyond.

For a split second, Heimdall stared at her in amazement. Though he'd speculated that there was a traitor in the royal court of Asgard, he never would have suspected Amora. He'd never spoken to her and had barely even seen her from a distance before he dared to approach the queen in her throne room, but by all accounts both Odin and Frigga trusted the sorceress and had given her considerable honors and responsibilities, and she'd served the Realm Eternal conscientiously and effectively.

Heimdall shook off his stunned astonishment. He didn't know what had drawn Amora to this place at this moment, but if he and Sif were to avoid capture, or worse, they needed to act and act now. The thought flashed through his mind that rushing a powerful sorceress might be tantamount to suicide, but Amora was only a few paces away. Perhaps he could reach her before she could cast a spell, or maybe she'd turn tail as she had when he'd charged her in the forest.

Leaving Mimir's head where it sat atop the pedestal, he drew his sword and dashed forward. Sif did the same.

But before they could reach Amora, she snapped her fingers, and a racing shimmer traced the black and red lines in one of the designs inlaid on the floor. Fire roared up to form a wall separating the enchantress from her foes.

Heimdall leaped. For all he knew, magical flame might incinerate him in an instant, but if the barrier was no hotter than ordinary fire, perhaps he'd make it through all right. There was an instant of dazzling brightness and searing heat, and then he landed on the other side, maybe a little singed but essentially unscathed. Sif sprang through a split second after.

Amora's green eyes widened in alarm. She clearly hadn't expected the Asgardians to brave the blaze.

"Surrender!" Heimdall said, advancing. Even knowing she was a dangerous mage, he was reluctant to strike down an adversary who didn't have a blade in her hand.

Unfortunately, his instinct to show mercy gave her the moment required to collect her wits. She thrust out her hand, spoke a word of power, and an unseen force bashed brother and sister and sent them reeling backward toward the flames. Amora scurried through the doorway and out of sight. Evidently, if the blaze failed to neutralize her foes, she didn't want to remain this close to their swords.

Heimdall caught his balance an instant before he would have stumbled back into the flames. He looked to the side, and Sif had recovered her equilibrium as well. They charged after Amora.

The sorceress wasn't in the next room, and it had two doorways leading out of it. Heimdall turned toward the one on the right while his sister pivoted toward the one on the left.

He heard a rustle and a startled curse at his back and knew it was Sif who'd gone in the proper direction. He spun around. A rug had reared up to wrap itself around his sister and carry her down to the floor, where she was struggling to free herself. Peering up at him, she yelled, "I'm fine! Get Amora!"

Meaning to do precisely that before the traitor could cast another spell, he raced across the room, but not fast enough. The ritual swords and staves flew out of the conjuration chamber, surrounded him, and assailed him.

Steel rang as, pivoting, Heimdall parried one weapon and then another. He was outnumbered and had no adversaries made of vulnerable flesh to cut at, but, he judged, his situation wasn't hopeless. The animated blades and rods made straightforward, rudimentary attacks, the level of skill perhaps reflecting the level of ability Amora would display if wielding one of them with her own hands. Maybe he could knock a hole in the ring, lunge through, and reach the sorceress before the swords and staves overwhelmed him.

He parried a slashing sword forcefully enough to slam it aside, and the way was open. At the same moment, however, Amora stepped into view, framed in the doorway opening into the next chamber. "Think carefully," she said, waving her hand.

Heimdall looked at the place she'd indicated. Not all the ritual swords had flown to menace him. Two were hovering over Sif, one poised to thrust into her eye and the other aimed at her throat.

Still trapped inside the rug, which writhed and bunched to counter her efforts to free herself, Sif said, "Get her!"

Amora smiled. "You *might* manage that," she said, "but not before the swords kill your sister. If you care about her, I recommend you drop your own weapon."

Heimdall tried desperately to think of an alternative, some unexpected action that would turn everything around, but his head was empty of everything but fear on his sister's behalf. He laid the two-handed sword on the floor and straightened up again. Sif cursed.

Amora shook her head in mock disapproval. "Some people just don't appreciate the things we do to help them. Now, we're going to do the same thing we just did only the other way around." Positioning themselves only a finger-width away from Heimdall's body, the swords poised themselves to deliver killing thrusts. "Now, Sif, the carpet is going to release you, and as you stand up, you'll leave *your* blade on the floor. Unless you want to try for me and sacrifice your brother as you seem to think he should have sacrificed you."

The rug stopped squirming and tightening. Sif extricated herself from it and rose with her broadsword left atop the shaggy pile.

"I thought you'd be sensible," Amora said. "Now, let's go back to the summoning chamber. It's roomier – roomy enough to keep a safe distance between us – and witchcraft is especially easy in a place of power. I know you wouldn't want me to get a headache."

Brother and sister returned to the space in question with the floating swords and rods herding them along and Amora sauntering in their wake. The wall of fire had disappeared without even leaving a smoky smell behind, and the two warriors halted by the head of Mimir. It was maddening, Heimdall thought, that they'd come so close to seizing it only to fail at the last.

"How did you find us?" he asked, partly because he was curious but mostly because while Amora was talking, she wouldn't be putting him and his sister to death, and maybe that would give him time to think of a way out of this situation. Fortunately, now that she was firmly in control, the enchantress seemed to enjoy gloating and preening. "Was it just bad luck?"

"No." The sorceress raised her forefinger. A bead of blood clung to the tip. "I helped Skrymir make the entity in the bowl. I put a bit of my life in it, and when you killed it, I felt the death like a pinprick. Now it's my turn for a question. Does anyone else suspect there's a traitor in Frigga's inner circle?"

Perhaps, Heimdall thought, he should lie. Maybe the right falsehood would keep Sif and him alive. But Amora's green eyes gazed into his, he felt lightheaded, and the truth slipped out before he could stop himself. "Not as far as I know. It was just a possibility that occurred to me."

Amora laughed. "Well, *that's* a relief. From the moment I sensed you trying to find signs of my enchantment in the vault of the Odinsleep, I've been fretting about who might suspect what and berating myself for not sealing the door when I slipped out with the head. You forget one little detail, and a whole elaborate plan threatens to unravel."

"But your magic sealed it after we came out again," said Sif, "so no one would believe we'd ever been inside."

"Yes," the sorceress said, "and I used my magic to kill the sentry you struck unconscious so everyone would be good and angry and even less inclined to listen to you."

Heimdall gaped at her. "*You* murdered the guard?"

Amora studied him for a moment, taking in his manifest surprise and relief, and then smirked. "This whole time, you thought you did it, didn't you? And oh, how it weighed on you. It must be awful to have such a tender conscience."

Though Heimdall certainly didn't forget that he and Sif were in dire danger, for a moment he felt a profound relief that he wasn't a murderer after all. Then came a surge of anger. "You'll pay for what you did."

"Seriously? Depths of Ginnugagap, what's the life of one little nobody in the middle of a war? Anyway, it's silly for you to threaten me when you're helpless."

He supposed she was right, and in any case he shouldn't bluster and berate her if his goal was to keep her talking while he tried to think of a way out. If he bored or annoyed her, she might respond by commanding the floating swords and staves to kill Sif and him immediately.

Though he was doing his best to come up with a tactic or trick, he was still bereft of ideas. It occurred to him that the head of Mimir could almost certainly supply one, and after being herded back into the conjuration chamber, he was standing right beside the relic. But of course he couldn't stretch out his hand to touch it, let alone converse with it, with Amora watching. Any attempt to do so would surely provoke a violent reaction.

"You're right," he said, "it's stupid to threaten you. But can I reason with you? Why side with the frost giants when you're an Asgardian? When the All-Father has given you so many honors?"

"The problem" Amora replied, "is that he's given about all he can, and I'm not content to be a mere lady of the court forever. I'm better than that. I want to be a queen, and the peace treaty that ends the war will carve out a piece of Asgard for me to rule."

"And for that," snarled Sif, "you'll betray your homeland and your oaths to the crown."

Amora laughed again. "You're so dramatic! This war isn't Ragnarok. That's still far in the future. So what does it matter if Asgard loses, cedes some territory, and, for an age or two, pays tribute in gold and slaves? What does it matter even if Odin has to bend the knee to Skrymir and call him master for a while?"

"What you're overlooking," Heimdall said, "is that an Asgardian like you can't trust the frost giants."

"Oh, I don't," Amora said. "Why do you think I didn't just murder Odin when I had the chance? Because I don't want Jotunheim to crush Asgard beyond any hope of ever regaining its strength. It's by playing one off against the other that I and my new realm will survive and prosper. Truly, there's only one thing I haven't quite figured out yet, and that's whether there's any point to keeping the two of you alive."

Heimdall had the ghastly feeling Amora was about to decide there wasn't. He'd chosen not to attack her at the cost of Sif's life, but if the sorceress was about to kill them both anyway, that had been a bad decision. He'd thrown away his only chance to avenge the murdered sentry and save the people of Asgard and Vanaheim from the misery that would follow upon defeat.

Or perhaps not. His furious promise that Amora would *pay* in full measure seemed a hollow boast, but maybe he and Sif could at least wreck the enchantress's scheme by depriving the Jotuns of Mimir's head and so changing the outcome of the war. It all depended on whether Sif could distract Amora long enough for Heimdall to make his move.

He looked at his sister from the corner of his eye. She was looking back at him, and from the set of her mouth and the general grim cast of her countenance, he perceived they were of the same mind. For whatever reason and despite the threat of all but certain death, she too had decided they must act.

With Amora standing within earshot, Heimdall couldn't tell his sister what he intended, but she didn't need to know he was planning to attack the sorceress. She was plainly aching to do that anyway. Telling himself he wasn't *absolutely* ordering her to her death, that she *might* survive the next couple seconds somehow, he gave her a tiny nod.

Sif dropped low, onto her hands. Startled, sure her prisoners were helpless, Amora took a moment to react. That meant the floating implements guided by her will were slow to act as well. Swords thrust and staves clubbed, some of the weapons clanging and clacking together, but all the attacks passed harmlessly over the white wings of Sif's helm.

Sif scrambled up and rushed Amora with the ritual weapons hurtling in pursuit. Unfortunately, they were flying fast enough to reach Sif before she laid hands on the sorceress.

Still, Sif had given Heimdall the distraction he needed. He raised his fist and slammed it down on top of Mimir's head, pulverizing the crumbling, desiccated relic. Blinding light exploded from the point of impact.

Twenty-Five

Heimdall reeled, fell to one knee, and, still blind, threw up his hands in what he expected would be a futile attempt to ward off thrusting swords and battering staves. In this instant, he didn't fear for his own life – at least he and Sif deprived Amora and the frost giants of Mimir's head before he perished – but hated it that his sister too had to die to accomplish their purpose.

To his surprise, nothing pierced or struck him, but after a moment came the loudest crashing he'd ever heard. Even the storm giant's thunder hadn't been as loud, and he reflexively clapped his hands over his ears. But even though the noise was painful, it didn't deafen him. He knew it hadn't because a moment later, he heard Sif's boots pounding the floor. That thudding was almost equally loud.

The dazzling glare before him coalesced into a view of the summoning chamber, his sister, and Amora, but to his amazement, he was seeing everything differently than before. He could make out the tiniest rotten flecks of Mimir's shattered head littering the floor, every individual strand of black hair sticking out from under Sif's helm, every minute scratch on her armor and Amora's green leather boots, dress, and headdress.

The onslaught of hundreds of what should have been imperceptible details made it impossible to comprehend the broad strokes of what was happening. But he *had* to understand to know if Sif was still alive. Trembling, afraid for both her sake and of the strange condition that had overtaken him, he struggled to make sense of what he was seeing. Finally, after what could only have been a moment or two but felt like an age, he did.

To his vast relief, Sif *was* still alive. He didn't know what magic he'd released by smashing Mimir's head, but the explosion must have in some measure affected Lady Amora as well. She'd fumbled her psychic grasp on the flying weapons whereupon all of them, those threatening him and Sif alike, had fallen to the floor. Apparently, that had been the prodigious crashing of a moment before.

Amora was still staggering, and Heimdall felt a surge of hope that Sif would close with the sorceress and dispose of her. But when his sister was nearly there, the witch collected her wits sufficiently to draw herself up straight and stare, and her green eyes glimmered with an inner light. Sif cried out as her limbs locked in position and her running momentum spilled her to the floor. As if the magic had taken a great deal out of her, Amora stumbled through the door and out of sight.

After several grunting, straining moments, Sif broke free of the paralysis and ran after the sorceress. Her footsteps thumped as she prowled from one room to the next, and the breath sighed in and out of her lungs. Heimdall found that the noises kept him aware of her exact location.

She returned to the doorway, spied Heimdall kneeling on the floor, and rushed to crouch beside him. "Are you all right?" she asked. Her voice was intolerably loud, and he flinched.

"Can you whisper?" he asked, doing it himself.

"Yes," she replied, her voice now hushed and likewise full of concern, "but what's wrong? Did Amora bewitch you too?"

"It wasn't Amora. From the sound of things, you didn't get her."

"No. She whisked herself away. Or turned invisible. Something. Brother, I can see you're not right, and I promise we'll find help for you. But we can't do that if we're still here when Amora sends the Jotuns after us. We need to take Mimir's head and…" Her voice trailed off as she noticed the scraps of broken bone and withered flesh on the stand and the floor around it.

"I didn't think we could get away with the head," Heimdall said, "so when you distracted Amora, I smashed it."

Sif gave a nod. "Good. Now it can't counsel the frost giants any more. But we still need to go. Can you walk at all? I can carry you if I have to."

"Yes," he said. "Walking's not the problem. When I destroyed the head, something passed from it into me."

"Amora too, I think. Suddenly she was weaker."

"As she has mystical perceptions, I think the release of magical forces pummeled her. But since she wasn't touching the head, I suspect she didn't get what I received. I hope not."

"What *did* you get?" asked Sif. "You make it sound like a boon, not an affliction."

"Well, it might be if I can master it," Heimdall said. "Mimir was said to be wise and likely was. But it turns out that many of his insights came from seeing and hearing what others couldn't, and I think his powers of sight and hearing have passed to me. As I look at you, I see every pore. Every tiny chip or dull spot on one of your teeth."

She snorted. "I must look ugly."

He smiled. "If it's any consolation, I always thought so anyway."

"This coming from a man with a face like a horse and a colicky horse at that." Her expression turned serious. "You said *if you can master it*."

"Mimir can't have walked around all the time seeing and hearing the way I am now. Life would have been unlivable. He must have been able to control his perceptions. Give me a moment, and I'll see if I can do the same."

Heimdall willed Sif's face to look as he was accustomed to seeing it and for all the sounds of respiration, heartbeats, and the whistling wind outside the tower to fade to inaudibility. At first, nothing changed, and, with an upwelling of anxiety, he wondered if the moment when he'd previously controlled his sight had only been a fluke. He insisted to himself that it hadn't, told himself that Sif couldn't possibly escape nursing a helpless companion along, and perhaps it was the desperation underlying that thought that finally helped him bring his perceptions under control.

"I think that's got it," he said in a normal voice, and it *was* normal, not a thunderclap buffeting his head.

"Thank the Fates." The first two words sounded as they should, but *Fates* was a bellow, and he flinched. "What's wrong?" his sister asked, her voice still booming.

"Nothing," he said, straining to hear normally. The effort succeeded. His own voice didn't sound painfully loud, and besides, they had to move regardless. "I just lost control for a moment."

"All right, then." Sif squeezed his shoulder and then helped him to his feet.

They hurried out of Amora's secret apartments into the frost giant-sized workroom beyond, recovering their swords as they went. At first, with every few steps, sounds swelled to an unbearable volume or vision and threatened to overwhelm him with intensity and detail, but he was able to reassert control, and the effort became easier and the moments less frequent with repetition. Sif kept a concerned eye on him until, he inferred, she decided he truly was able to function normally again.

He thought wryly that he could scarcely blame her for wondering. The abilities he'd acquired from the destruction of the head seemed miraculous, transcendent compared to the way ordinary people saw and heard. Difficult as it was, it surprised him that he was gaining control of them this quickly. He suspected that even though it had seemed to have no effect at the time, drinking from Mimir's Well had helped.

He and Sif circumvented the pit trap and, bounding along, descended the staircase. The small courtyard encircling the tower of sorcery was as deserted as before. The fugitives darted on into one of the adjacent buildings, one that, if they were lucky, would provide a relatively direct path to a way out of the citadel. Heimdall hoped stealth, their relative smallness, and the gloom of night would keep them safe from detection along the way.

His pulse ticking in his neck, he and Sif hid under a bench while two giggling frost giant children, embarking on some sort of clandestine late-night adventure, padded by them. As they waited for the young giants to pass, Heimdall took the opportunity to exercise Mimir's extraordinary hearing once again.

The chortling waxed louder, as did the Jotun children's footsteps. So too did Sif's respiration and heartbeat and his own. At the same time, he caught countless other sounds that had been inaudible before.

The trick now, he thought, was to sift through all the noises in the citadel and lock on to the one he wanted if, in fact, it existed. He heard giants snoring. Slumbering oxen wheezing in their stalls. Disgruntled because he thought he always drew the least desirable duties, a sentry grumbled to himself as he walked the battlements.

Then Heimdall caught Amora's voice, still musical but now strident with urgency. "… smashed Mimir's head!" she said.

Heimdall felt a pang of disgust that the sorceress was already reporting what had happened. Probably she'd run straight to Skrymir himself, the sorcerer king who knew all about the head and could quickly turn out the castle guard to search for the intruders.

The deep voice of a male frost giant snarled in response. "You swore it was safe! How did Asgardians even get into the citadel, let alone find the thing?"

"I don't know, but–"

"Well," said the frost giant king, sounding marginally calmer, "the war is all but won, and we have our own cunning and our own magic. Maybe we don't need the head any more."

"I trust not, Majesty," Amora said, "but you still must catch the intruders."

To keep us from denouncing you to Frigga, Heimdall thought. As I vow we will do, if we ever make it out of here.

"Oh, we'll catch them." Skrymir raised his voice back to a bellow. "Guards! Attend me!"

"Run," Heimdall said. "We're out of time."

He and Sif dashed through the citadel. Meanwhile, shouts boomed and echoed as frost giants relayed the warning that two Asgardian warriors had infiltrated the fortress. Using his augmented sight, Heimdall peered into the gloom ahead. Shadow slid, the slightest difference between one darkness and another encroaching on it, and he frantically motioned for Sif to stop. There was no cover within reach, so the intruders simply crouched.

A moment later, a frost giant warrior hurried into view with battle-axe in hand. Heimdall let out a sigh of relief when, intent on reaching some other part of the castle, the Jotun didn't turn or even glance in the Asgardians' direction.

Brother and sister ran on as soon as the Jotun warrior passed by. When he chose to hear them, Heimdall caught the sounds of beds creaking as giants rose from their slumbers, wood clattering as they pulled spears from the racks made to hold them, doors slamming and their bolts dropping.

The entire citadel was rousing to hunt the intruders. He took a long, steadying breath and told himself not to take fright at the noises but rather to assess what they revealed. When he did, he reversed course.

"What are you doing?" asked Sif. "The nearest way out is just ahead."

"The frost giants already have that exit secured. Trust me, I can tell. There's another in this direction."

But to his dismay, they had to stop shy of that door too, as Jotun warriors blocked it off as well. When he told Sif, she said, "If there's no way out, we'd better go to ground."

He considered the idea and then rejected it. "I don't think that will work. The frost giants are going to search thoroughly."

But what *would* work? Trying to come up with a plan, he cast about the space they were currently traversing, some sort of minor council chamber perhaps, furnished with a table and benches. When he looked thoroughly, well above the normal sight line of two Asgardians scurrying through the enormous hold like mice, he spied the high windows. On this overcast night, they admitted so little light that ordinary eyes might have missed them, but thanks to Mimir's gifts he could see them clearly.

He pointed, and Sif looked up at them. "Could you jump high enough to clamber onto one of those sills?" he asked.

"Not from the floor," said Sif, "but from the top of one of those benches, yes."

Taking opposite ends, they shoved a crudely made wooden bench up against the wall. The legs grated on the stone floor, and Heimdall winced at the thought that some Jotun would hear the squeal. But there was no sudden rush of pounding footsteps to indicate such was the case.

He and Sif clambered on top of the bench. From there, they leaped, caught the edge of a window ledge, and pulled themselves up.

To Heimdall's surprise, the windowpane was made of shaped and crafted ice. He and Sif battered a hole in it with their swords. He winced at the cracking, crunching noise that made as well, but, as before, no frost giant came rushing in response.

On the other side of the window was an iron grille. Sif squeezed through and jumped down to the ground underneath.

Heimdall tried to follow, but his broader shoulders jammed between the bars. He struggled to squirm onward. His cloak ripped, and the iron of the grille rasped against the steel of his armor, but after a moment the widest part of his body popped through. He heaved the rest of him out and dropped beside his sister.

They'd reached an outer courtyard, and Heimdall peered across the open space before him. A couple dozen frost giant warriors were striding about. That was far too many for safety's sake, but Heimdall was glad to see most were forming up into search parties, which then hurried toward one or another of the doors in and out of the central buildings of the fortress. The Jotuns plainly believed the trespassers couldn't have gotten this far yet. Yet, even so, the postern, the only gate anywhere nearby, was closed as it likely always was unless there was some particular reason to open it.

"What now?" asked Sif.

This time, an idea came immediately. Heimdall hoped that wasn't because it was a bad one. He pointed to stairs leading up the citadel's curtain wall. "We climb to the battlements and jump."

Sif cocked her head. "The fall won't kill us?"

"Maybe not if we jump in the right spot."

They ran across the courtyard to the steps, then ascended them in the same leaping, scrambling fashion that had taken them up the staircase in Skrymir's tower of sorcery. Every second, Heimdall had the terrible feeling that some enemy would surely notice their frantic clambering, but no one did.

Once atop the wall-walk, the Asgardians scurried along, and Heimdall peered out over the merlons and down at the ground beyond. Thanks to his enhanced sight, he was confident of recognizing what he sought at the foot of the wall. Finally he spotted it, but it was still a way ahead, and there was a Jotun sentry armed with a spear and shield tramping toward Sif and him from the same direction. The guard was on the far side of the object of Heimdall's searching, but likely to reach the jumping-off spot ahead of the two Vanir if they didn't make haste.

Heimdall sprinted again, and Sif dashed after him. After a few more moments, she too caught sight of the approaching guard, though likely only as a towering silhouette against the night sky. She growled an obscenity and reached for her broadsword.

"No!" Heimdall said. "We're here!" He turned toward one of the crenel gaps between two merlons... and hesitated.

Even the sight he'd taken from the head of Mimir had its limits. He'd been able to tell the Jotunheim-sized snowdrift heaped against the foot of the wall was an especially deep one, but he wouldn't know for certain whether it was deep enough to cushion his long, long fall until he plunged down in the middle of it. He might leap to his death, and Sif might follow him to the same end.

But the guard would see them in another moment. Heimdall told himself he'd made a plan, and now he needed to trust his judgment and carry it through. He sprang out into space.

Twenty-Six

Heimdall slammed down in the snowdrift and for a moment lay there stunned. When his mind resumed working, he tried to move and discovered that, though he was sure to be bruised and sore presently, all his limbs still worked. It was a relief and a bit of a surprise as well.

Now that he was thinking again, he realized Sif needed to jump too, and quickly, to avoid the sentry's notice, and he needed to make sure she didn't smash down on top of him. He floundered clear of the snowdrift, and she thudded down an instant later, the impact throwing white powder into the air. She then lay motionless, half buried.

Fearful for her, he rushed to her side. "Sif! Are you hurt?"

She groaned and sat up. "Have I told you before how much I hate all your ideas? But I think I'm all right."

He gave her his hand and helped her crawl out. She slapped clinging snow off her body, and then they ran away from the castle and into the city beyond.

They hadn't had to traverse Utgard proper before. The wagon in which they'd stowed away had done it for them. But they knew the port and the sea were downhill, and Heimdall's sharpened senses helped them avoid the attention of Jotuns abroad late at night as they made their way along.

He judged he and Sif had nearly reached the wrecked-ship shanties and the docks when he paused again to listen. To his dismay, at his back, the citadel's primary gate was groaning open and a company of giants was trotting through, feet thumping the frozen ground.

"They know we made it out of the citadel," Heimdall said.

"How could they?" asked Sif.

"Amora's sorcery? Skrymir's? I don't know, but they're venturing out into the city."

"So it's time to run again." Sif flashed a grin. "By now, I know the routine."

They dashed down to the street that ran alongside the docks and onward. In time, the street ended, and beyond it, the trail began its steep, zigzag course up to the crags. A howling wind blew veils of snow across the path. Heimdall shivered at the chill.

He and Sif started up. When he judged they'd climbed high enough, he stopped and surveyed the lower reaches of Utgard from above and felt a sinking feeling in the pit of his stomach. "They're going to overtake us," he said.

Sif turned and likewise looked down at the port and the streets and buildings bordering it. "How can you tell?"

He pointed at a particular bit of the city. Faint blue light gleamed on one wall then another as the source moved rapidly along the street at the base of the buildings. "Can you see that?"

"No."

"Well, it's the light of that cold blue fire on the ends of torches or inside lanterns, maybe. Either way, it shows the warriors didn't split up to search the town at random. The whole company is coming straight at us."

"Again, thanks to magic, no doubt, and there's no hope of making it to the horses before they catch up. But maybe the horses will come to us." She turned and shouted up at the crags looming overhead. "Bloodspiller! Golden Mane!"

The winged steeds didn't come.

"They can't hear you over the wind," Heimdall said.

Sif scrutinized the scarps and the unappealing prospect of trying to cling to icy treacherous handholds on a cold and gusty night. "Do your magic eyes see anywhere to hide?"

"Even if they did, I imagine the frost giants' sorcery would continue to point right at us."

Sif faced back down the trail and drew her broadsword. "This is it, then. Just as well. I'm tired of sneaking and hiding. You keep climbing and I'll hold the Jotuns back as long as I can."

Heimdall reached over his shoulder for the hilt of his own blade. "No. You never abandoned me."

"Don't be stupid. The mission isn't over. We deprived the frost giants of Mimir's head, but it turns out Amora's a traitor. Somebody needs to warn Frigga."

In the abstract he agreed, but found it didn't matter. "Then we'd better win," he said, gripping the two-handed sword, "because I'm not leaving you."

As they awaited the giants, however, that *we'd better win* felt more and more like the hollow bravado it was. Even two skilled Asgardian warriors had no hope of prevailing against an entire company of giants. But perhaps, he thought, Mimir's sight could provide a way out. He turned back and forth examining his surroundings with his newly honed senses for anything he and Sif could turn to their advantage.

There was nothing. But as he pivoted, the Gjallarhorn dangling from its leather cord bumped against his hip. He glanced down at it, and even though his preternaturally keen sight revealed nothing new about the way it was made, his mind abruptly grasped something that had eluded him before.

"I know why there's a stopper in the small end," he said, excitement in his voice. He took the ox horn in hand.

Sif gave him a wry look. "Is this really the time?" Below them, the pursuing frost giants started up the trail. At a distance, the torches some carried looked like blue fireflies.

"Yes. Mimir may have used the Gjallarhorn to drink, but its maker intended it to be a trumpet." Heimdall pulled the stopper out. A protruding ring of brass remained attached to the horn. It was a bugle's mouthpiece.

Sif grinned. "Bloodspiller and Golden Mane couldn't hear our voices, but they might hear that, and Valkyries use horns to signal back and forth."

"Yes, although I don't know any of the signals."

"Just blow!"

Heimdall filled his lungs, brought the instrument to his lips, and blew. Likely amplified by enchantment, the resulting note was loud enough to make Sif recoil in surprise.

It was also loud enough for the frost giants to hear. Their leader bellowed an order, and they charged. Now that they were running flat out, their long legs would carry them up the track in a matter of moments.

Heimdall peered up at the crags. There was still no sign of the Valkyrie steeds, so he sounded the Gjallarhorn again.

"It was a good idea," said Sif, "but if the horses still aren't coming, you might want to stop tooting that thing and ready your sword."

He wondered for an instant if he should, and then Golden Mane and Bloodspiller came to the edge of the ledge on which their riders had left them and peered over the side. Heimdall sounded the horn a third time. The mounts sprang off the edge and spread their wings as they plummeted.

Golden Mane and Bloodspiller were swooping down through the air while the giants were pounding up a mountainside on foot, but by now the latter had drawn so close that for a couple heartbeats Heimdall couldn't tell which would reach his location first. Much to his relief, it was the steeds.

As soon as they touched down, he and Sif flung themselves on their backs. He wished the horses still had their bridles and saddles, but their riders would just have to manage without them. He tapped on Golden Mane's neck as he'd formerly used flicks of the reins to tell the black steed *up* or *down*. Golden Mane sprang off the edge of the trail, lashed his pinions, and ascended. Bloodspiller and Sif followed.

Roaring, the frost giants threw their enormous spears. Golden Mane and Bloodspiller swooped and veered to avoid the missiles while their riders held on. One spear passed just under Golden Mane's galloping hooves like a tree trunk streaking by below, but after that the Jotuns at the forefront of the horde had flung all their spears, and the steeds and their riders were still climbing and still unscathed. One furious giant warrior followed up by throwing his battle-axe as well, but the weapon spun away into the night without coming anywhere close to either Asgardian.

Sif laughed. Plainly, she was certain she and Heimdall had escaped. For a moment he believed the same, and then a flicker of light on the battlements of Skrymir's citadel caught his eye. He peered at it with the sight of Mimir that rendered the darkness and the distance back to the fortress inconsequential.

The biggest frost giant Heimdall had ever seen stood on the battlements snarling words of power and sweeping a staff made of ice back and forth in ritual passes. The passes left wisps of blue-white glimmer in the air. The giant – King Skrymir, surely – wore a crown made of ice and had several other Jotuns hovering in attendance. Amora was also present and floating in midair at the height of Skrymir's head but otherwise not working any overt magic.

Heimdall tensed to see it didn't appear that Skrymir needed any assistance. Shadows writhed in the air above the frost giant ruler and congealed into a dozen huge black owls. The conjured birds flew fast as arrows in the fugitives' direction.

Heimdall now realized that if he and Sif simply fled across the face of Jotunheim, hostile magic was all too likely to bring them down. There was only one place to run if they hoped to evade their foes. "Follow me!" he called to Sif. He then shouted to Golden Mane. "Yggdrasil!"

A luminous portal opened in front of the black steed. Golden Mane and his rider hurtled through into the void they'd visited before, and Sif and Bloodspiller appeared a moment after.

Sif turned to her brother. "I agree we had to do this, but I'm not delighted to be back here."

"Nor am I," Heimdall answered. Yet as he regarded the spectacle before him, something struck him. "Wait, though. It's different for me this time."

The difference wasn't overt. Yggdrasil remained a colossal tree floating among stars and nebulae with whole worlds perched among the branches and roots. But his expanded perceptions could encompass the terrible grandeur of the spectacle without distress. The immensity of it no longer threatened his capacity for thought or sense of self. This, he inferred, must be how the Valkyries experienced it thanks to the training or initiation that prepared them for the vista.

"Does that mean you're not in danger of losing your mind?" asked Sif.

He smiled. "No more than usual."

"*I* should have smashed Mimir's head. But since you seized on the easy part of the task, find us a way out of here. With luck, Bloodspiller will follow you and Golden Mane even if I've fallen into a stupor."

"Right." He peered up at the high branch on which Asgard awaited, and the golden shimmering suggestion of a path appeared before him, twisting back and forth a little as it climbed toward the home of the Aesir. He surmised that this too was an aspect of the void outside the Nine Worlds as the Valkyries experienced it, and that following the pathways facilitated the passage from one to another. He started Golden Mane up the trail to Asgard and found the black steed negotiated the various turns without requiring any prompting. The winged horse also saw the path and expected his rider to use it. No doubt the stallion had been puzzled if not disgusted during their previous journey when Heimdall was oblivious to the tracks.

After a few moments, another luminous round portal opened before them. They passed through into a frozen landscape in which a whistling wind blew snowflakes bigger than the first joint of his thumb, the sky was gray with cloud cover, and whiteness blanketed the ground below.

"Are we back in Jotunheim?" called Sif.

For a moment, Heimdall wasn't sure either. He peered ahead, farther than she or any normal Vanir or Aesir could see, and found the remains of a longhouse sticking up above the snow. It was the right size for Asgardians to inhabit and looked as if passing frost giants might have smashed in the roof.

"No," he said grimly, "this is Asgard. The winter weather just shows the Jotuns have kept right on winning the war in the days we've been away."

Twenty-Seven

After two more days of travel, as Heimdall and Sif flew toward the citadel of Asgard, he found it easy to use his heightened sight to give any frost giants a wide berth and likewise determine the disposition of forces. To his disappointment if not his surprise, everything he saw confirmed his initial impression. There were no Asgardian armies still in the field. Any that survived had fallen back to defend the All-Father's city while the forces of Jotunheim were on the march to encircle the capital and lay siege to it.

He wondered glumly just how long the rout had taken. Not long, he suspected. Thanks to his sojourn in the Realm Below and the jumping between worlds, he didn't know precisely how long he and Sif had been gone, but he didn't think it had been more than a couple weeks.

He and Sif set down on a hilltop to give the winged stallions a rest. As he swung himself off Golden Mane's back, Heimdall said, "Skrymir was right when he told Amora the frost giants don't really need the head of Mimir any more."

"Not as things stand currently," replied Sif, rubbing Bloodspiller's flank. "But when the All-Father wakes and brings *his* wisdom and his power to bear, they'll wish they still had it. We just have to convince someone with magical abilities to enter the vault of the Odinsleep and break the spell Amora cast on him."

Heimdall smiled a wry smile. "Of course. Why not, when we were so successful last time?"

Sif laughed. "At least this time we know Lady Amora is a traitor. That ought to help."

"I hope so. Surely by now someone has grown suspicious of her mysterious absence. That should make it easier to convince people she's a turncoat. Before we can even denounce her, though, we have to enter the citadel and obtain a hearing in front of the queen without being summarily killed for our own supposed treachery."

"How do you think we should do that? By stealth?"

Heimdall thought about it and then said, "I'd rather not. I'd rather not do anything that reinforces the impression that *we're* the traitors. If everyone can see us approaching the city, and if we make our peaceful intentions obvious, we might fare better."

Sif nodded. "That makes sense… except, could the horses whisk us from here right into the throne room? Then we could be sure no one would kill us before we ever reached the presence of the queen."

"Interesting idea," Heimdall said, "but I doubt it. Their ability to flash from one spot to another seems to exist to shift them into the void where Yggdrasil stands and out again. I don't think they can use it to go a precise point in a particular world. Once they're inside Asgard, Jotunheim, or wherever, they depend on their wings to take them swiftly to where they need to go. Moreover, even if they could carry us straight into Frigga's presence without flying over the city and the castle walls first, we don't know how to tell them to do that."

"Approaching slowly and in plain view it is, then."

When they judged the horses were ready, they flew on. Though the giants were advancing on the city of Asgard, their various forces drawing tight around it like a noose, they were still some miles out from the perimeter, and brother and sister continued to avoid them as they had before. They still might die today, Heimdall reflected, but, if so, it would be at the hands of their own people.

When cold and snow grudgingly gave way to the warmth and green of Asgard's perpetual summer, which still prevailed in a circle around the city, Heimdall blew the Gjallarhorn and kept sounding it periodically thereafter to announce his and Sif's approach. They held the steeds to an aerial canter, not an all-out gallop, and they left their swords in the scabbards. Heimdall hoped that, taken all together, the display would proclaim peaceful intentions.

While he and Sif had been away, the effort to turn the part of the city that had spilled beyond the walls into defenses had continued and was ongoing even now. Warriors and common folk labored side by side to throw up still more walls and dig even more ditches and pits, to the point where the town beyond the towering ramparts of Asgard was scarcely recognizable as a one-time settlement any more. Dogged labor had transformed it into a maze of fortifications. The laborers raised up their sweaty, dirty faces as Heimdall and his sister passed overhead.

Sif called across the space between the horses. "No one's shooting at us."

"So far," Heimdall replied, feeling somewhat encouraged. He wondered if they should land in front of one of the city gates and enter the capital at ground level. That too might signal benign intent more clearly than soaring over the wall intended to keep intruders out. He was still thinking about it when a trumpet somewhat like the Gjallarhorn sounded from the ramparts. This one, however, was blowing the call that meant the forces of Asgard were under attack.

Below the riders and their steeds, warriors set down stones, dropped shovels, and scrambled for bows and spears. The guards on the ramparts ahead already had weapons in hand and used them, but they were too eager, and the first bowshots and spear casts fell short of the targets and arced down to the ground.

"Curse it!" said Sif. "What did we do to alarm them?"

"Nothing!" Heimdall answered, bewildered. "I don't understand!" But then, to his shocked dismay, he saw something that made it all clear.

A slender blonde figure in green had appeared among the warriors on the stretch of battlements directly ahead. She called orders, and artillerymen turned a catapult and a ballista in the flyers' direction and began to load the weapons. Archers nocked new arrows, and spearmen took up new spears. Satisfied that all the warriors were doing what should be done to kill her enemies, Lady Amora then took a long breath, raised her hands, and chanted the first words of a spell.

Heimdall had hoped that with the conquest of Asgard imminent, Amora would remain with the frost giants. Instead, she'd apparently used magic to make a swift return to Frigga's court and sabotage efforts at defense from within. Now that same sorcery had revealed Heimdall and Sif's approach, and the witch intended to kill them and make sure they never had the chance to speak to the queen.

His heart pounding with anxiety, Heimdall had no doubt the safe course was to turn and flee. A climb to a higher altitude or a shift into the void where Yggdrasil stood might save him and Sif if the steeds could manage it quickly enough.

But he suspected that if he and his sister ran now, they'd never get this close to Frigga again. Exercising Mimir's abilities, he frantically peered and listened for anything that could help them and, with an upwelling of hope, caught familiar voices and the clop of hooves sounding from the inner reaches of the citadel.

He turned to Sif. She'd drawn her sword and was plainly an instant away from urging Bloodspiller into a swooping charge despite the barrage of missiles likely to meet her halfway. "Don't!" he cried.

Sif glared back at him. "If we can't talk to the queen, Amora needs to die!"

"Just wait! Help is coming!"

After several more seconds, while the artillerymen were still readying the catapult and ballista and Amora was still declaiming the no-doubt devastating death magic she intended to unleash, a dozen Valkyries on their own winged steeds soared above the wall.

The one in the lead was Uschi, as before clad and armored all in black and with her raven hair and inky cape streaming out behind her. She used her flaming sword to wave the other Valkyries on toward Heimdall and Sif.

As she did, it occurred to Heimdall to thank the Fates for his luck. Given that Uschi had supposedly fallen asleep and been responsible for his and Heimdall's escape, she could have faced discipline, but evidently, in the midst of wartime, her overall record was impressive enough that her superiors had allowed her to remain in command of her company. Moreover, like Amora, she too had noticed him and Sif approaching, and, still grateful for their help against the frost giants, rushed to save them.

Unable to hurl missiles from the catapult and ballista, loose arrows, or throw spears lest they hit the aerial cavalry, the warriors on the ramparts simply stood and watched the Valkyries gallop through the air. Even Amora left off her conjuring. Evidently the magic she'd intended to unleash would likewise have struck the choosers of the slain.

The Valkyries wheeled around Heimdall and Sif. "Where are the saddles and bridles?" Uschi called.

"We lost them," Heimdall said. "Things took an unexpected turn."

"Well, at least the horses are alive. My warriors and I will escort you into the citadel." She smiled. "As our prisoners, obviously."

Heimdall smiled back. "This is twice you've helped us."

"You helped me and mine first, and even if you hadn't, back in the farmhouse you gave me much to think about. If someone had stolen Mimir's head, it might well mean there was a traitor at court, probably someone possessed of enough magic to counter the vault's defenses. And when Amora commanded the warriors to kill you immediately, even though you were clearly approaching peacefully, that fixed my suspicions on her. Oh, look, here she comes now."

Amora's magic floated her up from the battlements and on toward the warriors and winged stallions in the sky. "Don't attack her," Heimdall said. Even in the unlikely event that his sister could kill the sorceress despite the circle of Valkyries duty-bound to protect her, their ultimate objective was still to have someone wake Odin, and that wouldn't happen if they looked like blackguards now.

"Even though she's putting herself within reach?" Sif sighed. "Oh, all right." She slid her broadsword back into its scabbard.

Despite that, Amora didn't put herself within *easy* reach of Sif or Heimdall either. Probably, he thought, that was just as well. He'd warned Sif against attacking the sorceress, but now that she was close, he felt the same fierce anger his sister manifestly felt.

Perhaps because another enchantment was involved, he didn't need Mimir's powers of perception to hear Amora clearly across the space that separated them. "Heimdall and Sif are traitors already condemned to death," she said, addressing herself to Uschi. "You and your Valkyries, kill them, or if you're unwilling, withdraw and let the warriors on the battlements do their duty."

"I know they're accused of treason," the Valkyrie in black replied. "I have *not* heard they were to be killed out of hand even if they surrendered themselves for judgment.

Perhaps, Lady Amora, you have misinterpreted the queen's commands."

"I assure you, I haven't," the enchantress said, "and I also assure you that you don't want bad blood between us."

"I do not," Uschi said, "but now that the prisoners are *my* prisoners, my duty, as best I understand it, is to keep them secured and alive until someone with actual authority over me commands me to do otherwise. I trust you understand."

"I do," said Amora, "and I won't forget this." She gave Heimdall and Sif a poisonous smile. "It seems you *may* have the opportunity to babble your lies and excuses to Frigga after all. I promise, it won't matter in the end."

Heimdall turned to Uschi. "We *do* have to speak to the queen immediately."

The Valkyrie gave a nod. "I'll see what I can do."

The riders flew on into the precincts of the citadel with Amora flying along beside them. They all set down in a courtyard Heimdall hadn't visited before, one long and wide enough for winged horses to gallop, spread their wings, and rise into the air. He surmised that the surrounding buildings were the steeds' stables, the Valkyrie barracks, and likely the workrooms of the smiths, armorers, and saddlers required to keep the warriors and their mounts ready to fight. The air smelled of hay, and metal rang as a dwarf hammered a glowing red sword blade on an anvil.

Heimdall intended to keep an eye on Amora, but despite his vigilance and to his surprised dismay she vanished between one moment and the next without him seeing how she accomplished it. He hastily alerted Sif and Uschi that the enchantress was gone.

"So I see," Uschi answered. "My guess is that she wants to get to Frigga before I do and persuade the queen to order your execution before I ever have a chance to speak. I'll chase after her in a moment, but first we have to take care of the formalities. Prisoners, dismount and hand over your swords."

Heimdall and Sif obeyed.

"Good," Uschi said, passing the weapons to a subordinate. She then addressed herself to all her Valkyries. "Keep these two right where they are, out in the open. If evil magic sends a thousand spiders to kill them, or anything like that, I want plenty of witnesses. Now, I'm off to catch up with the sorceress." She wheeled her mount, kicked the stallion into a run, and the steed beat his wings and carried her back into the air.

After that, there was nothing to do but wait, and Heimdall experienced an odd mingling of trepidation and anticlimax. Grooms saw to the horses including Golden Mane and Bloodspiller. One Valkyrie brought a bench for the prisoners to sit on, another found them oat flatbread, cheese, and ale, and he discovered that at the end of his long journey, anxiety wasn't dulling his appetite. His stomach rumbled, and he attacked what he knew might be his final meal with gusto. Beside him, Sif ate just as ravenously.

Until, her repast finished, she covered a burp with her hand and said, "I wasn't expecting to sit around. I imagined that once we reached the citadel, one way or the other, everything would happen quickly."

Heimdall smiled. "It's almost as if a monarch preparing her city to defend against armies that are nearly at the gates has other things to do besides listen to outlandish stories from two miscreants wandering in from the cold."

Sif chuckled. "I'm not complaining, exactly. Not considering what awaits us if we fail to convince Frigga."

"At least the frost giants don't have Mimir's head any more. We accomplished that much. Not that I assume we *won't* persuade the queen." He told himself they had the truth on their side, and surely that mattered.

"That's good to hear," said Sif. "But if it becomes clear she doesn't believe us, I'm going to rush Amora. The Jotuns shouldn't have *her* any more, either, and if the giants do defeat our people, she shouldn't be alive to share in the spoils."

"She'll be expecting an attack," Heimdall said, "and the guards in the throne room will be ready for one as well."

Sif shrugged. "I'm still going to try."

Heimdall realized he couldn't talk her out of it any more than he could stand by passively while she fought her last fight alone. "Obviously, if you go for Amora, I will too. But at least give me a chance to make our case."

"I already said I would." Sif smiled. "Do you remember when Father would sit in judgment and sort out disputes that happened on his lands?"

Heimdall grinned. "Wardell the poacher. His excuses were so comical that Father couldn't bring himself to punish him. Like when he claimed the hares he'd trapped were dark elf sorcerers who'd changed their shapes, and he'd saved the fief from a terrible invasion."

Brother and sister continued reminiscing about their childhoods. While there was nothing to do but wait,

Heimdall appreciated the distraction from the current situation, and he suspected Sif felt the same.

Finally, Uschi set her winged steed down in the courtyard once again. Although the respite and the nostalgic conversation had done Heimdall some good, as he stood up his pulse beat in his neck, and his nerves felt taut as bowstrings. Because he knew it was time.

Uschi dismounted and gave her steed over into the keeping of one of the grooms. She and her warriors then formed up around the prisoners and marched them among the lesser buildings of the citadel toward the central keep.

"I hope," Heimdall said, "we're headed for the throne room."

"As opposed to the dungeons or the block," said Sif.

"The queen will hear you," Uschi said. "Sly as she is, Lady Amora couldn't come up with a convincing reason why she shouldn't. The rest is up to you."

The splendor of the throne room reminded Heimdall of his and Sif's dirty, disheveled appearances. The scowls on the faces of the guards and the way the grips tightened and shifted on their spear shafts attested to their conviction that the prisoners were dangerous traitors who'd already murdered one of their comrades.

This time, although Amora was present as expected, there were no scribbling clerks or gaggle of petitioners in attendance, presumably, Heimdall thought, because Frigga hadn't planned to be here today. The mud on her shoes and the hem of her gown suggested she'd spent her time outdoors inspecting troops and the ongoing efforts to bolster Asgard's defenses. He and Sif each dropped to one knee before her and the All-Father's empty throne, and she frowned down at them.

"My inclination," Frigga said, "was to throw you in a cell and deal with you after the war ends. But Uschi tells me you saved her and the company, which I admit is odd behavior for traitors. She's also under the impression you have something of importance to tell me. Stand up, then, and speak."

"Thank you, Majesty," said Heimdall, rising. "I know you have urgent matters to attend to, but I ask that you give us sufficient time to tell what happened when we entered the vault of the Odinsleep and some of what happened after."

"And so the lies begin," Amora said. "You couldn't get into the crypt. We know because the warriors who discovered you standing over the sentry you murdered saw that you couldn't."

"We'd already been inside," said Sif. "We couldn't open the door a second time because your witchcraft sealed it."

"Ridiculous," Amora said, "I wasn't even there."

"We didn't see you," Sif replied, "but then, people don't always see you unless you want to be seen, do they?"

The sorceress turned to the queen. "Majesty, I don't mind if the traitors slander me and tangle me in their web of falsehoods. No one will heed them. I've proven my loyalty time and again. But I believe the instinct that warns you there are better uses for your time than listening to this nonsense is telling you only the truth."

Amora's lies brought more of Heimdall's anger boiling up in his mind. But he judged that agitation would serve him poorly in the effort to convince the queen, and he took a deep, steadying breath before speaking again.

"Please, Majesty," he said. "Sif and I will be as brief as we can, but it's vital that you hear us. Let us tell our story as it unfolded. Perhaps it will make the most sense that way."

Frigga frowned. "I promised Uschi I'd give you a hearing, and I will. Just get on with it."

Grateful that the queen would at least listen to the story, Heimdall first offered an account of what had happened in the vault of the Odinsleep. Amora took the opportunity to declare once again that the two warriors couldn't possibly have entered, but that simply by trying and by murdering the sentry, they'd committed treason and sacrilege and deserved to die.

Still holding his anger in check, Heimdall ignored her and went on to relate some of what had happened after he and Sif fled the citadel of Asgard. He greatly abridged such matters as their wanderings in the Realm Below and omitted entirely the hnefatafl game with Nidhogg, but still, as he heard the tale coming out of his mouth, he heard unlikelihoods that put the extravagances of Wardell the poacher to shame.

To his dismay, he could see scornful, skeptical smiles or doubtful expressions appearing on every face, even, eventually, Uschi's. He wondered grimly if, the fight outside the farmhouse notwithstanding, the Valkyrie leader now regretted the gratitude that had prompted her to insist Frigga give the fugitives a hearing.

Sif plainly sensed the mood in the hall as well, and Heimdall could see her gathering herself for a suicidal charge at Amora. He could scarcely blame her and would join her if she did, but he had the same sense he'd had when the frost giant envoy and the trolls trapped him in the cave. He and Sif shouldn't throw their lives away on an empty gesture, especially when it would let the enemy win. There had to be a way to turn this situation around. Somehow. While he strained to think of it, he gave his sister a glance intended to convey, *not yet.*

Once Heimdall's account reached the encounter with Amora in Jotunheim, the enchantress sneered and said, "At last the lies break down completely. Your Majesty knows I've been at your side almost constantly, lending aid and counsel as required."

"You have magic to whisk you back and forth between Asgard and Jotunheim," Heimdall answered.

"And why was such an important lady of the court personally leading the effort to catch two fugitives when we were running away?" asked Sif. "Why were you so eager to see us killed before we ever had a chance to reenter the city and talk to anyone?"

"I was merely," Amora said, "attempting to deal with traitors and murderers as they deserve."

"Majesty," Heimdall said, "I beg you. If we open the vault, you'll see that all the defenses are as we described them. You'll see the head of Mimir is missing. All of that is proof that my sister and I are telling the truth."

"We can't," Frigga said. "Odin's command forbids it."

Even now? Heimdall thought. He felt a fresh surge of anger and struggled again not to let the emotion show in his voice or on his face. Still, his fists clenched tight.

"Majesty," Amora said, "you've suffered this rubbish patiently. I have as well, even though the traitors tried to make me the villain of their tale. But there isn't a shred of proof to support anything they've said. I know not why they aided Uschi's company, but we do know they came away with stolen Valkyrie stallions to speed their flight from justice. I likewise don't know what madness prompted them to return to Asgard. Evidently they were foolish enough to imagine their lies persuasive. But whatever they were thinking, it's time to put an end to this."

Frigga grimaced. "You're right, my lady." She turned to Uschi. "I understand you wish to believe the best of the man and woman who saved your company. But *you* must understand that people can't defy the All-Father's commands and defame a royal counselor without evidence. I accordingly sentence–"

Sif took a step forward, and, if the prelude to her attack turned a key in Heimdall's mind, and, desperate to save her, he suddenly knew something more to do and say. He grabbed his sister's wrist to hold her in place. "I *have* evidence!" he said.

The queen frowned in a way that suggested she wasn't accustomed to being interrupted. Still, she said, "What is it?"

Smiling with the confidence he'd only just regained, Heimdall pointed. "That tapestry hanging on the far wall. There are twenty-nine little white catsfoot flowers on it. I doubt you can see them all from here, but I can. It proves Mimir's powers have passed to me."

"It proves nothing," Amora said, "except that at some point you had the chance to count them."

Heimdall turned. "The guard standing all the way at the

other end of the hall to the left of the doorway. He has a loose thread hanging from the end of his right sleeve."

"Which you took note of coming in," the sorceress said.

"Right now, there are three men walking on the other side of the door. Two of them are chaffing the other for mooning over a woman who doesn't want him."

"Let's see," Uschi said. She ran down the length of the hall, disappeared through the door, and in due course returned with three servants who, awestruck and stammering that the queen herself was paying them any mind, confirmed that they had indeed just been saying what Heimdall had overheard.

Surely now, he thought. Surely now the queen believes me.

"All right," said Amora to Frigga as the servants filed out again, "It's plain some magic has sharpened Heimdall's eyes and ears. But so what? Did the All-Father ever tell Your Majesty that keen sight and hearing were the source of Mimir's wisdom?"

"No," said the queen. "Odin kept some things secrets even from me."

Heimdall felt his momentary confidence start to crumble.

Amora smiled. "Then there's *still* no evidence to back up any of the traitors' lies."

"By the Tree!" Sif cried. "Majesty, isn't *anything* you've heard strange or suggestive enough to put doubt in your mind?"

Frowning, one hand to her chin, Frigga sat silently for several heartbeats. Finally she said, "The one thing we can be absolutely certain of is that Odin ordered that no one is to enter the vault. Accordingly–"

"Please!" Heimdall said. "Wait! The future of our people depends on it!" At that instant, he had no idea what he'd say if she did wait, but his every instinct screamed that if he let the queen go ahead and pronounce her judgment, that would be the end of everything.

"I'll listen once more," Frigga said. "Then it will be time to bring this matter to a close."

For a horrible second, Heimdall's head was empty of everything but desperation, and then a final idea came to him. "Odin can't have commanded that no one look at the hallway and the outer face of the door leading into his crypt. There's a sentry there, and other people pass by from time to time. If we go there now, I'll show you the proof you need."

"Majesty," Amora said, "you've been to the door already. You've seen there's nothing there. The traitor is simply stalling in the hope that something, anything, will happen to save his life."

"You may be right," Frigga replied slowly, "but there *are* things here that make little sense to me, and even with the defense of the city to attend to, I won't send these two to the headsman without giving them a chance to prove their innocence. Not if they can do it without violating Odin's decree." She looked around the throne room. "Uschi, you and your Valkyries are still in charge of the prisoners. Guards, Lady Amora, you'll accompany me as before."

The queen, Amora, and two royal bodyguards headed up the procession. The Valkyries marched behind with Heimdall and Sif in the middle of them. As they all made their way through the citadel, and those they passed saluted Frigga and peered curiously after her, Sif whispered, "Do you truly think you'll find something to prove we're telling the truth?"

Heimdall's mouth was dry with anxiety and anticipation, and he had to swallow before he could answer. "I don't know, but Mimir's gifts *might* reveal something no one else can see. It was one last throw of the dice."

Sif laughed, drawing surprised looks from those around her. "Well, if it doesn't work, at least we'll finish as we've been going all along."

After another minute, they arrived in the proper hallway. Two guards now stood outside the doorway to the vault where Odin slept, but other than that, on first inspection, the gloomy passage was no different than on Heimdall's previous visit.

Heimdall looked to Frigga. "If the guards step away from the door," he said, "that will help me find what I'm looking for."

"Do as he asks," said the queen, whereupon the spearmen with their shields bearing Odin's two-ravens emblem moved farther down the corridor. When Heimdall then advanced to the spot they'd vacated, Uschi and another Valkyrie followed a pace behind. He couldn't imagine what desperate act they thought he might attempt with both ends of the passage blocked and warriors still surrounding Sif, but evidently hovering close was part of their duty as they understood it.

The dimness was no impediment to the sight he'd inherited from Mimir. On the wall were minute flecks of blood left behind when he'd punched the sentry back into it and evidently cut his head. Tiny droplets likewise speckled the floor where the warrior had fallen. There were also particles of soil that people had tracked in.

But to Heimdall's disappointment, none of it represented any sort of exoneration. Knowing his new gifts made it unnecessary but impelled by desperation nonetheless, he went down on one knee for a closer look at the floor. Still, he found nothing helpful.

"Majesty," Amora said, "I say again, it's time to bring this matter to a close."

"I haven't examined the door yet," Heimdall said. "That's where the proof is." He hoped. If not, there was nowhere left to look.

When he peered with the vision of any common Asgardian, the door was as he'd seen it before, arched, heavy, possessed of a golden handle, and nothing more. He felt an upwelling of excitement, however, when his new sight revealed symbols indenting the grain of the oaken surface. It was as if something had pressed against the panel with great force and precision but only stamped marks as deep as a hair was thick.

"There are runes here!" he said.

Frigga squinted. "I see nothing."

"I'll trace them for you." His forefinger ached as he did so, an indication, he surmised, that the enchantment retained its power.

"Those *are* some of the mystic signs," said the queen.

"But once again," said Amora, "it proves nothing. We already knew that when it's time for the Odinsleep, the All-Father uses magic to seal himself up in the crypt."

Whatever Sif and I say, Heimdall thought, finally giving

in to despair, whatever my new eyes and ears can discover, it's never going to be enough. Amora will always know what to say to deflect.

Which, he thought grimly, meant Sif had been right before. The two Vanir needed to try to kill Amora. They'd almost certainly fail, and even if they succeeded, the Valkyries and guards would strike them down a moment later to be reviled as traitors and a shame to their kin forever after. But it was the only play left.

Or so he imagined. But as he gathered himself to lunge and shove through all the warriors separating him from the woman in green, Frigga said, "My husband doesn't share all his secrets with me, but he has shared many. We've worked magic together often enough that I know his preferred methods. I never knew him to use these particular runes."

"With all respect, Majesty," Amora said, "you're a skillful mage, but the king is the greatest of us all. I daresay he's mastered *every* rune."

"I have no doubt," Frigga replied, and Heimdall felt elation because it appeared to him that she was at last regarding Amora with a hint of doubt in her eyes. "But it's a matter of… style, I suppose. I doubt Odin would use this particular spell to seal a door when others would work equally well. Whereas I am *skillful* enough, as you put it, to know Karnilla of Nornheim frequently relies on this system of runes. I also recall that Karnilla was your first mentor in sorcery before the two of you had a falling out."

"Majesty," Amora said, all wounded innocence, "*surely* you aren't accusing me. Not on the word of these two murderers. Not on the basis of a single coincidence."

"I am not," the queen replied. "Certainly not yet. But there *are* too many curious aspects to this matter. I won't risk making a wrong judgment when simply looking beyond this door will make all things clear."

Amora's eyes widened. "Odin's command–"

For the first time, Frigga looked impatient not with her prisoners but with her sorceress, advisor, and lady of the court. "Perhaps I've been too respectful of my husband's decrees. *I* rule Asgard while he sleeps, and I must do as *I* think best to protect the Realm Eternal. If I'm wrong and this angers him, it will be on my head." She smiled wryly. "And if anyone can mollify him, surely it will be his loving wife."

Amora bowed her head. "As you command, of course, Your Majesty. Perhaps, since, as you say, you are the one the All-Father will forgive most easily, you should also be the one to dissolve his enchantment."

"Very well." Frigga faced the door.

"No!" Sif shouted. "Don't turn your back on her!" She rushed toward Amora, and Heimdall sprang after her. Startled and confused, some of the Valkyries jumped in the way while reaching for their swords.

Meanwhile, Amora stared into the eyes of one of the equally surprised royal bodyguards. Frigga's other guard spun toward them, and the sorceress did the same to him. The enchantress then murmured, too softly for anyone but the two warriors and Heimdall to hear, "Kill the queen."

Bewitched, the two men drew their blades.

Twenty-Eight

Heimdall knew what was about to happen, but he was too many strides away from Frigga and had too many Valkyries in his way to do anything about it. But, to his relief, Sif was closer, facing in the same direction, and saw the threat. She bellowed, "Vanaheim!" and bulled through the Valkyries blocking her.

Afterward, she faced two warriors with swords in hand while she had none. To keep them from cutting down Frigga – who was turning back around but too slowly for it save her – Sif whipped off her grubby cape and whirled it to entangle the weapons in its folds.

The cloak could only snare the swords for a moment before the entranced guards jerked them free. Sif used that second to shift in close to the warrior on the right and punch him in the face. The warrior lurched backward and fell.

At the same time, his comrade stepped behind Sif and poised his sword to run her through. Then, however, Uschi and the two other Valkyries who'd belatedly recognized the threat to the queen swarmed on him, twisted his arm till he dropped his sword, and bore him to the floor.

Meanwhile, Amora raced back down the hallway and rounded the corner at the end.

The Valkyries let Heimdall through. He charged after the traitorous sorceress and turned the corner just as she flourished her hands to complete a spell. With a flash of green light, a doorway appeared before her. Her conjuring chamber in Skrymir's castle was on the other side, and she hurried across the threshold.

Heimdall lunged after her but was an instant too slow. The portal vanished before him, and he staggered on through the space it had vacated. Amora was gone beyond his reach. He sought to console himself with the thought that at least her overt treachery had finally made it clear to all that he and Sif were telling the truth.

As he tramped back to his sister, Frigga, Uschi, and the others, the queen was declaiming the words of a spell. When she finished, the bewitched guard who was still conscious closed his eyes and slumped in the grip of the Valkyries restraining him. The fellow Sif had struck unconscious let out a snore that suggested the magic had affected him as well.

"They'll sleep for a time," Frigga said, "and when they wake, their minds will be clear." She turned to Sif. "I owe you my life. Thank you."

For once, Sif looked shy, albeit only for an instant. "I just did my duty, Majesty." She looked to Heimdall. "I take it Amora got away?"

"Yes," he said. "Magic whisked her back to Skrymir and the frost giants."

"Once again," Sif said, "it's plain I have to do *everything* myself."

The gibe made the queen smile, but only slightly and only for an instant, after which her expression became serious once more. "Heimdall and Sif, I pardon you for invading the chamber of the Odinsleep and declare you innocent of all other charges laid against you. Now it's time for *us* to invade the vault and set things right."

With that, Frigga faced the door, raised her hand, and recited another spell. One by one, the runes Heimdall had detected became visible as symbols that glowed like red-hot iron, then crumbled into embers and ash that vanished as they spilled toward the floor. When the last of them were gone, Heimdall took hold of the golden handle and opened the door on the shadowy flight of stairs beyond. Frigga spoke a single word, and a floating orb of silvery glow appeared to light the way.

At the bottom of the steps, Sif pointed. "That's where the spikes jump out and you have to crawl underneath."

Frigga smiled her flicker of a smile once more. "Let's hope the Queen of Asgard doesn't have to sacrifice her royal dignity to that degree." She spoke more words of power, and Heimdall could see the sections of wall that housed the spikes shiver ever so slightly. At the end of the spell, she walked confidently forward, and nothing stabbed at either her or the warriors who scurried after, frantic to go first to protect her but prevented by the unthinkable disrespect implicit in elbowing the queen out of one's way.

Heimdall was pleased to see that Frigga's magic also quelled the lure of the shackling chairs and poison feast and the power of the silver mirror. The first double seeking to emerge was a replica of the queen herself, but it convulsed and vanished halfway through when her spell crushed the sorcery of the looking glass.

Avoiding the counterfeit Odin as he had before, Heimdall opened the hidden door that led to the real one. Here, too, all was as he and Sif had seen it last. Barrel-chested and white-bearded, the All-Father lay slumbering atop his bier, and the long table nearby held the threepronged Uru spear Gungnir and the king's other remaining treasures.

Most of the Valkyries fell silent at the sight of a sacred mystery they possibly felt on some level that they ought not to be seeing, and never mind that the queen had ordered them here. Heimdall remembered the feeling well. Even after all he and Sif had experienced, he still felt a twinge of it himself.

Plainly not sharing the general feeling of reverence and awe, or unwilling to show it if she did, Frigga turned to Heimdall. "Can you find the marks of Amora's sorcery in this chamber as well?"

He pushed away his lingering awe to perform the service she required of him. "I hope so, Majesty." He stared at Odin and the bier and beheld the runes impressed on the sides of the block of stone, once again sharply defined but so shallow normal vision would never have noticed. "Yes! Walk with me, please, in case they run all the way around the pedestal."

As it turned out, they did, and sketching each with a forefinger for the queen's benefit made the digit burn and throb. When he and Frigga completed their circuit, she frowned and said, "Give Amora credit. *That's* a curse."

"But Your Majesty can break it?" Heimdall asked.

"I think so. Stand back by the doorway with the others. It will be safer for you."

He did as she'd commanded and, despite the implied warning, smiled with anticipation. This moment was the culmination of all his and Sif's dogged struggles, the fulfillment of all their desperate hopes, their victory. In a moment, Odin would wake and set things right.

Frigga raised her hands over her head and chanted. The phosphorescence of the floating orb turned green, after which verdant shoots erupted from the stone floor. In moments, they bloomed into yellow poppies and orange hawkweed flowers or swelled into pine, birch, and willow saplings that kept growing into trees that shot upward fast as a person could run, their upper reaches somehow existing and visible despite the ceiling that should have prevented it. Heimdall and the other spectators dodged to keep the leaping, thickening trees from bashing them, and Heimdall feared Odin or Frigga would suffer injury in the midst of the chaos, but both the King and the Queen of the Gods remained untouched.

At the conclusion of the spell, all the riotous growth vanished in an instant, and a seething green radiance gloved Frigga's hands. No warlock, Heimdall could only guess what was happening, but he suspected the queen had gathered the power of life itself to counter the curse that bound her husband in something approaching a deathlike state. She thrust out her hands, and the emerald light leaped from them to shimmer over the All-Father and his bier for several moments before guttering out.

To Heimdall's surprise and dismay, Odin slept on. He felt relieved, however, when it became apparent the queen wasn't finished yet.

Frigga drew herself up straight and began another invocation. The light of the floating sphere turned gray, and everything began to shake. Valkyries cried out in surprise as they, like Heimdall and Sif, stumbled and sought to regain their balance. Dust and bits of stone fell from the ceiling, and cracks snaked across the floor, widening as they came.

Until the quaking stopped and the damage disappeared as suddenly and completely as had the runaway plant growth. A long-hafted mace made of granite-colored light appeared in Frigga's hands – all the violence of the angry earth, Heimdall surmised, concentrated for her use – and she once again circled the bier smashing at each rune in turn.

The blows failed to damage the marks, and Odin slept on.

At the end of the futile battering, the mace faded away, and Frigga stumbled a step. Uschi started toward her, and the queen raised a trembling hand to order her to stay back. She then took several deep breaths and began whispering a third spell, this one sibilant as the hissing of a snake.

This time, Heimdall told himself, the magic will work. In nursery tales and sagas, it was always the third effort that succeeded. He knew full well that life didn't always adhere to the rhythms of a story, but in this moment, he clung to the hope anyway.

The glow of the floating ball had reverted to white after the failure of the second spell, and it didn't change color now. Instead, it dimmed, ever so slowly but steadily, dying by almost imperceptible degrees.

As it did, aches pained Heimdall's joints and back. Alarmed, he peered at his hands, which were gnarled and withered, the knuckles swollen. He looked at Sif. His sister's hair was grizzled, her face etched with new lines, the flesh loose under her chin, and he realized that old age had sunk its claws even into long-lived Asgardians.

Only for a little while, though, even if it seemed longer. To his relief, when the whispering ended, Sif, the Valkyries, and Heimdall all became youthful and strong again. With the sight of Mimir, he could tell as much even though the chamber had gone entirely dark.

He could likewise see that Frigga had cloaked herself in the aspect of something murky and gaunt, something that gave him an instinctive pang of dread even though he knew that the object of all her conjuring was only to help her husband. He wondered if she'd become the personification of time itself, time that obliterates everything in the end. She clenched her claw-like fingers into fists as though crushing something inside.

Amora's runes glowed orange and crumbled to nothing like the marks she'd left on the door above. Any awe or fear forgotten, several of the onlookers gasped and babbled to one another that the counter-magic was working. When the last vestige of the traitor's spell casting turned to ash and vanished, the hovering orb glowed back to life, and a couple Valkyries started to cheer.

But then they stopped, because Odin slept on. Once again, Heimdall understood just how they felt. He too was aghast.

Frigga hobbled to the All-Father's side. The semblance of some ghastly wraith had fallen away, but she still wasn't herself. She had a stoop, wrinkles on her face, and her hair looked sparse and brittle. She laid her hand on Odin's shoulder. "Husband!" she quavered. "Wake up! Your people need you!"

Odin slept on.

Horrified that the magic had failed, that the All-Father hadn't roused to save his kingdom, that he and Sif truly had fallen at the last, Heimdall forgot deference and strode back to Frigga unbidden. "Can you tell why it didn't work?" he asked.

Blue eyes rheumy in their pouches, the queen gave him a rueful look. "You see me. The forces I invoked took a toll, and at the moment I have little magic left. Still, I have to keep trying, don't I? Stand there quietly and let me work."

She muttered to herself, and in due course used a forefinger to write runes on the air. For just a moment, his improved sight allowed Heimdall to see the signs as streaks of rippling distortion, as though the ambient light were passing through water. At the conclusion of her divination, Frigga slumped and said, "Oh, no."

"What is it?" Heimdall asked.

"I *did* lift the curse of endless sleep," said the queen, "but it appears Amora cast it just a day or two after the All-Father entered the vault. With it dissolved, the natural Odinsleep still has the better part of a week to run."

Heimdall felt as if someone had kicked him in the stomach. "The frost giants will be here in a day or two."

"I know," Frigga said. "We meant well, but in terms of the war, all we've accomplished is to deplete my magic when Asgard needs it most."

"Majesty, I am so sorry–"

The queen raised her hand to silence him, and if youth wasn't yet returning to her countenance, resolve did. "I thought this was a good idea the same as you did. Now we must manage with the resources we have. I've squandered my sorcery for the time being, but the royal mages – the loyal ones – haven't. Odin can't help us, but the talisman he depended on for secret wisdom lives on in you. You'll advise me as I direct the defense."

"Me?" Heimdall asked, shocked. His confidence in his own judgment and battle prowess had grown considerably during his journey, but this sudden elevation still felt like far too much. "Majesty, it's true I now see and hear things better than before, but I'm not an experienced commander. I'm only–"

"Shut up," said Sif. "Now's not the time to be modest. My brother has a sharp mind, Your Majesty, sharp as anyone you'll find, and now these new gifts as well."

The words eased Heimdall's mind a little. Sif knew him better than anyone, and if she believed he was equal to this challenge, perhaps he actually was. It was at least true that he did have Mimir's abilities to draw on.

"If Your Majesty truly does want me," he said, "I promise to do my best." He took a breath. "I actually do have an idea or two about how to defend the city."

"Then it's decided," Frigga said.

Twenty-Nine

The frost giants hadn't quite brought snow to the city of Asgard, but the day was overcast, and a wind colder than the Realm Eternal's perpetual summer should have permitted gusted out of the north to lash the banners. War bands of Jotuns stood at a safe distance beyond the outer defenses waiting for Skrymir's signal to attack and giving the defenders ample time to take in the demoralizing spectacle of their hugeness and manifest power.

Feeling strange in the fancy armor and garments befitting his new status, Heimdall stood with the queen on the highest ramparts of the central keep of the citadel, which afforded them an unobstructed view of the entire city and the ground beyond. Also present were a half dozen royal guards and a mage. Among other duties, the warlock would instantly transmit Frigga's orders – and Heimdall's, too, apparently – to Asgardian commanders wherever they might be fighting.

He hoped those orders, and the advice he'd already given

in the two days since the return to the vault of the Odinsleep, for that matter, would prove useful. The Gjallarhorn still hung at his side, and he touched it as if it might bring him luck. That was irrational, he knew, but having the instrument provided a trace of comfort nonetheless. It had, after all, saved his life and Sif's back in Jotunheim.

Just as he'd intended, he'd asked a couple of the royal mages to look at the trumpet, and even though they were working as frantically to prepare for the Jotun onslaught as everyone else, they'd given it a cursory examination. As far as they could tell from that brief assessment, its only magical property was to sound very loudly when required. Since it hadn't turned out to be the devastating weapon Heimdall had hoped it would be, he'd seen no particular reason he shouldn't retain possession.

He looked for Sif and found her where she'd been before, crouching with other skirmishers behind one of the houses that still stood in the very outermost defenses. Even though nothing was happening yet, he kept having the impulse to check on her. But his task was to peer in all directions and observe everything, and after a moment he turned his gaze elsewhere.

Evidently sensing his restlessness, Frigga said, "It won't be much longer." Though she didn't look as old as she had immediately after lifting Amora's curse, her face was still lined, and she carried herself as if her gilded armor and the tall ornate headpiece that was half helm and half crown weighed on her. Heimdall had little doubt that, just as she'd warned, any major works of magic – or mighty feats of arms, for that matter – were currently beyond her. Even so, he thought with a flicker of humor, he was the one who was nervous.

"I'm ready, Majesty," he answered. He stood up straight and tried to look as calm and confident as she did.

"Do you still see Skrymir?" Frigga asked, eyes narrowing as she peered out at the enemy forces.

"Yes." Heimdall pointed. "He's still over that way with some of the biggest giants."

"What about Amora?"

"So far, there's no sign of her."

"For all her powers and ambitions, she's never been keen to fight in the forefront of a war. It wouldn't surprise me if–" The clouds overhead churned and thickened, and the day grew nearly dark as night. A shaft of lightning blazed down to strike among the outer defenses, and thunder crashed an instant after.

Heimdall wasn't surprised. He'd predicted Skrymir would bring storm giants to the actual siege of Asgard, and though the creatures were staying well back from the front lines, he'd had little trouble spotting them.

Because Heimdall had warned his fellow Asgardians to expect them, Thor had taken upon himself the task of countering the storm giants' powers with his own. It was plain he'd set about his work when further blasts of lightning fell not on the defenders but among their foes, and even as it blew stronger and stronger, the wind gusted outward from the city into the giants' faces.

But even the God of Thunder couldn't simultaneously invoke the powers of the storm and clear the sky. As he pitted himself against the storm giants, the day grew darker still, and, possibly hoping the confusion of gloom split by dazzling lighting bursts and full of booming thunderclaps would work to his advantage, Skrymir bellowed and ordered a wave of attackers forward.

Fortunately, neither the darkness, the glare of the lightning, nor the roar of the thunder befuddled Heimdall's senses. Even so, when Skrymir brandished his staff of ice and cast a spell, he didn't see any effect and cast about frantically in an effort to determine what had changed.

It took several moments before he realized he saw the change but at first hadn't registered it. There were dozens more frost giants advancing than there had been before their ruler cast the spell, and the figures of the new ones lacked detail. As compared to those that had been pounding along previously, it was the difference between a sketch of a warrior and the warrior himself.

Heimdall turned to the mage. The latter was a frowning, cadaverous fellow with a pointed goatee, dangling mustachios, and a star-bedizened high-collared cloak who looked like he'd modeled his appearance on that of the wicked warlock characters in many a pantomime and puppet theater. "Some of the advancing giants are illusions meant to divert attention from the ones that are real!"

The sorcerer frowned and squinted. "I don't see it."

"I do!" Perhaps Heimdall was lucky that, conjuring so many phantoms at points all around the city, Skrymir's magic fell short of the perfection it might otherwise have achieved.

"If Heimdall says it," Frigga snapped, "it's so. Relay his instructions."

The task of telling the many thanes on the towering city ramparts and beyond which Jotuns were real and which were not took a while. By the time Heimdall and the sorcerer finished, the fighting had begun.

Heimdall looked for Sif and the warriors Frigga had placed under her command. Three Jotuns were advancing on them, one real, two illusory. Guided by the information he'd provided, the Asgardians were loosing arrow after arrow at the true frost giant and ignoring the phantasms.

The shafts provoked bellows of rage and pain, but the frost giant kept coming despite the barrage. Sword in hand, Sif darted from behind cover to stand on guard in front of the Jotun. Sneering, the giant quickened his trot to reach her, and his leg plunged into what had been a concealed pit. He screamed as a stake at the bottom stabbed into his foot. He then tried to pull his extremity free but abandoned the effort when it proved unbearably painful.

Sif grinned and ran back to rejoin the other skirmishers. They'd all but exhausted their supply of arrows, and she ordered them to fall back.

Heimdall wrenched his attention back to the battle as a whole. Throughout the outermost defenses, giants had run afoul of the various snares that had been laid for them while the skirmishers who baited them onward made a fighting retreat. Meanwhile, catapults and ballistae discharged their missiles from the city walls, and Valkyries wheeled and shot arrows from on high.

The illusory giants were mostly gone – maybe Skrymir realized they served no purpose and was conserving his power – although a couple fading phantoms remained to flail impotently at Asgardians, who continued to ignore them.

There were still plenty of real attacking giants, though, ones who'd escaped serious injury among the first round of traps and continued their advance on the city walls. To swell their numbers, Skrymir ordered forth a second wave of attackers who trod heedlessly on the bodies of slain or injured comrades in their eagerness to close with their foes.

Heimdall waited until all the skirmishers had fled inside the gates and all the frost giants were well within the ring of outer defenses. Then he said, "Now," and the sorcerer in the high-collared cloak relayed the message to the warlocks and witches waiting along the city walls, all of whom had been conserving their power in preparation for this moment and all of whom raised their voices to chant a single mighty spell. At the conclusion, the entire town beyond the city wall, all the surviving houses and all the hastily erected fortifications made of wood exploded into flame.

Asgardians had for a while possessed some understanding that frost giants were leery of fire, but until Heimdall's foray into Jotunheim, he hadn't realized they liked it so little that regular hot yellow flame was present nowhere. It was the cold blue substitute that lit the Jotuns' dwellings and cooked their meals. Amora, moreover, had prepared fire to leap forth from the floor of her conjuring chamber. As she'd had no reason to believe anyone but Skrymir would ever enter the space, she had, lest the Jotun king betray her, readied the weapon a frost giant dreaded most.

Or so Heimdall had inferred. Now he felt a surge of elation to see himself proven right.

The frost giants in the ring of fire weren't burning as Aesir or Vanir flesh would burn. They were, however, shrinking, their substance melting like snow under a hot sun. Panicking, some sought to blunder back the way they'd come. Others rushed on to the city wall, but when they smashed at it, their blows were no longer strong enough to inflict significant damage, and, their height diminished, they could no longer reach the defenders on the battlements. The Asgardian warriors rained spears, arrows, and cauldrons of boiling oil down into their upturned faces, and all the while the fires kept burning at the Jotuns' backs.

Across the city, warriors began to cheer as frost giants perished or fell back and the Asgardians judged they'd won the day. Perhaps, Heimdall thought, the time for celebration had indeed arrived, but he himself wasn't ready to join in yet. There were still a goodly number of Jotuns surrounding the city including some who had yet to venture close.. They still posed a significant threat even if they presently seemed little inclined to brave the fires, and he suspected their sorcerer king wasn't ready to retreat.

It was a suspicion quickly proved correct. Now wearing a steel helm in place of his crown, Skrymir gripped his staff of ice in both blue hands, raised it over his head, and bellowed an incantation with a pause after each line. Though he wasn't sure anyone else could, Heimdall heard Amora's dulcet voice filling in the spaces with a contrapuntal spell of her own. His brief elation withered into foreboding.

An arching glimmer appeared. It was like the gateways the Valkyrie steeds opened but broad as a longhouse was long and taller the walls of Asgard. On the other side was a benighted place of glaciers and drifting veils of mist, superficially like Jotunheim but somehow even bleaker.

A creature even bigger than Skrymir strode out of the fog and across the threshold between worlds. Two more followed. Each was a colossus made of glinting ice with jagged protrusions of the substance sticking out of its limbs. Smirking, Amora flew alongside them, and when they'd all come through, she and the frost giant king allowed the luminous doorway to contract out of existence.

THIRTY

Heimdall realized the enormous things could only be ice giants of Niffleheim, kindred to the frost giants, recruited to aid in their war, and held in reserve like the storm giants until the final battle. He tried to believe their arrival would change nothing. Frost melted in the presence of flame. Surely, so too would ice.

Yet the ice giants tramped closer to the ring of fire with no signs of wariness or distress. They stared at the burning structures before them, and a mass of ice appeared at their feet. Rising and thickening as it came, it pushed its way into the circle of flame.

At first, fire did indeed melt ice, but that produced water, which began to extinguish the blaze. As the flames died, the ice continued to mass, building a sort of ramp the frost giants might eventually use to charge the ramparts. Meanwhile, possibly in obedience to some arcane principle Heimdall didn't understand, even the fires elsewhere in the circle burned lower. Encouraged, Jotuns who'd previously fallen back in disarray readied themselves for new runs at the city walls.

The various Asgardian sorceresses and witches pushed back against the ice giants' power and sometimes succeeded in making a chunk of ice break away from the incursion or causing flames that were dying to leap up anew. But one by one their mystical strength was failing them, and they left off their conjuring, slumped, and gasped for breath, while the might of their opponents seemed without end. Artillerymen on the ramparts turned all the catapults and ballistae that could be brought to bear to hurl stones and bolts at the ice giants, but the shots merely chipped their exteriors and glanced away. The colossal creatures didn't even react.

Heimdall hoped for a moment that perhaps Thor would intercede and prevail where everyone else had failed, but as the ongoing flashes of lightning and thunderclaps attested, the Prince of Asgard was still busy opposing the efforts of the storm giants. If he stopped, *they'd* put out the fires, and either way, Skrymir and his forces would overrun the city.

Frigga turned to her new advisor. "If you can see or hear anything else to help us, now would be a good time."

Heimdall peered at the ice giants. It appeared to him that there might be fault lines, planes of relative weakness, running through the huge creatures' bodies, but what did it matter? If the faults weren't vulnerable enough for the stones from catapults and the bolts from ballistae to inflict significant wounds, what mightier weapon could the defenders bring to bear? Bowing his head and rapping his knuckles on his temples, he strained to think, and finally a notion came to him.

"I think I have the one weapon that might work against the ice giants," he told Frigga. "I just need to get close enough to try."

"I can order a company of warriors to accompany you," said the queen.

He thought about it and then shook his head. "Thank you, Majesty, but no. I don't need them to wield the weapon, and if it doesn't work, I would have led them to their deaths to no purpose." He then turned to the thin, pale warlock. "I need Golden Mane, the black Valkyrie horse with the yellow mane and eyes. The warrior riding him will be in Uschi's company."

This time, the wizard didn't argue. He repeated the message, and it became clear Uschi had heard when Golden Mane and his rider winged their way toward the citadel from the spot where her band of Valkyries was doing battle. The Valkyrie's lance was bloody and her round metal shield crumpled, proof she'd already done her fair share of fighting, but even so, her glower made it clear she didn't like being ordered out of the fray to hand off her mount to another. Still, as Golden Mane furled his pinions and set down on the highest ramparts of the central keep, she offered no objection. She simply swung herself out of the saddle and held the bridle while Heimdall climbed up and took her place.

"Now," he told the sorcerer, "tell the warriors on the wall to stop the catapult stones. I don't want them to hit me." The warlock relayed the order, and Heimdall urged Golden Mane into motion.

Golden Mane galloped down the wall-walk, reached

a corner, and leaped over the merlons into space. The winged stallion plunged down toward the tiled roofs of lesser buildings and the cobbled courtyards of the citadel for a moment. Then his spread wings caught the air, and he leveled out and climbed.

Heimdall rubbed the horse's neck. "Good. Now let's make the ice giants sorry they came."

Their fighting concluded for the moment, the sweaty, weary warriors and mages on the city wall gazed up at him as he soared overhead. No doubt they were torn between hope he could do *something* against the new threat and doubt that one lone rider who wasn't Odin on eight-legged Sleipnir, Thor, or even Frigga could succeed when their own concerted efforts had already failed.

One frost giant threw a spear, then another, and Golden Mane dodged each huge missile in turn. Most of the Jotuns, however, made no effort to stop the stallion and his rider. Maybe they didn't even notice the approach of a single warrior on a black steed galloping across the stormy sky, or perhaps they too assumed there was nothing Heimdall could do to harm the ice giants.

Heimdall knew they might be right about the latter. But on childhood hunting trips into the snowy mountains of Vanaheim, his father had warned him to be quiet lest he bring an avalanche rumbling down on their heads. Similarly, scholars had told him that sustained powerful sounds could rattle and ultimately shatter certain substances. He was gambling that the faults he'd discerned in the ice giants' bodies bespoke a comparable kind of brittleness.

Golden Mane bore him close to the nearest colossus.

He brought the Gjallarhorn to his lips and blew with all his strength. The note that blared from the enchanted instrument was prodigiously loud. It had no effect on the ice giant, however, and the creature didn't even appear to notice the rider circling its body like a gnat. Like its fellows, it just kept staring and adding its strength to the effort to quench the ring of fire and build the ramp of ice.

Heimdall told himself not to be discouraged. During the journey across Jotunheim to Skrymir's royal city, he'd experimented with the Gjallarhorn enough to discover that if he varied his embouchure, it was capable of producing several different tones. He sucked in a deep breath and sounded another one.

This time, his sharpened sight detected a shivering as the trumpet's call assailed the ice giant's body. No matter how loudly he blew, however, and no matter how closely he dared to approach, the enormous creature suffered no real damage.

This time, though, he'd captured its attention. It turned its head to regard him and Golden Mane, and a crudely shaped war hammer made of ice grew upward out of its fist. Once armed, it pivoted and struck.

The black steed lashed his wings, dodging, and the giant's weapon swept on by with a *whoosh*. Heimdall had to depend on Golden Mane to keep evading as his foe continued striking. He needed to concentrate on finding the right tone.

He blew a different note, and it *wasn't* right. He sounded yet another, the final tone of which the Gjallarhorn was capable.

A piece of the ice giant's head broke off and fell bumping

down its torso, and as Heimdall continued blowing, more pieces cracked away from the whole until finally the ice giant's entire body sheared and slipped apart along the fault lines like the edge of a glacier giving way and falling into the sea.

Heimdall rubbed Golden Mane's neck. "You see, friend? We *can* kill them!" His surge of fierce satisfaction gave way to renewed determination as the two remaining ice giants turned in his direction, and they too grew weapons, one a battle-axe and one a sword, from their hands.

Golden Mane wheeled around the ice giants, evading the sword and axe strokes by swooping, climbing, and dodging. Meanwhile, Heimdall sounded the Gjallarhorn again and again.

Chunks of the ice giants' forms crunched, cracked, and fell away, but the sort of catastrophic harm the horn had inflicted before was slow in coming. Maybe, Heimdall thought, gasping in more air, it was because he was dividing his attacks between two targets.

Meanwhile, no doubt responding to the will of his adversaries, huge spikes of ice, like the stalagmites on the floor of a cavern, shot upward from the ground. At first the thrusts seemed simply efforts to spear Golden Mane in the belly or, failing that, to provide vertical obstacles to his dodging. Then, however, horizontal lengths of ice grew from one spike to the next and made it even harder for the winged horse to maneuver. Heimdall felt like a fly with a pair of spiders spinning a web around it.

He blew the Gjallarhorn, and finally, *finally*, the face of the creature before him broke away from its head, leaving it eyeless and presumably blind. He sounded the trumpet a second time, and its sword arm and much of its torso fell in several pieces, a third time, and the rest of its body crumbled into fragments. He grinned, started to suck in a fresh breath, and then Golden Mane screamed as he slammed into an obstacle.

Additional lengths of ice sprang into being to close around the horse and his rider too. The remaining giant had willed still more horizontal bars to shoot from one vertical spike to another and surround Golden Mane so thoroughly that finally not even a Valkyrie steed could escape the trap.

The lengths of ice thickened, steadily exerting more pressure on the prisoners caught inside. Half crushed, Heimdall couldn't draw in enough air to sound the Gjallarhorn to any effect, nor could he even point the trumpet in the direction of the third giant. Golden Mane heaved and shuddered as he fought to break free, but the ice held fast.

In what he took to be his final moment of life, Heimdall realized he wasn't afraid. He simply hoped he'd accomplished enough for the other defenders of Asgard to somehow do the rest. He hoped Sif would survive the battle and regretted Golden Mane was dying with him.

Then other horns sounded as a company of Valkyries wheeled around the ice giant's head. Half the riders were blowing them, the other half loosing arrows and hurling spears. Heimdall realized they must have been watching from above the city and flown to his aid when his colossal adversary caught him.

The ice giant turned away from him and flailed at the

Valkyries. Heimdall doubted the creature feared their archery and spear casts, but maybe, thinking them possessed of the same magic as the Gjallarhorn, it feared the bugles.

Someone cried, "Hold on!" From the corner of his eye, Heimdall saw Uschi swooping down to his level. The flaming sword burned brighter and brighter as she made her approach and then, leaning far out of the saddle, cut thrice.

Ice shattered and fell in pieces, and Golden Mane heaved at the remaining bonds that held him. They snapped as well, whereupon the horse fell right along with the fragments. It was as if the press and chill of the ice had so injured him that he'd lost the ability to fly.

"Come on!" Heimdall called. "You can do it!"

Golden Mane tossed his head. The ice had frozen fast to strips of his wings, and he'd left feathers and scraps of the hide under them behind. But despite the bloody welts, he unfurled his pinions. The plummet became a swoop, and then he was racing along just above the ground but parallel to it, no longer in danger of smashing down to his death.

Heimdall bade the winged horse land on the ground and swung himself out of the saddle. "You're hurt and you've done your part," he said. "Now get yourself to safety."

Golden Mane hesitated, but only for a moment. He then turned, galloped, unfurled his wings, and flew back toward the city walls.

Heimdall pivoted to find the third ice giant turning toward him as well. Apparently, despite the Valkyrie's attack, it had decided he was the one true threat.

A single stride brought the ice giant into striking distance. It was like seeing a mountain leap across the face of the land.

The enormous axe chopped down. Heimdall dodged out from under the blow, but the impact of the weapon striking the ground threw him off his feet. He scrambled back up, and another axe chop missed him but jolted him to the floor once more.

Heimdall rolled to his knees, pulled the Gjallarhorn to his lips, and blew. The ice giant's leg trembled and then shattered underneath it, and the creature fell. Chunks of ice dropped all around Heimdall, and he threw his arms over his head. Fortunately, none of the bigger fragments smashed down on top of him.

Ice grated against the ground as the crippled giant pulled itself around to threaten him anew. Falling back, Heimdall sounded the enchanted trumpet repeatedly. Sections of the creature's body cracked and crumbled away until a final blaring note blasted it into shapeless, motionless rubble.

His heightened senses notwithstanding, Heimdall had been so focused on the last ice giant that it was only now he registered the shouting, thudding, and shaking as frost giants came charging forward. They were too late to prevent the destruction of the ice giants but not too late to avenge them.

Thirty-One

At that moment, Heimdall had no doubt the frost giants would accomplish their bloody purpose, but he resolved to make them pay a cost. Breathing heavily, he dropped the Gjallarhorn to dangle from its strap and pulled his two-handed sword from its scabbard.

Before the frost giants in the lead quite reached him, though, Valkyries swept over him to assail them. Some hurtled and wheeled well over the blue-skinned creatures' heads loosing bowshots. Others swooped lower to thrust with lances or chop with axes and swords. Uschi was one of the latter although her blade no longer burned. Apparently she'd used up all the fire magic striking at Heimdall's icy bonds.

The onslaught of the Valkyries checked the frost giants' charge. Next, bellowed battle cries and the drumming of countless running feet sounded at Heimdall's back. He glanced around, and other Asgardian warriors were racing toward the Jotuns. Seeing the ice giants fall, Frigga must have ordered an all-out attack on that portion of the enemy army where king Skrymir stood casting spells and giving orders.

Heimdall grinned and took a deep breath. When the first running Asgardian warriors came up even with him, he ran alongside them and hurled himself at the vanguard of the frost giants.

For some time after that, he had no idea which side was winning. He had no time to spy with his heightened vision when he was hacking and dodging, dealing death or evading it every second, and even if he had, he couldn't have assessed the progress of the battle as a whole with a forest of blue legs towering on every side. But the circle of fire had killed or weakened many a Jotun, the destruction of the ice giants had surely demoralized others, and while the Asgardians might be small in comparison to their enemies, there were far more of them and on average they were the more skillful fighters. He hoped all that would tilt the balance in their favor.

"You!" A huge voice roared.

Heimdall turned. His face twisted with rage, Skrymir was striding toward him. The king of the frost giants had set aside his staff of ice in favor of a single-edged sword like a cleaver. The blade dripped with the blood of the Asgardians it had already butchered.

Heimdall glanced around seeking help, but at that moment every comrade within reach was busy with some other foe. He thought of running and losing himself in the chaos of the battle, but his blood was up, and so he stepped forward with the two-handed sword at the ready. He realized just how reckless he was being when his adversary grinned at his folly and abruptly there were half a dozen Skrymirs surrounding and stalking toward him.

Heimdall knew he'd just been looking straight at the one real Skrymir and believed that should allow him to distinguish his actual foe from the phantoms. He wasted a precious moment trying, before realizing there was something about the magic that kept that commonsense measure from working.

He then peered with Mimir's sight, looking for the lack of detail that had enabled him to pick out Skrymir's illusions before. This time, however, the frost giant king hadn't created dozens of phantoms all around the city of Asgard. The effect was far more circumscribed and thus perfect enough to bewilder even Heimdall's eyes. He stared and squinted and still could find no flaws in any of the enormous figures closing in around him.

"Ready to die?" The leering Skrymirs asked.

Perhaps it was the sound of frost giant's voice that made Heimdall decide that if his eyes couldn't save him, he should try listening. He used his enhanced hearing, and the thousand noises of the battle swept over him. Arrows whizzed in flight. Warriors on both sides cried taunts and insults at the enemy or exhortations to their comrades. Asgardians and Jotuns screamed as weapons pierced them, and the wounded lay groaning and whimpering. The feathery wings of Valkyrie horses rustled high overhead.

In the moment or two remaining to him, Heimdall sifted through the cacophony in search of sounds that might save him and at last found the flaw in the illusion Skrymir had created. All the phantoms had voices, they'd all spoken in unison, but only the real Jotun ruler had feet that audibly brushed the earth as he stepped.

Heimdall turned his back on the actual Skrymir and advanced on one of the phantasms. Because the real frost giant king and the illusions were moving as one, each mirroring the actions of the others, he could tell when the true attack swept down at his back.

He leaped out from under it, whirled again, and rushed the real Skrymir. His charge took him through two of the illusory sword blades seemingly embedded in the ground. He felt something too slight to be called resistance as he plunged through, like cobwebs breaking across his face.

He cut deep into the frost giant's leg just above the ankle. He yanked the sword free, blood gushed from the wound, and the phantoms winked out of existence. At once he circled behind the Jotun king's foot and slashed again. Skrymir, Skrymir ran forward to escape the punishment and stumbled and nearly fell when the foot of the wounded leg came down awkwardly. Heimdall laughed and started to give chase, and a mass of hissing serpents with darkly glittering scales, dozens coiling and crawling over one another, appeared on the ground between him and the giant. He halted just shy of their striking fangs. A woman laughed.

As Heimdall backed up a step, he spied Amora. The sorceress finished making her way behind several embattled giants to take up a position a few paces beyond Skrymir. She evidently expected that, limping or not, the Jotun king would hold Heimdall back until she brought the Vanir down with a spell.

Heimdall feared she was right. She kept chanting, and one tangle of snakes after another appeared on the piece of earth where he and Skrymir were fighting. The Asgardian didn't dare step within reach of the serpents, and that constrained his movements more and more. Meanwhile, the frost giant set his feet wherever he liked knowing the resulting snakebites wouldn't pierce his thick leather shoes.

Skrymir's enormous sword whirled down. Heimdall dodged, ran, and – exerting the full measure of his Asgardian strength – jumped over the tangle of serpents immediately in front of him. He then dashed on toward the space between the frost giant's feet and the sorceress on the other side. If he disposed of her first, maybe he could deal with the Jotun after.

Amora's green eyes widened in alarm. Unfortunately, though, reacting quickly to Heimdall's charge, Skrymir took a step backward and slashed repeatedly, the horizontal cuts flashing scythe-fashion back and forth low to the ground. Heimdall had to retreat lest the cleaver-like blade split him in two.

As Skrymir began to pursue him, Heimdall caught a glimpse of Sif rushing in on Amora's flank. For an instant, he hoped the witch didn't notice, but then she pivoted, made a sinuous mystical gesture, and spoke a word of power.

The sword in Sif's hand twisted into a serpent longer than a man was tall. She tried to cast the snake away but was an instant too slow. The serpent lashed its coils around her, tangling her limbs and dumping her on the ground. Teeth gritted, she caught hold of the snake below the wedge-shaped head. Meanwhile, Amora raised her hands and started reciting another spell, one likely to slay Sif before she could fight her way free of the reptile's embrace.

"Stop!" Heimdall shouted. "I'm laying down my sword!" Stooping, he did so.

Grinning, Skrymir left off attacking, but Heimdall had little doubt as to the frost giant king's true intentions. He'd pause for a moment to let his foe believe surrender would save his life, then laugh and hack him to pieces.

Ever cautious, Amora gave Heimdall one quick glance but then returned her attention to Sif and the spell casting intended to destroy her.

But that was all right. It meant Amora wasn't looking when Heimdall grabbed a fist-sized chunk of ice – a piece of one of the ice giants the Gjallarhorn had crumbled – straightened up, and threw it at her.

The sight of Mimir sharpened his aim, and Asgardian might carried the missile across the intervening distance. The ball of ice smashed Amora in the temple, interrupting her magic and sending her reeling.

Startled, Skrymir gaped at Heimdall for a moment, then, still hampered by the wounded leg, reflexively turned to see what harm, if any, the throw had inflicted on his ally. Heimdall snatched up the two-handed sword and charged.

Skrymir hobbled back around before the Asgardian quite closed the distance, but not in time to protect himself. Heimdall swung the great sword and carved a gash in the leg that had been unwounded hitherto.

The frost giant bellowed, and the cleaver-like blade swept down. Heimdall dodged behind Skrymir's foot and cut again.

As he did, so he glimpsed Sif and Amora. Blood streaming down her profile, the sorceress raised her arms to begin another spell. Sif scrambled free of the dead snake's still-writhing coils, sprang to her feet, and grabbed hold of the enchantress's right arm. She twisted the limb, and Amora screamed as it popped out of the socket.

Meanwhile, limping worse now that both legs were bleeding, Skrymir slashed down at his foe. Heimdall sidestepped and counterattacked with a stroke that gashed two of the Jotun's fingers to the bone. The frost giant stiffened in shock, and the Asgardian slashed again at the creature's leg. Blood spurted from a severed artery.

Skrymir fought on for a few more moments before recognizing how serious that last leg wound actually was. When he did realize, he sought to stumble away from the fight. Heimdall rushed after him, cut the other leg, and the Jotun finally fell.

Skrymir rolled onto his side, brought his leg up, clutched with both hands to stanch the spurts of blood, and bellowed for help. Other frost giants started forward to succor him, but hesitated when Heimdall raced into position to poise his sword at their monarch's throat.

"Your side has lost," Heimdall panted. "You can either tell your warriors to surrender and some healer can attend to your leg, or you can order them to come at me and we'll see how much more harm I can do you in the moments before they reach me."

Skrymir snarled an obscenity.

"It's up to you," Heimdall said. "If watching me die is worth bleeding out shortly thereafter, say the word."

Skrymir repeated the obscenity. Then, however, he called to his warriors, "Stop fighting and get me some help!"

As the word traveled across the battlefield, most of the giants quickly laid down their weapons, often also raising their hands on dropping to their knees. Judging that the fight truly had gone out of Skrymir as well, Heimdall risked another look in his sister's direction.

Sif had Amora prone on the ground and was kneeling atop her. She yanked off the sorceress's headdress and jammed it into her mouth. "Spit that out, and I really will kill you."

Heimdall smiled to see his sister taking the precaution. She was making certain that, with her voice silenced, Amora was incapable of the recitation most of her magic required.

Sif shoved the cowed, bloodied prisoner toward Heimdall. Leaving the Jotun healer to his work, he walked to meet them. "We did it," he said.

Sif grinned. "Mostly, I did it. But I suppose you helped a little."

Thirty-Two

At the end of the afternoon, Queen Frigga came out of the city onto the battlefield to accept Skrymir's formal surrender. A company of her warriors and a gaggle of advisors attended her. Heimdall supposed that, for the moment, he still qualified as both. Striding along beside him, Sif rested her hand on her sword hilt as though expecting frost giant treachery.

Heimdall was watching for signs of trouble as well, but he didn't expect them, nor did he see any. The Jotuns towering before him looked sullen but cowed.

That was certainly true of their king. His bandages bloody, hobbling with the aid of his staff of ice, Skrymir kneeled clumsily before the Asgardian monarch. "I yield my person and my army," he rumbled.

"I accept your surrender," Frigga said, "but I'll be more assured of your peaceful intentions when you shrink down to Asgardian size. Two of my warriors assure me you can."

Skrymir grimaced at what, Heimdall suspected, his

subjects were likely to see as a profound humiliation. "Must I?" he asked.

"Yes," Frigga said. "Look at it this way. You're going to stay in Asgard until Jotunheim sends a hefty ransom. Enough to pay for all the trouble you've caused. Would you rather spend the time with a roof over your head or chained up outdoors like an animal?"

Skrymir closed his eyes and muttered under his breath. At the end of the incantation, he did indeed shrink and shrink to Heimdall's height while his fellow Jotuns looked on. Some blue faces reflected shame, others disgust, and the Asgardian suspected that none of the onlookers would be eager to follow their ruler to war again anytime soon.

"There," Skrymir growled, "it's done. And what of my warriors? Will you make slaves of them all?"

"No," Frigga said, "Asgardians don't keep slaves." Besides, Heimdall thought, a horde of resentful frost giant thralls would pose a danger to Realm Eternal forever after. "They can have tonight to tend the wounded, but come sunrise, I want them marching back to Jotunheim."

There was a little more back-and-forth after that. Then guards escorted Skrymir into the city, and, watched by other Asgardian warriors, the demoralized giants set about making camp for the night.

"And that," said Frigga, satisfaction in her voice, "is that." She turned to Heimdall and Sif. "Except for the matter of rewarding the two of you. What would you like?"

Sif smiled. "Amora's head on a platter?"

The queen laughed. "You don't have to ask for that. When Odin wakes, her punishment will be severe. What else?"

"Golden Mane and Bloodspiller," Heimdall said. "The winged steeds we, uh, borrowed from Uschi's company. They served us valiantly, and we've grown fond of them."

"Yes," said Sif, "that, please."

"No one but a Valkyrie has ever possessed a Valkyrie horse before," Frigga said, "but I'll see to it. What else?"

"Truly, Majesty," said Sif, "that reward coupled with the restoration of our honor is more than enough. We fought for Asgard, not for personal advancement. But, that said, like any of your warriors, we *hope* to improve our fortunes."

"And so you shall," Frigga said. "From this day forward, Lady Sif, you are a thane of the realm with your own company of warriors to command."

Sif beamed. "Thank you, Majesty!"

Frigga turned to Heimdall. "You too are a thane, and you should stay on at court as an advisor to the crown."

Heimdall blinked in surprise and some consternation. "Thank you, Majesty, but that office would elevate me far beyond my capabilities. I look at the counselors surrounding the throne, and I see wise old sages. I'm just a callow young swordsman. What could I contribute?"

"As I recall," Frigga said, "you were the one who insisted on entering the vault of the Odinsleep and the one who thought to slip into Jotunheim and deprive the frost giants of Mimir's head. You're also the one who proposed engulfing the Jotuns in fire and who realized he could wield the Gjallarhorn to slay the ice giants."

Inwardly, he recognized she had a point. He did occasionally hit on a notion that had occurred to no one else even if those notions didn't always work out as expected, and in addition, he now possessed the gifts of Mimir. Still, he didn't *want* to be a royal counselor and spend his days in a council chamber pondering weighty matters of state. Someday, perhaps, but not yet.

For now, he realized, he'd had more than enough of bearing the responsibility for the fate of Asgard. He wanted to live the life of a simple warrior again and perhaps explore more of the Nine Worlds. What he'd seen so far had nearly killed him repeatedly, but, by all accounts, there were wonders waiting as well.

He strained to think of some way to make a tactful refusal, but Frigga spared him the necessity. "Never mind," she said. "I can see from your expression that you truly don't want the office. Go command a company like your sister, then, but rest assured, the All-Father and I will remember both of you. You never know when we'll require warriors of your caliber for some special errand."

Heimdall felt a stirring of anticipation at the prospect that such *special errands* would likely to take him to the far corners of the realms. With his new gifts, and his sister by his side, the future held a great deal of excitement.

Epilogue

The sun was sinking westward by the time Volstagg finished his tale. Shadows were lengthening, and the competitors, tutors, officials, and spectators of the tourney had finished their business and gone their separate ways, leaving only the chalk dueling circles on the grass. The food vendors were pouring water on the coals in their grilles, putting away unused flour, spices, and the like, and generally closing up their stands, a loss he sought to bear with equanimity. He'd turned to them for refreshment twice more while relating the story and savored their offerings each time, but he took comfort in knowing a bountiful and equally tasty meal awaited him and Bjarke at home.

"And," he finished, looking down at the copper-haired boy seated beside him on the bench, "that's pretty much the end. Frigga meant what she said. Over time, she and the All-Father gave Heimdall and Sif new responsibilities and new gifts to go with them, until they grew into a true god and goddess of Asgard. When the king eventually had a wizard – the same gloomy fellow who stood with Heimdall and Frigga atop the citadel, as it happens – create the rainbow bridge to facilitate travel among the Nine Worlds, he figured someone had better stand watch over the thing, and Heimdall the All-Seer was the perfect choice. So, he's been the sentinel ever since." He stood up. "Now let's head for home."

"But there's something you didn't tell me," Bjarke said.

Volstagg frowned. "I didn't? Well, then, ask your question as we walk. You don't want to be late for supper and let your brothers and sisters to get all the best cuts of that pig your mother is roasting."

Bjarke grinned. "You mean *you* don't want to be late."

For a moment, Volstagg wondered if he should scold the lad for impudence, but ended up smiling back. "Whelp! I'll have you know, I eat like a bird. Barely enough to keep up my strength for when Thor calls on me to fight alongside him once again. Come on." They headed across the field, Bjarke with his helm tucked under one arm and his practice sword canted across the opposing shoulder. "And tell me, what did I leave out?"

Bjarke hesitated in the manner of a child who worries he's about to pose a question his elders would rather not hear. Eventually, though, he asked, "What about Amora? The queen was going to punish her. Cut off her head or something. But I've seen her walking around the city like some great lady."

Volstagg grunted. "This is a grown-up thing and may be hard for you to understand. But at the moment, she's once again a lady of the court. After all she'd done, there was talk of executing her, but she offered the murdered warrior's kin a huge amount in wergild, and afterward Odin settled for banishing her. She spent a century in exile, and then the All-Father allowed her to come home. No doubt he had his reasons even if we lesser folk couldn't understand."

In truth, Volstagg considered it a terrible decision, one they would all have cause to regret when the sorceress turned on the Realm Eternal yet again. But meanwhile, there was no point in fretting over it, or in encouraging the lad to doubt the wisdom of his sovereign.

Bjarke brooded over that for a few paces, then, his expression brightening, said, "Well, at least Lady Sif beat her up."

Volstagg chuckled. "Yes, there is that." It occurred to him that he'd gotten so caught up in relating Heimdall's adventures that upon reaching the end, he'd neglected to underscore the moral that had prompted him to tell the tale in the first place. "Anyway, do you understand the point of the story?"

Frowning, brow wrinkled, Bjarke thought it over. "Heimdall didn't just win because he was brave and a good swordsman. He had ideas, just like Frigga said."

Volstagg beamed down at his son. "That's it exactly. He *thought*."

"And I should be like him?"

"Right again."

"Well, then, here's what *I'm* thinking. Before the next tourney, can uncle Fandral be my teacher?" Fandral the Dashing was Volstagg's comrade in the Warriors Three and generally regarded as the finest swordsman in Asgard.

Once again, there was a moment when Volstagg might have taken offense, but as before, he saw the humor. “First chance I get,” he said, “I’ll ask him.”

Acknowledgments

Thanks to my editor Charlotte Llewelyn-Wells and to Marc Gascoigne, Anjuli Smith, Vanessa Jack, and everyone at Aconyte Books for all their help and support. I especially appreciate it since we worked on this novel while the COVID-19 pandemic was underway, and, as they were working from home, all their tasks were that much more complicated.

And thanks, obviously, to Stan Lee and Jack Kirby who together created the Asgardian part of the Marvel universe. I hope my book reflects the spirit of wonder and adventure they brought to their tales of the heroes and villains of the Realm Eternal.

Author's Note

This novel draws from both the magnificent vision of Asgard found in Marvel comics and "real" Norse myth and real Viking culture. With regard to the latter, *hnefatafl*, sometimes called Viking Chess, is a real game, and you can purchase sets and find rules and strategy tips online. Please just be aware that Marvel and Aconyte Books assume no liability if you choose to play against the dragon Nidhogg.

About the Author

RICHARD LEE BYERS is the author of over fifty fantasy and horror novels, including a dozen set in the *Forgotten Realms* universe. A resident of the Tampa Bay area, the setting for many of his horror stories, he spends much of his free time fencing and playing poker.

twitter.com/rleebyers

Return to the Realm Eternal

The God of War must explore a terrifying realm of eternal fire to reclaim his glory, in this epic fantasy novel of one of Odin's greatest heroes.

ASTOUNDING TALES OF MARVEL'S ICONIC SUPER HEROES IN EXCITING NEW PROSE NOVELS

XAVIER'S INSTITUTE

LIBERTY & JUSTICE FOR ALL by Carrie Harris

Two exceptional students face their ultimate test when they answer a call for help, in the first thrilling Xavier's Institute novel, focused on the daring exploits of Marvel's mutant heroes.

MARVEL UNTOLD

THE HARROWING OF DOOM by David Annandale

Our thrilling new line presenting tales of Marvel's heroes and villains begins with the infamous Doctor Doom risking all to steal his heart's desire from the very depths of Hell.